SOMEWHERE IN BETWEEN

Dawn Hosmer

ISBN 978-1-7374695-3-7 (paperback)

First paperback edition June 2020

Second paperback edition July 2021

Edited by: Bambi Sommers

Dedicated to my husband, Steve
Thank you for always supporting this crazy dream of mine and
believing in me each step of the way.

Sometimes the strength of motherhood is greater than natural laws.

— BARBARA KINGSOLVER

CHAPTER ONE
NOW

Bright lights and the heavy, sickening scent of flowers assault me. I'm lost. I went from complete and utter darkness, the most restful of sleeps, to this. I scan the room, trying to figure out where I am, what is happening. Rows of chairs. Flowers everywhere. Elegant paisley wallpaper. A man, dressed in a black three-piece suit, glides in the room from a side door, moving soundlessly.

"Excuse me? Sir?" I shout.

He makes no acknowledgment that he's heard me. I try again, "Sir?"

Again, nothing. I'm astounded at people's rudeness nowadays. Everyone tends to be so lost in their own worlds that they don't even realize when they're being spoken to. I could be jumping to conclusions. Maybe he's deaf. Perhaps a touch will make him realize I'm speaking to him.

I reach out to touch his arm. My hand settles on it, but, again, there's no reaction from him. It's as if he can't feel me. He's so cold, I wonder for a moment if he might be ill.

"Sir," I say a bit louder and with a definite edge of frustration. But again, I get no response from him.

I glance around the room, hoping someone else is nearby who will help me figure out where I am when I see it. An elegant white casket with a floral spray on top reading, Mother, Wife Daughter. I'm in a funeral home. But how did I get here? Whose funeral is it?

I search my memory for something, anything, to tell me how I got here and whose funeral it is but come up blank. I watch as the man reaches in to straighten the emerald green dress worn by the woman in the casket. He is expressionless, almost robotic. I crane my neck to see around him. I scream and fall to my knees, unable to process what I just saw. My mind is whirring, trying to make sense of it. But I can't. It doesn't make sense.

My body is in the casket.

It's my funeral.

MY SCREAMS FALL on deaf ears, unable to enter this dimension from whatever realm I'm stuck in. The man adjusts a wisp of my chestnut brown hair and shuffles off toward the back of the room, opening the double doors. It's then I see the sign with my name on it, hanging next to the door. Mackenzie Bartholomew: April 10, 1980 – December 29, 2019. Bile rises in my throat. I died four days after Christmas. What? How? My kids!

Guests begin pouring in. I try to study the faces, but I'm lost within a sea of question+ns. Why am I dead? I try to pull up some memory of my death, but all I find is blank space. How did I die? Why am I here? I'm obviously dead, so why am I here in spirit? Why did I get awakened from my peaceful slumber to come back to this place? I see them walk in, and I know. Matt's hands are linked with our daughters'. An intense rage fills me at seeing him. But then my heart melts, and regret washes away the anger when I look at my beautiful girls. Avery is on his right, dressed in one of the outfits I bought her for Christmas. Vera is on his left and skips as though she doesn't have a care in the world. Hanson, dressed in a suit I've never seen, trails behind them, with his eyes downcast and devoid of emotion, like a statue.

Suddenly it becomes clear. I'm here to make sure that my children are okay. I'm stuck in this place, somewhere in between life and death, until I know my children are safe. I'm here to make sure the truth comes out about my death.

But what exactly is the truth?

CHAPTER TWO
NOW

My mother stands guard by my casket, playing her part beautifully. Her artificially brown hair has been styled in an updo as though she's attending a fancy cocktail party, not her daughter's funeral. That woman should've been an actress. She would do an excellent job of playing any role which requires a high level of drama. She's mastered the art for sure. She sobs inconsolably as people make their way forward to examine me. Anyone meeting her would believe my death has destroyed her world, that her life will never be the same without me here. I know that's complete and utter bullshit. Just like the many men who have come and gone in her life, I am replaceable.

I know for a fact that she absolutely loves every bit of attention and pity she's getting by being the star of this show. Well, maybe not the star—I guess that role goes to me this time. Like always, she's managed to make it all about her. She loudly proclaims that she doesn't know how she'll go on and whether life is still worth living. The obligatory comforting responses always follow her declarations. People try to convince her that she'll be okay and offer whatever help they can. I wish I could tell them not to waste their breath. She'll be fine. She always is. And for God's sake, never offer my mother anything. If they offer support, she'll bleed them dry.

It sickens me to listen to her. I wish I could escape this. I try to move my focus to others, but for now, it's stuck on her.

"I don't have any idea why she would do this. I had no idea she was hurting so bad," my mother says, before breaking down into another crying fit, forcing two young gentlemen I've never seen before to rush to her side to hold her up.

"Really, mother?" I shout. "You had no idea I was hurting so bad? Really? Of course, you didn't because that involved you getting out of yourself long enough to notice that other people exist in the world." I'm screaming, but no one can hear me. Exactly like when I was alive. My hands tremble with rage. Years of pain and frustration over not being believed or heard, course through my body.

The first time I remember feeling so invisible was when I was six years old. It was then that I realized how alone I really was and how there was no one in my corner to protect me.

We lived in the house on Burley Street. The one that was never warm enough, no matter how many layers of clothing I piled on. I hated that house from the moment we stepped foot into it. It never felt like home. I was so confused about why we had to leave our old house, my old bedroom, my friends in the neighborhood. I asked my mother over and over again but never got a response, or at least never one that contained any truth. Back then, there were only two of us. Dad had been gone for four years by then, so long I held no memory of him. Mom always had a man ready and willing to fill the role in his absence, but none of them stuck around for too long.

Then, she met Jake. I wouldn't say we were happy before Jake's arrival, but we definitely had a rhythm, a somewhat comforting routine. We knew what to expect and what was expected of us. That all changed when he arrived.

Jake and mom met at the gas station in town. Yes, the gas station because the town was so small that it only had one, along with a lone traffic light. He moved in within a week. I didn't meet him until he was lugging his trunk full of belongings up the front steps. I hated him upon first sight. Perhaps it was the way his greasy hair fell into his eyes. Or the fact that he reeked of booze, stale cigarette smoke, and body odor. Or, maybe because his first words to me, were "Get out of the way, kid."

By the age of six, I was cynical enough to know that he wouldn't be around long, so I would just ignore him and, eventually, he'd disappear, like all the others. When he was still with us after a month, I decided to open up to my mother to tell her how I felt.

She was tucking me into bed one night. "Mommy?" I whispered.

"What?" she snapped.

"I don't like Jake. When's he leaving?"

She slapped me. "I don't want to hear you say that about your new daddy!"

Tears sprung to my eyes. "He's not my daddy!"

"He is now!" she shouted and left my room, slamming the door behind her, even though she knew I was terrified to be in my room at night with the door shut.

I cried most of that night, unable to sleep. My mother had never slapped me before and had never insisted I call any of her men, up to that point, "daddy." I figured that meant Jake was there to stay.

My mother must've told Jake what happened because, after that, he insisted I call him daddy, and, every time I was home alone with him, he would lock me in the basement without any lights on. I tried several times to tell my mother, but each time she'd stop me because she didn't want me "bad-mouthing my daddy."

Jake was with us for two long years.

I'm pulled back from my sea of memories to now by the sound of Matt's voice. A chill creeps up my spine as I raise a hand to my neck, remembering his hands there.

CHAPTER THREE
NOW

The warmth of the room, combined with the constant thrum of voices beating inside of my head, is nauseating. The room is packed, with every seat full and people milling about making idle chit chat. There are so many memories with each of the people here...well, most of them anyway. Some I've never met. Maybe they're Matt's colleagues or friends of my mother. I suppose I should feel loved that so many people came to offer their goodbyes, but instead, I just feel exposed. Are any of them plagued with the same questions I am? How did I die? Is anyone trying to get the answer to that question?

It's funny how everyone wears the same sullen expression when they enter the room, knowing they must make an attempt to look sad, whether or not my death had any personal impact on them. Eyes downcast, faces scrunched with concern, as they walk timidly through the door. They maintain their stance as they move past the casket and offer hugs, handshakes, and words of condolences to my family. As soon as they've done their duty, they quickly make their way to a group of acquaintances, leaving their sadness and worry behind. They laugh and chat as though they're at a party, celebrating with friends, not mourning the life of a thirty-nine-year-old, healthy, mother of three who mysteriously died.

My babies. My poor, poor babies. My attention was so stuck on my mother that I was unable to look after them, as I should have been doing. I search the room. Avery stands diligently by Matt's side. Always my sweet, sweet girl. Even at fifteen, she's stayed so kind, always taking care of everyone else and trying to fix everything. How I wish I could fix this for her! She shouldn't have to be the one to try to hold everything together. She glances at my body now and again, unable to keep from reaching out to touch my face, my arm, my hand. How I wish I could feel her warmth. I would love to be able to take her in my arms and comfort her, tell her it's okay to not always be so strong. Tell her she's allowed to fall apart once in a while. Her tears refuse to fall even though they're always there. She's a master of keeping them at bay.

People always say you shouldn't be friends with your children, but Avery was my friend. I enjoyed her company. We'd laugh, talk about movies or books, take walks together. Of all my children, Avery and I are most alike. She's always seen me as a person, not just her mother. Perhaps it's because I had her at one of the happiest times of my life.

Matt and I were married when I was twenty-three. I was pregnant with Avery within three months, and I was ecstatic. It was like my life was finally coming together into the perfect picture I'd always imagined. Happily married to a gorgeous husband. A new home. A new baby on the way. A job that I loved. A better environment to raise Hanson in, who was four at the time. Everything was coming together. I loved every minute of my pregnancy, much different than the first time around.

Hanson was so excited to be a big brother. Some of my best memories with him were of preparing for "his" new baby as he referred to Avery. I let him help me pick out toys, books, and clothes for her. We got him his own baby to practice with while my belly grew. He'd lug that baby around everywhere; it was the cutest thing. He'd make sure she "ate" and napped. He'd read her books and tell her bedtime stories. Once Avery arrived, things changed, though. That excitement waned quickly.

When Avery was about three months old, I came downstairs after laying her down for a nap and found Hanson in the kitchen standing by the trash can with a scowl.

"What's wrong little buddy?" I asked, touching him on the back and leaning down to look in his eyes.

"Nothing," he said, but the tears pooling in his eyes told a different story.

"Do you want to cuddle while your sissy sleeps?"

"No."

Hanson never refused cuddles. "Okay. Do you want to play?"

His bottom lip came out. "No!" he shouted. "I wanna be alone." He sprinted off towards his bedroom.

That was a first. Hanson never wanted to be alone. Even at night, he'd often find his way into our bed. I decided to respect his wishes and give him some space. I wipe down the kitchen counters to give him a little time before I pried him for more information. When I opened the trash can, I gasped. Lying inside was his baby. Her face was completely darkened with marker; her arms covered with holes that he'd poked into them with something. I pulled her out of the trash, not sure what to do about it. One thing was clear, he did not like being a big brother.

I SCAN the room and find Hanson, sitting in the corner by himself. Many of his friends and former teachers are here, but he's not making any attempts at conversation. He doesn't seem particularly sad, just sullen. Lost. Alone. Oh, Hanson—still my baby boy even though he's now a man. I wish so many things could've been different for him. What's going to happen to him now that I'm gone? I wish I could offer him some comfort, but he hasn't let me do that, without a fight, for years.

Vera runs up to him, giggling.

"Hanson, will you play hide and seek with us?"

"Vera. No. You need to sit down," he says with a scowl.

"Daddy said I can play," she announces as she puts her hands on her hips. Her baby-soft brown hair is flying everywhere, loosened from the ponytail I'm sure Avery tried to make earlier today.

"Well, Daddy's an idiot. Our mom is dead. You shouldn't be running around here like you're at a party." Hanson bolts up from his chair.

"I'm telling. You called Daddy a bad name."

"Go ahead. I don't really care. I'm going for a smoke." Hanson pushes past her as her voice raises a few decibels, shouting for her daddy.

My baby girl is only seven but going on twenty. She's such an assertive little thing; has been since day one. She came into this world making her presence known, and nothing or no one was going to get in the way of her plans. She marches up to Matt, tugging on his arm until he finally stops his conversation and turns his attention toward her.

Matt puts his hand on her head. "Yes, Vera?"

"Hanson said you're an idiot," Vera announces.

Matt turns to his colleague and chuckles, acting like he doesn't care one bit. The red creeping up his neck leaves no doubt that he does. "Well, that wasn't nice. He's probably just upset."

"Idiot is a bad word. Mommy says I'm not allowed to say it."

"You're not allowed to say it. Hanson shouldn't either. I'll talk to him later. You go play." He smiles, but I see the fury behind it. Sixteen years of marriage allows you to see the truth, even when you don't want to.

Vera runs off, and Matt resumes his conversation, but his eyes scan the room. I'm certain he's searching for Hanson. I hope he forgets by the time their paths cross.

A whooshing sound fills my head, and everything around me melds into a swirl of color. I can no longer hear the voices in the room. Nothing holds its shape. The world sways beneath my feet. I close my eyes and cover my ears, trying to block out the noise, the colors. What is happening? I fall into a vortex of color and an explosion of sound, carried away from this dreadful place full of sadness.

CHAPTER FOUR
THEN

The whooshing sound slowly leaves as my surroundings come into focus. I sway on my feet and whip my head around, trying to figure out where I am. Dark paneling, candlelight, classical music, and the smell of something delicious cooking. I'm in Victoria's, the upscale steakhouse where I worked while putting myself through college.

The doors fling open, and my chest tightens—I'd forgotten how handsome Matt was. How carefully he hid his cruelty behind his blue eyes and confident smirk. He approaches the hostess stand with a quirky, lopsided smile, shaking rain off his jacket as he removes it. My younger self peeks out from the backroom as the host escorts Matt to the table. My breath catches at the sight of myself. I'm so young! I'd forgotten how shiny my hair was, how my brown eyes sparkled. If only I knew at twenty-two that love should have stayed the furthest thing from my mind. My eyes are so bright with goals and the ability to ignore life's challenges. That youthful face still so full of hope and promise. Younger me stacks dirty dishes with steady hands, still empowered with the energy to hold down a full-time job, go to school part-time, and raise a two-year-old alone.

Even though I see the hope and promise in my younger self, I know

I felt like I was failing back then. Because, in my mind, by the age of twenty-two, I should've already had my undergraduate degree and been working on my Masters. I should've had my own apartment, not being forced to live back at home where I'd wanted to escape for as long as I could remember. I'd always been a goal-setter and have worked my butt off to achieve whatever I set my mind to. I wasn't going to play the part of a victim like my mother. I was in control of my life, and I had no intention of giving that power to anyone else.

At least that's what I always believed until the whole incident, resulting in an unplanned pregnancy and having a baby so young, interfered with my plans. For a year after Hanson was born, my life felt completely out of my control, but once I realized how much I was acting like my mother, I pulled myself together and got back on track towards achieving my dreams.

I shake my head to clear it of the memories. How am I here right now? Why am I back to this day when Matt and I met? A day I wish I could go back and erase. Surely, I can't change anything about it now.

This day that I've been somehow transported back to finds me working the dinner shift, which was always my favorite because I earned the most money during the evenings. I'd been working at Victoria's for about six months before the day Matt walked in, attempting to save money so that I could get out of my mother's house and into my own place. It is eight, and the dinner rush is over when Matt arrives. Kristin, the hostess, hurries back to former me, interrupting me from finishing my closing duties.

"Mackenzie, I just seated you. A very handsome single guy!" She giggles.

"Damn it! I wanted to get home to see Hanson before bedtime!" Former me throws down the rag I'd been using to wipe the counters.

Kristin shrugs. "Sorry. Did you hear the part about handsome?"

Younger me shakes my head. "I couldn't care less about handsome. I care about homework, my son, sleep. Handsome is nowhere on my radar right now." Younger me grabs a tray and heads towards the table.

Younger me forces a smile, despite the irritation. "Good evening!

Welcome to Victoria's. I'm Mackenzie and will be your server. Have you dined with us before?"

He looks up from his menu, studying me a moment before he speaks. "Oh, hi! No, I haven't. This is my first time to the area. And I'm Matt, by the way."

He rises from his chair and holds out his hand to shake mine.

I remember thinking what a nice change it was to be greeted this way. Now, I see it for what it is—a way to suck me in and make me believe he's a charming, kind man. My younger self's eyebrows raise in surprise. We never got many downright rude customers, but many of them made it clear that we were there to serve them and that we were definitely lower on the totem pole in terms of human existence than they were. It takes younger me a moment to reach my hand out.

"Nice to meet you," younger me says as he takes his seat again.

"Anyway, what do you recommend?"

Younger me rattles off a list of my favorite dishes on the menu when he interrupts, telling me to surprise him. After ensuring he doesn't have any allergies or aversions to food, younger me heads towards the computer, completely stunned by his request. I'd never been asked to surprise a customer before by ordering for them. Younger me glances at him from over the monitor. I turn as well to try to only focus on what I saw in him that day, what captivated my attention. It's hard to see him through those same young eyes, without the last sixteen years of history. Of pain. He is young, probably late twenties to early thirties, casually, but nicely dressed, handsome. A smile works up the corners of my younger self's mouth while typing in his order.

"Walk away. Serve him his food and move on!" I whisper to my younger self, hoping the words somehow get through.

Younger me delivers his cup of Lobster Bisque and a glass of Pouilly-Fuisse. He gives a slight smile as he raises the glass to his lips. "Excellent choice. I can't wait to see what else you've selected." I once found that smile so handsome, so charming. Now, I want to slap it off his face.

"I hope you enjoy it." My younger self refills his water glass and leaves him to enjoy his bisque, which he finishes quickly.

Younger me watches, from behind the computer, as his main course is delivered—Surf 'n Turf with a side of steamed asparagus, a loaded baked potato, and Victoria's famous pretzel bread. Matt raises his eyebrows as the runner delivers his two glasses of wine. Younger me smiles as she explains that the Chardonnay is to enjoy with his Lobster tail, and the Bordeaux is to pair with his filet. His eyes scan the restaurant for younger me as the runner walks away, but I duck behind the wall to the bar. Younger me sure pulled out all the stops to impress this unworthy man.

"What are you grinning about?" Sal, my manager, asks as he walks by.

My younger self quickly fills him in on Matt's request and rushes off before Sal has the chance to respond. I used to get so angry at Sal because he was always trying to set me up with customers. Knowing what I do now, perhaps I should have let him. Why did I get swept off my feet by a charming man with a handsome smile?

My younger self puts on a mask of professionalism, hiding the giddy smiles, as we approach the table. "How is everything tonight, Sir?"

"Don't smile! Don't flirt! Just serve him his meal and let him go on his way!" I reach out my hand and try to clasp it around the arm of my younger self. While I'm unable to grab hold, my younger self must sense something because my arm twitches slightly forward away from the grip.

"Sir? I told you my name is Matt," he smiles. Of course, he has to have dimples in each cheek, which are impossible to ignore. And the candlelight makes his blue eyes dreamy.

"Yes, he's handsome. But don't forget your goals. Your dreams!" I say.

"Sorry. How is everything tonight, Matt?"

"This," he says, spreading his hand out toward dinner, "is fabulous. You know your wine well. Serving two glasses—pure brilliance. And the food is divine. I need to trust my servers more often, I think."

Divine? Brilliance? I want to gag. But a blush works its way up my younger self's neck towards my cheeks. "I'm glad you're enjoying it. Can I get you anything else?"

Seeing myself so smitten by a few charming words and a handsome smile makes me want to vomit. While looks alone may not have been enough, my hormones and wishful thinking about possibly having a normal life, closed the deal, burying my life goals and dreams far, far beneath. Damn, after living with my mother, I should've seen how lust and desire led to destructiveness.

"You tell me. You're the one in charge here. Will I be getting anything else?"

"We shall see, although I'd definitely save room for dessert if I were you." My younger self saunters away, turning back to give a smile.

I smack my younger self on the arm. "Stop swaying your hips and flirting. He doesn't deserve you!"

Younger me continues to sneak glances at Matt now and again, enjoying the pleasure on his face as he eats. After the busser clears his dinner plates, my younger self serves him the dessert.

The entire time we walk toward the table, I raise my voice, trying to force younger me to listen. "Mackenzie. Please! Don't do this. Don't fall for this act. It's a lie. He's not who he pretends to be."

My voice fails to reach the living, though. Oblivious younger me places his dessert on the table in front of him and smiles.

"That looks delicious. What is it?"

"It's our most popular dessert. The Chocolate Ganache Tart with Fresh Raspberries. And a glass of Vin Santo del Chianti, which pairs nicely with it."

He sits back and crosses his arms as a slight smile lifts the corners of his mouth. He doesn't say anything, just nods slightly. I would love to punch that smug grin off his face.

I remember how long that silence felt and being plagued with fears of what it meant.

"What's that look for? Is this okay?"

"This dinner has been perfect. I couldn't have picked better for myself. You, Kenzie, are something else! Although, if I didn't know better, I'd think you were trying to get me drunk with all this wine."

My younger self's cheeks flame bright red. Former me turns to leave and bumps into the chair behind me. I know what's coming next. The one thing that will change absolutely everything. The event that will start the whole ball rolling with Matt and me. I remember being shocked by what I was about to do. My gut screamed out to me not to do it, but I didn't listen. How I wish I would've listened. I pace as the inevitable is taking place. Along with his bill, former me writes down my name and phone number.

Tears stream down my cheeks as he smiles and tucks the slip of paper with my number on it into his wallet. The whooshing sound fills my mind as swirls of color again take over my vision. As I'm whisked away to another time, another place, I think about all that has changed through the years with Matt, but one thing remained the same. He still calls me Kenzie—he is the only person that ever did.

CHAPTER FIVE
NOW

The whooshing sound stops as suddenly as it started. I plant my feet firmly until the swaying stops, and the colors fade. Flowers. People. Casket. I'm back in the funeral home. Aunt Lillian's voice snaps me fully back to now, directing my gaze towards the front of the room.

"She looks so lovely. Like she's sleeping," Lillian says, putting her hand on Avery's arm and dabbing her eyes with a tissue. "They did a wonderful job."

I study Matt closely, trying to gauge his reaction. "She was always the prettiest girl in the room. Still is." He doesn't look at my body when he speaks, rather his eyes shift around the room as though he's searching for someone or something to distract him.

I step forward to study my body a bit more closely. What in God's name does Aunt Lillian see that I can't? I look absolutely nothing like myself. In life, rarely was there a day that I wore make-up. Unless, of course, it was a special occasion. Now, it's caked on so thickly—like I've grown a second skin. Of course, whoever worked on me, probably had to do this to cover my injuries, my bruises. My hair has always been poker straight, much to my dismay. I'd accepted it over the years and usually had it cut with long layers to give it some body and just let it be or threw it up in a messy bun. But, now, my usually shiny, dark chestnut hair is curled, with tendrils falling softly around my face. It reminds me of hairdos from the seventies when the feathered look was in style. And what am I wearing? A dress? I can't even remember the last time I wore a dress. My eyes move down to my hands that are neatly folded across my stomach, the left hand lying on top of the right. Someone took the time to make sure my wedding rings made it back on my finger. I can't recall the last time I wore them.

"I don't understand any of this. She shouldn't be gone. This all feels unreal," Aunt Lillian sobs.

I chuckle as Matt shifts his weight from one foot to the other and clenches his fists. He looks so uncomfortable, like he wishes the floor would swallow him whole. I'm sure he's not the only one who wishes he'd just disappear. My mom walks over and wraps Lillian in her arms, letting Matt off the hook. Why does everyone always let Matt off the hook so easily? He's always been such a charmer. I'd developed the ability to see through his façade over the years, but others still get sucked in.

Mom leads Aunt Lillian to a chair and sits next to her. I can't help but listen in. My heart breaks for Aunt Lill. She's been more like a mother to me than my own mom for most of my life. She was the one that hung my art projects in her home. She took me shopping for prom dresses and bought me ice cream whenever my heart got broken. She was the first one I told I was pregnant and the person who attended birthing classes with me.

As a little girl, I used to imagine that I was really Aunt Lillian's daughter. Age-wise, it could've worked —if she'd had me when she was fourteen. Which I convinced myself wasn't entirely impossible. I created a whole scenario where she had a romance with a boy who was a bit older and accidentally got pregnant. Because she was so young, she knew she wouldn't be able to raise me, so she gave me to Linda. I decided that this was why she never moved away from her hometown —because she wanted to stay close to me, her daughter.

Seeing her and my mother together, it is crystal clear why I'd hoped such a thing. Anyone watching and listening to the two of them would think the same. Lillian sobs, not caring who hears her.

"It just doesn't make sense, Linda. How can they think she did this to herself?"

"You know she's always had a bit of depression," my mother says with nary a tear.

"Yes, but she'd never kill herself. She'd never leave her kids. She wouldn't do something like this without telling me." Aunt Lillian wraps her arms around herself.

Mom's eyes go wide, and she glares at Lillian in silence.

Finally, Lillian must sense the iciness being sent her way. "What? What's wrong?"

Mom shakes her head and then spits out, "You always have to make everything about you, don't you? She wouldn't do something like this without telling me. You. Are. Not. Her. Mother. I am." Mom's shouts quiet those milling about the room, and many stop to stare. Mom stands to walk away, but Aunt Lillian reaches out and grabs her hand.

"Linda, I'm sorry. I didn't mean anything by that. Please…"

Mom yanks her hand away and has tears in her eyes. But they're not tears of sadness. They're those filled with rage. She always cries when she's pissed off. "You never mean anything when you take your jabs. Do you, Lillian?"

Mom stomps off before Lillian has a chance to respond. Aunt Lillian buries her face in her hands and loudly sobs, her entire body shaking with the effort.

I sit in the seat next to her and wish so badly that I could reach out and comfort her, as she's done for me countless times throughout the years. It's so painful seeing her so broken, so hurt, yet again, by my mother's cruelty.

"Aunt Lillian. Don't cry. I'm right here," I say, knowing she can't hear me. I try to wrap my arm around her to comfort her. I rest it on her shoulder, hoping she feels an ounce of the love I carry in my heart for her. "I wish you were my mom. I always have. I love you."

How is it possible for my heart to be breaking even though it's no longer beating? Even though I'm no longer real?

Perhaps I never was.

CHAPTER SIX
THEN

A gain, the whooshing sound explodes in my brain while I'm swept away into a kaleidoscope of colors. The funeral home and the visitors disappear, all blending together to form an indistinct pattern. Even though I don't know what lies ahead, I can't say I'm sorry to be leaving that dreadful place. As drastically as it started, it ends. It takes me a bit less time to regain my steadiness. I'm on the sidewalk in front of one of our old houses. The one I lived in when I was nine or ten. I walk toward the house as a bus pulls out front, screeching to a stop. Ten-year-old me bounces down the steps and immediately bolts toward Aunt Lillian, who has just stepped onto the porch with my suitcase in hand.

Oh! This was one of Mom's dark times when she had to send me away.

Many times, throughout the years, I'd had to stay with Aunt Lillian for extended periods of time. The day I'm witnessing now was the time I went away with her to live for most of my fourth-grade year. This was one of the times Mom was between men, which never sat well with her.

I didn't understand much at the time. All I knew was my mom

cried a lot, rarely got dressed, and was angrier than usual. I had to fend for myself in terms of food, getting to and from school, and homework.

"Aunt Lill," ten-year-old me yells, dropping my backpack on the sidewalk and running to her with outstretched arms. This time in my life was absolute hell. It terrified me when my mom was so emotionally and physically unavailable. I always thought I hid it well. But, looking at it from my current point of view, I can see the sadness in my eyes that I hid behind a smile that didn't quite reach them.

She pulls younger me into a hug and kisses me on top of the head. She always smelled so good, like flowers on a warm summer's day. I move closer, hoping to catch a whiff of her scent and feel its comfort.

"Hiya, kiddo. How are you?" She lets younger me go and sits back down on the porch, patting the stoop next to her.

"I'm good. Whose suitcase is that?" ten-year-old me says, pointing.

"Well, it's yours. I thought it might be fun for you to come stay with me for a while. Would that be okay with you?"

"Yay! I mean, yes," my younger self shouts. The excitement brightens my face before the confusion settles in with a scrunched forehead. "But why? Is it okay with Mommy?"

"Your mom and I have talked, and we think it'd be better for you to stay with me for a bit. You know your mom…," she pauses a moment and looks to the sky as if hoping the words would fall from there instead of from her mouth. "Anyway, your mom has been having a rough time lately and isn't able to take care of you the best right now."

Tears fill my ten-year-old eyes. Blinking to keep them from falling, younger me nods and picks at the skin by my thumb, as I always used to do when I was upset.

"Hey. It'll be alright. I promise."

Ten-year-old me nods, but Aunt Lillian wraps her arm around me, pulling me close anyway. Her embrace was always so comforting. Who knows how long it had been since someone had comforted me instead of the other way around? A few tears fall, from both versions of myself, despite my best efforts.

"I'm sorry I didn't come sooner. I didn't know how bad things were," Aunt Lillian says and sniffles. "I wish you would've called me. You can always call me."

"I know, but Mommy told me not to. She kept saying she was almost better," younger me says. "But, she's not, is she?"

I can't believe I was ever naïve enough to believe anything my mother said. I can't remember ever having trusted her, so hearing my younger self say this is a shock.

"No, honey. I don't think she is." Sadness weighs down her voice. "But, until she is, you are going to hang out with me! We will have so much fun!"

I remember wanting to match her excitement because, really, I would have always much rather been with Aunt Lillian than at home. But I also recall the intense fear that bubbled up in my chest. "But who will take care of Mommy? Will she be okay without me?"

I feel like I've been punched in the gut. Now that I'm a mother, I realize exactly how messed up my childhood was. Why, as a ten-year-old, did I have to be the one to worry about taking care of her? What a heavy burden to dump on a little girl!

Younger me pulls away and gazes into Aunt Lill's eyes for reassurance. I don't know what I saw as a child, but what I see there now is pain. She quickly hides behind a smile and says, "That is for the adults to worry about. You, my dear, are ten, and it is not your job to take care of anyone. Your only job is to be a child. And that's why you are coming to stay with me."

Relief settles into my ten-year-old body as my shoulders drop from my ears, and my younger self sighs deeply. But I also recall how confusing the concept of being a child was to me back then. I didn't know how to do that. Calmness flooded me, but confusion crept up right beside it. It was something I hadn't gotten much of a chance to do.

"Can I say bye to Mommy before we go?"

"I don't think that's a good idea today. But you can call her later. Okay, gator?" She laughs.

"I'll call her after a while, crocodile."

I can't help but smile because that is a saying I carried on with my own kids.

I hated leaving my mom without saying goodbye but knew that I could trust Aunt Lillian. She was one of the few people in life who'd never let me down. Even in my current state, she still is.

I STAY SEATED on the porch and watch as Aunt Lillian and younger me drive off. Part of me wants to go inside and see my mother. The other part of me knows exactly what I'll find. She'll be laying in the dark, doped up on some kind of pill that will supposedly take her pain away. I should've gone with my younger self and Aunt Lill, not stayed here.

Whoosh! Colors assault me from all directions, and then nothing. Everything stops. I force my eyes open, expecting that I'll be back in the funeral home but, instead, find myself inside Aunt Lillian's store, Brews and Books. This always was, and still is, one of my favorite places. The smell of coffee brewing, along with the scent of old books, wafts through the air. It is a smell I have always associated with comfort, love, and home. I scan the store, trying to figure out when I am. The store hasn't changed much over the years, but when Marlene's voice rings out from the back of the store, I know this must be around the same time as when I went to live with Aunt Lill. Marlene, one of the staff, retired shortly after that time.

At first, I don't see Aunt Lillian or myself, and I wonder why in the world I've been brought back here. I make my way through the store, running my hands along the dusty mahogany shelves—it used to be my job to dust them, and it appears I've been slacking. I finally find my younger self, still around ten, I think, curled up on one of the large velvet couches with my nose buried in Anne of Green Gables.

The bells on the front door jingle, making both my current and younger self whip our heads around to see who has come in. It's my mother, and my stomach drops. It's that day. Why did I have to come back here to this particular day?

At this point, my ten-year-old self had been with Aunt Lillian for eight months—long enough to give me a taste of what childhood should be like. And I loved it. Aunt Lillian lived across town from my mother in a small two-bedroom bungalow. Most days, after school, I would go to the bookstore where she always stopped whatever she was doing to give me a big hug and talk with me about my day. If I didn't have homework, I would help her with things around the store, which I absolutely loved. I got to know some of her regular customers, and that's when my nickname, Mack, started. At first, I hated it, thinking it sounded like a boy's name but grew to love it over time.

Aunt Lill cooked most nights, and I loved to help her in the kitchen. She was insistent that we try a new recipe each week, so I got to experience foods I'd never tasted before. Evenings were spent talking, reading, and occasionally watching TV. Aunt Lill's house was so much more peaceful than home. Mom always had the television on, blaring so loud that it was hard to hear my own thoughts, even when no one was watching it. I could actually invite friends over, without embarrassment or fear.

Back then, I usually talked to Mom at least once per week on the phone. She always cried and said how much she missed me. Yet, every time I asked if she could come to visit or if I could see her, she would say not yet.

This day that I'm being forced to re-live was the first time I had seen my mother in seven months. I left home in September, and now it's March. Younger me runs to her and gives her a hug. Her once brown hair is now dyed a deep auburn color, and it's grown out into long waves. She has make-up on and a lovely tight-fitting, green dress.

"Mommy!" ten-year-old me yells and wraps my arms around her.

"Mackenzie, hi!" She stiffens and doesn't pull me into a hug. "Not so tight. I've got an important meeting and can't have a wrinkled dress."

"What a bitch!" I shout as my younger self's shoulders slump in defeat. "She, I mean I, was so happy to see you, and you act like I don't matter. Hug your daughter, you callous, cold-hearted hag! "The heat of rage floods my cheeks.

Younger me takes a step back and bites my lip. "How are you? I've missed you."

"Getting better. So, where's Lillian? I need to talk with her a minute."

"She's in the back. Do you want me to get her?"

"No, no. I'll go back and talk with her. You just stay out here a minute, okay?"

Younger me nods and returns to the couch with my book. I stand between the couch and the door to the backroom, knowing what's coming next. I'm confused about whether to move towards my younger self and try to offer comfort from the blows about to come or go back to be with Aunt Lill, hoping to give her the strength she needs to stand up to her sister.

Raised voices spill out into the store. My younger self rises and inches closer to the back room. I put my arm around younger me and walk alongside.

"You can't….not fair…" Aunt Lillian shouts.

"…mother…not you," Mom shouts.

A few more angry bursts are exchanged before Mom pushes out the door to the backroom, barreling towards the front door with tears streaming down her cheeks.

"Mommy, are you okay?" Ten-year-old me runs to catch up with her, with outstretched arms.

"Don't touch me. Go hug your Aunt Lill," she yells and pushes out the door.

My younger self's arms drop and chin quivers. She seemed angry with me, but what did I do? Younger me slumps into one of the armchairs as tears spill down my cheeks. I sit next to ten-year-old me and whisper words I wish my younger self could hear. "It's okay. It's not your fault. She's the one that's messed up, not you!"

After only a few minutes, Aunt Lill comes out and pulls younger me onto her lap as she sits.

"Shhh…Shhh…it's okay, Mack," she says as she rubs my younger self's back in small circles, just as I always liked. Ten-year-old me turns towards her, with tear-soaked cheeks. Her face is blotchy, and her mascara is smudged.

"What happened? Why's Mommy mad at me? I heard you yelling," younger me spits out past a sob.

"Your mom is not mad at you. She's mad at me, and she took it out on you, which is not okay. You didn't do anything wrong," she says

"Why is she mad at you?"

"Remember what I said your job was? To be a child? Your mother and I will work out the rest, okay? Don't worry."

In my naivety, I believed that if Aunt Lill said everything would be okay, then everything would be okay. She'd never lied to me before.

WHEN I'M WHISKED AWAY this time, I pray that I get to go back to now. To the funeral home. As dreadful as it is there, I hate re-living all of this. It was hard enough the first time around. Back then, I felt pain and sadness, but now, I'm filled with rage towards my mother. As soon as I open my eyes, it's obvious that my prayers haven't been answered. I'm back in the store, and I know what day it is without even looking. May 7th, a day I'll never forget. I hadn't talked to my mother since the fight with Aunt Lill two months prior.

The bell on the front door jingles. My ten-year-old self glances up from a book and sees my mom, standing next to a tall man I'd never seen before.

Mom smiles bigger than she has in years and opens her arms, rushing to pull my younger self into them. "My sweet Mackenzie. I've missed you so, so much." She kisses younger me on the cheek.

"Leave me alone! Let me stay with Aunt Lill! Just go be with your man and live your life!" I shout and try to shake her but can't get a firm enough hold on her to make an impact.

Younger me stiffens in her arms. Her affection has the same confusing effect on me now as it did then. She rarely hugged me warmly, let alone kissed me. My younger self can't speak past my shock.

I pound my fist into her back. She lets go of younger me, whipping around and looking me dead in the eye. A shudder works its way through her body, and then she stiffens, plastering on another smile.

Did she just feel me? Could I really have made a connection? I expect this moment to change somehow since she sensed my presence, but she just extends her arms toward the man standing off to the side and carries on as if nothing happened.

"Mackenzie, this is Greg, my new husband. We've come to take you home."

With so few words, my mother once again shattered my world, stole my happiness.

Whoosh! The colors and sound carry me away.

CHAPTER SEVEN
NOW

I am welcomed back to the present by her shrill voice filling the room. I snap around to see where she is. Of all the nerve! How dare she come here and act like she cares that I'm gone! She's no doubt come to comfort Matt.

I wish I could come back from the dead long enough to strangle Chloe Martin. Nothing would bring me more pleasure. Well, perhaps, watching Matt squirm as she approaches him with her outstretched arms is pleasure enough. Chloe, as usual, has drawn so much attention to herself that almost every eye in the room is on her. She has on a bright red, low-cut dress that screams look at me. Leave it to her to wear bright red to a funeral home. She's obviously had another boob job—those bad boys, or perhaps I should say girls, are trying to bust out. She is ridiculous. She's far too old to have bleach blonde hair and to be dressing like she's a twenty-year-old headed to the club, especially when she is headed to a funeral home! Based on the men's responses in the room, with their eyes bugging out of their heads and their mouths hanging open, perhaps I'm the only one that feels this way.

"Matt, darling! I'm so sorry for your loss!" she says way too loudly and pulls him into an embrace. An embrace that seems more like she's trying to do a pole dance with my husband's body serving as the pole.

At first, Matt stiffens in her arms, but soon, too soon, relaxes into them when she whispers something in his ear. Perhaps she gave it an indiscreet nibble. That sounds like something that would excite the crap out of both of them. Doing something overtly sexual in front of everyone's watchful gaze, right next to my dead body.

I am so engrossed in their disgusting display that I don't notice Aunt Lill barreling towards them until she reaches out and grabs Chloe's arm.

"How dare you!" she shouts, and every person in the room quiets. "Get the hell out of here. Now!"

"Lillian," Matt says quietly and takes her arm, his eyes scanning the room.

"Get your hands off me, Matt. And Chloe, you get out. You have no right to be here."

Chloe puts one hand on her hip and puts her other arm around Matt. "Excuse me. Matt is my friend, and I am here to support him."

Matt, smartly, squirms away from her, putting distance between the two of them. "Matt, tell her to leave right this instant, or I swear to God…" Aunt Lill's face is flaming red and spittle flies as she speaks. I don't think I've ever seen her so angry.

"Chloe, I think it's best if you go," Matt says quietly.

Tears fill Chloe's eyes, and she recoils as though she's been punched. She dramatically raises a hand to her chest before speaking. "Oh, Matt, honey. You don't mean that. I know you don't."

Aunt Lillian is clenching and unclenching her fists like she's warming up for a boxing match. Now that I would love to see. "Chloe, go. Please," Matt says.

She saunters away with an extra sway in her hips, which, of course, draws Matt's attention straight to her ass. She's halfway to the door when she stops and turns back to Aunt Lillian, shouting for the whole room to here. "You know, you can blame me all you want, but it takes two to tango, as they say. It's not my fault."

Lillian lunges towards her, but Hanson, thank God, has returned to the room, and manages to stop Aunt Lill in her tracks, pulling her into a hug. "It's okay, Aunt Lill. Calm down!"

Chloe laughs her hyena cackle and walks out the door. Matt rushes off in the opposite direction, toward the restroom.

Except for how upset Aunt Lill is, this whole thing has been the highlight of my day thus far. It may even make being stuck here worth it. Of course, as bands of color engulf me and the whooshing resumes, I realize being stuck here also means facing memories I'd rather not deal with.

CHAPTER EIGHT
THEN

This time I come to and instantly recognize my surroundings, Vera's kindergarten classroom at McMillan Elementary school. Based on the copious amounts of pumpkins and leaves decorating the room, it's the day of the Fall Festival. The first time I ever met Chloe.

Vera and Chloe's daughter, Sunny, were best friends and attached at the hip during the school day. Sunny was the only person Vera ever talked about; she made it seem like the child could walk on water. It was her first girl-crush, and I'd thought it was cute. I had signed up to be one of the room mom's for Ms. Tullen's class; Chloe was the other room mom. We had communicated via email and text during the planning phase of the festival, and I couldn't wait to meet her in person. I didn't have a lot of friends, so I'd hoped that perhaps she and I could form a bond.

I'm reminded now, as she enters the room, how much I hated her from the moment I saw her. After everything, hate isn't a strong enough word. Despise would be more accurate. She is everything I never was. Loud. Attention-seeking. Blonde. Dressed fashionably. Curvaceous.

"You must be Vera's mommy. It's so nice to meet you in person," she shrieks and pulls former me into a hug.

I laugh, watching my former self tense within her arms, recalling how uncomfortable it was to be crushed against her boobs, inhaling the scent of her way too heavily applied perfume.

"Hi! Yes, I'm Mackenzie. You must be Chloe," former me says as I free myself from her clutches.

"The one and only." She flips her long blonde hair and twirls in a circle. Former me clamps my mouth shut to keep from busting out laughing. I thought it at the time, and I know it now, she is ridiculous. I shout it out now. Even though no one can hear me, it feels better having said it.

Somehow, younger me makes it through the party and comes to the conclusion that she wasn't quite as annoying when she had a focus—like a roomful of five-year-olds demanding our attention. My goal was to escape after the party clean-up without much further conversation but, as soon as the children were dismissed for lunch, former me again becomes the focus of her attention.

"So, sorry for the short notice, but Sunny would really like to have Vera come over tomorrow after school, and I thought it'd be great fun if you could come, too. We could get to know each other."

The suggestion makes me want to vomit, both then and now. But I knew how much Vera loved Sunny, and I didn't want to hurt my daughter. Our house rule was that the kids couldn't go to someone's house unless we knew the parents and had been to their home. So, despite my nausea, former me agrees to the "play date." You would've thought younger me had just agreed to be Chloe's new BFF the way she jumped up and down, her big breasts taking on an entire life of their own. As she wiggles and whoops, I chuckle, wondering if anyone has ever been knocked out by their own boobs. If not, this could very well be a first!

WHOOSH! Swirls of color engulf me, and then, magically, I'm transported to the next day after school. This time travel thing would be pretty cool if a) I was alive and b) it would take me somewhere I actually wanted to be, instead of to all the parts of my past I'd just as soon forget.

Five-year-old Vera squeals with excitement, which helps ease my discomfort a tiny bit. Chloe lives in the posh section of town, full of four thousand plus square foot homes and lawn crews. Her house is stunning. Of course.

Without an audience, Chloe is much less animated and actually a good host. I wondered back then if perhaps I'd judged too quickly. Now, I find that idea laughable. My assessment of her couldn't have been more spot on.

Vera and Sunny scurry off to play as Chloe fills generous glasses of wine for each of us. I'd give anything to be able to have a glass of wine now but, then, I was not a heavy drinker and never had alcohol that early in the day. Former me relaxes a bit more as I drink the wine. At the time, I thought Chloe became more tolerable but, watching the scene replay itself in front of me, I see that the wine didn't change her one bit.

Over the next two hours, I learned of Chloe's entire life history, or so it seemed. Listening to this the first time around was a bit entertaining. Now, it's just grueling. She was thirty-seven, like me at the time, and was married to a man twenty-five years her senior. Dr. Martin was a prominent plastic surgeon in the area—I could've guessed that one—and they'd been married for six years at that time. She swore me to secrecy but admitted that they'd met at the upscale strip club where she was a performer. She claimed it was love at first sight. I couldn't help but think perhaps it was lust at first sight for Dr. Martin and a lottery ticket for Chloe. Dr. Martin (aka Stu) had been married twice previously and had four grown children, who were very close in age to their new step-mother. Chloe talked at length about the trouble she'd had garnering their respect. That didn't surprise me one bit, especially if his children knew the circumstances surrounding the couple's initial meeting. As she shares all this information with my alive self, I pace back and forth, wondering why of all days, I had to be brought back here. To her. Maybe it's because I should've seen the truth of her during this visit, but I didn't. I gave her the chance to play a part in my misery.

Chloe freely shared information I wouldn't be comfortable telling my Aunt Lill. She shared details about their investments, her surgeries, and their sex life. I didn't realize it at the time, but she didn't give me the chance to speak much at all in the three hours we were there. Even though I detest her now, former me decides that, though she's obnoxious, perhaps I can tolerate her for Vera's sake. That turned out to be one of my many mistakes.

As Vera and younger me drive away, I think back over our friendship. During the four months after our first visit, I saw more and more of Chloe, both with and without the girls. She actually convinced me to step out of my shell a bit and take yoga classes with her, which I enjoyed. I was stunned she could stay quiet and focused for so long, though. We even had a couple of dinners with the husbands, too. Stu was handsome for his age and had a great sense of humor when he had a moment to speak, that is. Matt seemed to enjoy our time together with them as well.

It was a friendship that worked for me for so many reasons. The biggest being that Chloe didn't require much from me in terms of bearing my soul or my secrets. She did enough of that for both of us.

When the whoosh and colors invade me this time, nausea fills me, knowing where I'm going to be taken. Why? Why? Why? I shout as I'm carried away.

I know I'm right when I open my eyes and find myself sitting in my car next to my former self in the parking garage at Matt's work. It's April twenty-sixth—a day when everything changed. Former me had decided to surprise Matt at work with lunch, something I hadn't done for a long time. I tried to find a spot near his car so that I could be there waiting when he came out, but not finding it in his usual spot on floor two near the elevators, I kept driving. That's why we're now parked on level six, where I eventually found it.

My former self gets out of the car. I try to remain seated, not wanting to see this whole scene again. It was bad enough the first time. It's as though there's some unseen tether connecting me to my former self, though, which is new. I'm quickly pulled forward, forced to keep up the pace alongside.

Both of me hears them before we can see them—that screechy, high pitched moan was hard to miss.

"Just turn around and walk away! You don't need to see this!" I shout at my former self. But, of course, former me can't hear my pleas.

We are four cars away when we see Matt's face pressed into Chloe's big boobs, bared for all the world to see. My former self's body goes rigid and pauses a moment before barreling toward the car. Even though a large part of me wanted to turn and run the other way, pretending I never saw anything, the other part of me won and pulls alive me towards them by some unseen force. My younger self's eyes widen with shock as my mouth gapes open. Alive me cannot comprehend what I'm seeing—Matt had repeatedly made fun of Chloe and her obviously altered body, saying he preferred the real thing when it came to breasts. He had often talked about how insufferable her voice and laugh were.

My former self peers in the window as Chloe rides my husband. I'm just as sickened now, as I was then, by the look of pure ecstasy on his face as he sucked on her breast. Chloe's moans of pleasure echo in the parking garage. I try again to tell my former self to turn away, but I know younger me won't. Can't.

Finally, after what seems like a lifetime, Chloe's body stops bucking, and Matt frees his face from her chest, as they relax into one another. What happened next hurt me the most, creating a wound that would never heal. He takes her face in his hands and kisses her tenderly, passionately. He hadn't kissed me like that in years.

My former self's widened eyes fill with tears as my chin trembles. Former me raises my fisted hand and pounds on the window, interrupting their kiss. Both of them startle when they see my younger self standing there. Matt pushes a naked Chloe off of him, trying to get to the door before former me can walk away. Matt chases alive me across the parking garage, his pants only partially pulled up. Chloe sits with a satisfied grin, her breasts still wettened with Matt's saliva.

I know I am probably unable to do anything in my current state, but I can't help it. I lunge in the door and focus all of my rage into my fist as it flies towards Chloe's smug smile. Her hands fly to her mouth, telling me she felt something. I hope to hell it hurt. I raise my fist again, and then I'm sucked into the spiral of color, headed towards somewhere new. Hopefully, somewhere far, far away from here. From them.

CHAPTER NINE
NOW

The now-familiar setting welcomes me from one hell to this fresh one. The flames of prayer candles dance erratically as Hanson guides Aunt Lill past them to a seat. He drapes his arm around her shoulder. Avery finally leaves her post next to my casket and sits on the other side of Lillian. I join them, wishing they could see me, know that I'm with them.

"I'm so sorry, kids." Aunt Lillian's chin drops to her chest. "That was not okay for me to do. I shouldn't have acted that way."

"Yes, you should have. She shouldn't have come here," Hanson says through clenched teeth.

Avery scrunches her brow, and her mouth hangs open in surprise. It seems as though she's trying to hold her question back but finally blurts it out anyway. "Why? What did Chloe do? She and mom were friends for a long time. She should be here."

Oh, dear, sweet, innocent, Avery. She doesn't have a clue. Perhaps her denial is one of the traits she inherited from me. If only I could've kept Hanson as protected from the truth.

"It's a long story…" Aunt Lillian starts before Hanson cuts her off.

"They used to be friends. Not anymore. Not since your precious daddy and she…"

Now it is Aunt Lill's turn to interrupt. "That's enough, Hanson. I mean it. Stop." She uses a tone I've only heard a couple of times in my life. It must surprise Hanson because he actually stops talking and slumps back against his chair, folding his arms across himself.

Normally, Avery would've let this drop given the seriousness in Aunt Lill's tone, taking in Hanson's reaction, but not today. "No. I want to know. Why does everyone always keep secrets from me? Obviously, something happened that made you so angry, Aunt Lill. What was it?"

"Please, Avery. Please. Not today," Aunt Lill shakes her head as tears fill her eyes. "I'm so sorry. I shouldn't have acted that way."

Avery's face turns beet red. She stands, puts her hands on her hips, and shouts through the tears streaming down her cheeks. "I'm so sick of this. I'm not a baby. She's my mother. I have a right to know." To make her point, she stomps her foot.

Aunt Lillian and Hanson both rise, trying to coax Avery to sit back down. She pushes away and runs to the hallway leading to the bathroom, locking the door behind her. I'm as shocked as they are. I can't remember the last time Avery had such an outburst. Perhaps it was when she was two, and I wouldn't give her another cookie. I pause for a moment. Long enough to hear Hanson apologize to Aunt Lill.

One of the benefits of being dead—and some kind of weird ghost-like creature—is that I can witness things I normally wouldn't be privy to, like going through the bathroom door to where my daughter is locked inside, losing her shit. She stands in front of the mirror with tears streaming down her cheeks, ruining the make-up she worked so carefully to apply. She peers into her own eyes, saying I hate you, over and over again, with such venom in her voice. Is she directing it towards me? Does she hate me because she thinks I killed myself, left her on purpose? I wrap her in my arms, trying to provide comfort. But I can't. I will never be able to do so again.

Just when I think she'll never be able to receive comfort from me again, she leans into my embrace for a moment, and her chanting stops. She digs in her purse for something. I watch as she moves her hand around inside the bag. I think she's looking for make-up to fix what's been ruined by her tears but, instead, she pulls out a safety pin and lifts her shirt. She runs the point of the pin across her stomach, releasing tiny trails of blood with each pass.

"Stop it, Avery! Stop it right now! What are you doing?" I shout, but no words make it into the atmosphere. I grab hold of her arms, hoping that I can stop her, but this time, my hands go through her, unable to latch on. What in God's name is she doing? Why is she doing this? Why is she hurting herself?

I feel so helpless. I want to run and get Aunt Lill, to make her force Avery to stop hurting herself. But it's pointless. I force myself to look at her beautiful, flat stomach and see her pain. It's then that I see this isn't the first time she's done this. There are hundreds of tiny scars peeking out from her otherwise perfect skin. Some have been there so long that they are barely noticeable, others are freshly scabbed over.

I stumble backward and into the door—my head in the hallway and my feet still in the bathroom with Avery. I quickly yank my head back into the bathroom, my thoughts raging out of control. My God! How long has she been cutting? How could I not have known? Guilt assaults me as my image of Avery crumbles around me. The hidden pain she carries must be deeper than I could've ever imagined for her to repeatedly hurt herself like this. I assumed she was balanced and doing fine with everything because she always outwardly handled her emotions and stress in such a calm and collected way. But, inwardly, her pain must be monstrous. So big that she didn't know how to deal with it other than marring her otherwise perfect body. Why didn't she feel she could talk to me? Did she not think I'd understand? It appears my denial went far deeper than my marriage. It was thick enough to cover my children, too.

Finally, she drops the safety pin back in her purse and studies herself in the mirror again, her shirt raised to reveal all the new ways she's defiled herself. Blood drips like trails of tears down her stomach. A bone-chilling, eerie smile works its way across her face as she sticks her finger in the blood and touches it to the mirror, leaving a fingerprint of her pain for all to see.

She grabs toilet paper and wipes the blood off her stomach before lowering her shirt and leaving the room. She's once again the Avery I know, as she marches to Aunt Lill and apologizes for her rudeness. Her mask of obedience once again covers her pain.

CHAPTER TEN
NOW

As the guests mill around the room, I'm sucked into memories. Perhaps seeing my daughter intentionally hurting herself has transported my mind to a different time and place. Not only was my pregnancy with Avery a pure delight, so was everything about her. As a baby, she rarely cried other than for the obvious reasons like hunger or needing a diaper change. She started sleeping through the night at four months old and never had an issue with going to bed in her own crib. She and Hanson were opposites in almost every way. Hanson tried to sneak in our bed almost nightly until things got particularly strained between him and Matt. But, not Avery. Half of the time, as she got older, we wouldn't even have to tell her it was bedtime—she'd just announce she was tired and go to bed.

Her toddler years were pretty much the same, with only one or two outbursts that I can recall. Everyone used to laugh, saying that all her kindness would disappear once puberty struck, but that didn't happen. The only way she changed was she became more tearful during PMS, but she never lashed out or backtalked. She was indeed the perfect child, or as close to perfect as one could get.

Everything about her seemed to drive Hanson nuts, and he loved to torment her, trying to get some kind of reaction from her. But her kind

heart always won. She never met his meanness with anger or retalia-
tion. From even a young age, she'd peer at him with her big blue eyes
and say, "I love you, Hanson. Even when you're mean to me. I still
love you."

That usually sucked the wind right out of his sails, and he'd be
stunned into silence. Or, the times he was especially harsh, she'd burst
into tears and run off to her room to cry in silence. She wouldn't tell on
him nor put on a show for Matt and me. She'd simply go cry in peace
until she worked through it and then emerge from her room with a
smile, the cruelty forgotten.

Since I was an only child and always longed for siblings, I usually
was able to ignore most of the things Hanson said or did to try to rile
her up. I knew that it was simply what siblings did and figured as long
as they worked it out in the end, I should stay out of it and let them
resolve it themselves. But Matt was a different story. He'd get enraged
about Hanson's treatment of Avery, at times resulting in spankings. Of
course, Hanson would never cry regardless of the discipline he
received. Be it a spanking, a time out, being grounded, he met each
instance with the same scowl that seemed to shout, I don't care what
you do. I win because it doesn't matter to me. Most of the time, Avery
would end up more distraught than Hanson during his punishment.
Hanson would get spanked, and Avery cried. Hanson got a time out,
and Avery would be the one begging for him to be able to get out early.
Hanson would be grounded, and Avery would sneak him snacks or
games to play.

I loved all my kids equally, but I'd be lying if I said I liked them all
the same. I liked Avery— who she was as a person, a sister, a daughter,
a student, a friend. She reminded me of the person I should've been—
the one I always was deep inside even though the world forced me to
change, to harden. Yes, I loved Hanson, but he wasn't always easy to
like and even harder to enjoy. He was just always a bit too much. Too
intense. Too needy. Too demanding. Too loud. And Vera was a good
mixture of the two of them. Loving and cuddly one minute, a tyrant
throwing a fit and wreaking havoc, the next. Depending on her mood,
I'd sometimes call her Hanson Jr. and other times call her little Avery.

Matt and Hanson together were not a good combination. I think I knew this from the beginning, even before we were married, but I refused to acknowledge how much it would matter. At that point in my life, I was so desperate for love. For security. For freedom from my mother's home. I dismissed all my concerns about Matt's feelings toward Hanson. Perhaps I should've kept some things secret from Matt instead of handing him my heart, trusting that he'd keep it safe. That turned out to be a mistake I made with him, time and time again. I was constantly thrust in between Matt and Hanson playing the mediator, the negotiator. Constantly being torn in two having to choose sides. I overlooked so much with Hanson because Matt refused to let even Hanson's smallest infraction slide. Matt's overreaction forced me to underreact. If I could go back in time and change it, I would. I didn't do Hanson any favors by dismissing so much.

Avery began gymnastics when she was four and was a natural. She advanced quickly and poured her entire heart and soul into it from that first lesson. Nothing made her happier than when she was on the mat, lost in a world of tumbling. Her dedication and talent were admirable. She was competing and winning trophies by the time she was seven. I loved watching her perform because the quiet, easy-going child in her was gone. A fierce, determined beast emerged from within. It felt like she was allowing all the parts she kept hidden deep inside to escape whenever she was in competition.

Once she hit middle school, her love of gymnastics shifted into a passion for cheer. Seventh graders never made the cheer squad. Knowing this, I tried to discourage her from trying out, not wanting to see her heart get broken. She insisted, though and, to everyone's surprise, she made it. She was the only seventh-grader on the team, and she was better than most of the older girls. For as much passion as she had for gymnastics, cheer was where she was truly at home. It just fit her, and her personality, like a glove.

My heart breaks for my precious daughter because now it's clear that despite her smiles, her kindness, and her gentle heart, on the inside, she's been slowly dying.

CHAPTER ELEVEN
NOW

I'm snapped out of my memories, back to the funeral home as Matt makes his way towards Hanson, who is standing by the casket. Hanson sees him approach and takes a few steps away before Matt reaches out and grabs his arm.

"Get your hands off me," Hanson says through gritted teeth, yanking his arm away.

"We need to talk. Not here, though." Matt uses his don't question me voice.

"I got nothing to say to you, man. Nothing at all." Hanson throws his arms out to his sides and takes a few steps back.

"We can do this here or outside. Your choice." Matt's voice raises a bit, drawing attention from the visitors.

What a fiasco this is turning out to be! I guess I shouldn't be surprised since I'm nowhere near to intervene. Well, at least not in a way that I can influence anything.

Hanson pauses a moment before turning around. "Outside. Not here." He makes his way to the outer door, pulling a cigarette from his pocket as he goes.

A few other visitors mill around outside, smoking and chatting.

This whole affair reminds me of a cocktail party or a celebratory dinner.

Hanson leans against the brick wall and takes a deep drag on his cigarette. I hate to see him smoking. He'd quit up until the recent stress of everything. I guess I can't really blame him. I'd smoke, too, if I could.

"Why the hell are you smoking?" Matt shouts from the doorway.

"Why do you give a shit?" Hanson responds, not even glancing in his direction.

Matt stands directly in front of Hanson and lowers his voice before continuing.

"We need to get through this funeral and be decent to each other. Then, I don't give a shit about what happens between us. We don't ever have to talk again as far as I'm concerned," Matt says through gritted teeth.

Hanson bursts into a fit of laughter and then starts clapping. "Whoa, Matt. Watch out. You might get nominated for Father of the Year if you keep this up."

"You need to watch your mouth." Matt points a finger in Hanson's face.

"Or what, Daddy? You gonna ground me? Spank me?" Hanson sticks out his lower lip before breaking into a grimace. "I'm not scared of you anymore, man."

"Shut up, Hanson. Just stop!" I scream into the void.

"First of all, I'm not your daddy. Second of all, you're a man now. I'll deal with you as such," Matt says with venom but, surprisingly, takes a step backward. It's not like him to back down. Ever.

Hanson laughs but doesn't say anything. They both stand in silence for a minute. I wish I could will them to just go back inside. I hate them being out here. They've never been good together under the best circumstances, let alone under such stress.

Matt takes a deep breath. "Anyway, I just want us to get through all of this without putting any extra stress on the girls. Can we do that?"

"I'm trying my best but, I gotta be real with you," Hanson pauses, takes a drag of his cigarette, and blows the smoke directly into Matt's face. "I know about everything. All of it. So, you can go in there, shake hands, and act like a loyal, devoted husband, but you're not fooling me. And Chloe showing up? Really? That took some class. Is there gonna be a whole parade of your tramps coming to visit your dear, dead wife and offer you consolation?"

As Hanson speaks, Matt's neck and cheeks grow redder, and his right eye starts to twitch. He's going to blow his top. I see it. I'm sure Hanson does too, but, as usual, he doesn't stop talking.

"Maybe one of them can be my new mommy." Sarcasm drips like honey from Hanson's mouth.

Matt lunges at Hanson, flattening him against the brick wall and raises his fist. "Shut your fucking mouth, you little punk."

"No! No! No!" I shout. "Stop it!" I try to wedge myself between the two of them, but I'm air. I'm nothing. They can't feel me.

Hanson's reactions are quick, and he somehow manages to twist Matt around so that he's the one backed against the wall. The two of them are tangled together, grunting and shouting, drawing the attention of everyone outside. Punches fly. Matt lands one on Hanson's cheek. Hanson responds with a hit to Matt's nose. Blood immediately gushes, splattering droplets all over both of them.

"What the hell are you doing?" Aunt Lill shouts as she bursts out the door with Avery and Vera trailing behind.

"Stop fighting. Daddy. Hanson. Stop fighting!" Vera yells as she runs up, wraps her arms around Matt's leg and tries to pull with all of her might.

Avery grabs Hanson's arm, mid-swing, and pulls as hard as she can. Matt throws another punch that lands on Avery's chest, instead of Hanson. The wind is knocked out of her, and she slumps to the ground, bringing their scuffle to a stop. Finally.

"Oh my God, baby girl. I'm so sorry." Matt stoops, blood still gushing out of his nose. "Are you okay?"

Avery cries and holds her chest, still unable to catch her breath. She's such a tiny thing, that punch had to hurt. I hope nothing is broken. I sit and put my arm around her, hoping she feels at least a tiny

bit of comfort. Dammit! Why is my heart breaking? Shouldn't I be free
from this pain?

Hanson opens his mouth to speak, but Aunt Lill holds up her hand
to stop him, as she pulls Matt to his feet.

"I don't know what the hell is wrong with you two, but you need to
get your shit together. Look at you. Both of you covered in blood.
Matt, you punched your daughter! I've got Avery. You two go clean
yourselves up and stay the hell away from each other."

Mom walks out the door while Aunt Lill is talking. "Oh, my Lord!
What happened here?"

"Nothing you need to worry about, Linda. Just go back inside. It's
all under control," Aunt Lill shouts without even turning to her.

"This doesn't look like nothing," she says and pulls a tissue out of
her purse. She rushes toward Matt, acting as if her one little tissue is
going to help stop the waterfall of blood. Then, with all the dramatic
flair my mother can muster—which, trust me, is a whole lot—she
collapses to the ground, "fainting" from the sight of the blood.

I don't know whether to scream, laugh, or cry. Dying doesn't even
give me an escape from this craziness and these looney people.
Perhaps I'm in hell.

When again, my head explodes with a whoosh, and I'm lost in a
swirl of color, I know that I am most definitely in hell.

CHAPTER TWELVE
THEN

I come to at Windmill Park, to a much younger me and two-year-old Hanson clinging to my leg for dear life. Matt leans down to Hanson's level and tries to hand him a stuffed shark. Hanson was going through a phase where he was obsessed with sharks. The more effort Matt makes, the harder Hanson cries. Eventually, younger me picks him up and comforts him. My younger self tells Matt we'll be back and walks over to a swing with Hanson. My arms ache with the desire to hold my little boy again.

As the swing goes back and forth, my thoughts spiral backward, to this time I'm now stuck in. Why couldn't I see how much Hanson hated Matt from day one? Why did I so easily dismiss it? I know exactly why, even though it still pains me to admit it. Before Matt came along, it was just Hanson and me. Sure, we were living with my mom, but she was always locked away in her bedroom or hunting for her next victim. She didn't devote much time, energy, or interest in Hanson. When I wasn't at work or school, he had one hundred percent of my focus. I assumed back then that his reaction toward Matt was one of jealousy because he took away my time and attention. How I wish I could go back in time and trust Hanson's instincts, instead of my own faulty ones.

In the beginning, Matt made genuine efforts with Hanson. He tried to spend time with him and develop a bond. Hanson resisted at every turn, though. If Matt wanted to read a book to him, Hanson wanted to sing songs. If Matt tried to snuggle on the couch with him to watch a movie, Hanson wanted to lay on the floor. If Matt joined him outside in kicking a ball, Hanson suddenly wanted to blow bubbles instead.

I'll give credit where it's due—Matt tried. For a while. His efforts started waning about three months after we got married. I pointed it out to him, and he explained that he was just trying to give Hanson some time and space to see if it helped. It didn't. The chasm between them only grew wider. Once Avery was born, Matt no longer made any efforts. All his time and attention were focused on Avery. His anger was directed towards Hanson. And, boy, did that man have a lot of anger. He'd kept it hidden well from anyone outside of the four walls of our home.

I was always stuck in the middle. I knew how difficult Hanson could be and saw him thwart every one of Matt's efforts through the years, so I understood Matt's feelings of rejection and despair. But I also saw how differently Matt treated Hanson compared to Avery. The way his eyes lit up whenever he looked at her or mentioned her name versus the furrowed brow and scrunched up face he made whenever Hanson was in the room, or the way his right eye would twitch whenever I said Hanson's name.

Even though I saw it with my own eyes, I somehow managed to deny it—the fact that my husband, whom I adored at that point, couldn't stand my son. My baby boy. Maybe that's why I'm being sucked back to all these different times and places—to be forced to face all the parts of life, and myself, I tried to deny over the years. There seems to be a mountain of them.

Whenever the two of them were in the room together, I was wrapped in knots. Always waiting for the blow-up to occur. Why was that not a big enough sign for me? Why did it have to get to this point…the one where I'm looking back on my life from the other side of death? In the beginning, the blow-ups came in the form of Matt stomping out of the room, usually picking up Avery on the way, and locking himself in the den, isolated from Hanson and me. Or Hanson erupting into a crying or screaming fit, demanding I remove him from the situation to try to calm down a bit.

I'm mesmerized by the rocking back and forth of the swing, lost in my memories when I'm sucked away. The park, the swing, and two-year-old Hanson vanish in an instant. I'm back at our home now, witnessing a particularly tense family meal, and I wonder if I'll be shown anything good in one of these scenarios. It takes me only a moment to figure it won't be this one. I know which dinner I've been transported back to. My stomach drops when I realize.

All of us sit at the table, eating in silence. Twelve-year-old Hanson wears a scowl and refuses to look up from his plate. Avery isn't her usual bubbly self. Younger me has hardly touched dinner, and I'm pushing it around my plate. I'd been feeling ill for about a week prior to this particular night. And Matt is letting it be known through every bite that he had a bad day at work. His silverware clanks too hard against the plate. He slams his beer on the table after each drink.

As usual, whenever things got tense, Avery goes on a personal mission to lighten the mood and turns into a jokester. Avery must decide that she's had enough of the tension and starts chattering away, while Vera bangs her spoon on her high-chair tray. Avery breaks out a joke.

"What did the traffic light say to the car?" She grins.

Usually, Matt entertains her by at least trying to make a guess, but not tonight. He doesn't even make eye contact.

Younger me says, "I don't know. What, honey?"

Avery giggles. "Cover your eyes! I'm about to change!" She bursts into laughter.

Younger me says, "That's a good one."

At the same time, Hanson mutters under his breath, "Shut up, stupid." He says it so quietly that Avery doesn't even catch the remark.

But Matt does. Matt jumps from his chair, knocking his plate to the floor in the process, and pulls Hanson up by the front of his shirt, backing him against the wall. Only inches from his face, he screams, "What'd you say, you little punk?"

Instead of apologizing or keeping his mouth shut, Hanson repeats his exact words. Vera, Avery, and younger me sit in stunned silence until Matt raises his fist. Why did I just sit there? Why didn't I do something?

"Don't you ever call my daughter stupid." He swings his fist. The crunching sound it makes as it connects with Hanson's jaw is one I will never forget.

"Oh my God! Matt, what the hell…" younger me doesn't have time to finish the question before Hanson lunges toward Matt.

Hanson pushes back, making Matt stumble on his feet, sending him backward into the table, causing dishes to clatter to the floor. Instead of taking the opportunity to run to his room and slam the door behind him, Hanson lunges towards Matt and punches him. Avery and younger me both rise. Former me wraps my arms around Hanson and tries to pull him back, but he's so much stronger than me. Avery grabs hold of her father's right arm, but he doesn't even seem to notice she's there. Vera's screams echo through the kitchen. God, I wish I could shake myself. Why in the hell did I wait so long to intervene? Why did I let it come to blows?

"Stop it, Daddy! Stop it. You're hurting him!" Avery shouts, still clinging to Matt's arm.

Younger me finally pulls Hanson into a bear hug from behind, trying to keep him away. Avery's touch draws Matt away from his anger and re-directs his focus toward her, his sweet angel. The touch from former me does nothing to calm Hanson. Seeing Matt retreat doesn't lessen his anger either. He fights and pulls against younger me, trying to get to Matt.

"Hanson, calm down! Please just calm down!" younger me screams as tears race down my cheeks. He's unable to hear my pleas past his rage.

When I see that younger me is making no difference, I plant myself in between the two of them, hoping and praying I form an invisible barrier that they're unable to penetrate.

Of course, it doesn't work. Hanson breaks free of younger me and lunges again at Matt, going right through my body. I feel his fury within myself as he passes through. Matt's face scrunches in rage. His arm pulls back, and he thrusts his fist into Hanson's side. Air rushes from Hanson's mouth in an unbelievably loud oof as he doubles over. Matt reaches out and shoves Hanson's shoulder as my baby boy falls to the floor, gagging and unable to bring air back into his lungs. I throw myself on top of Hanson, hoping I can spare him from what's to come. Knowing I can make no difference now. Why didn't I do more when I could? Matt kicks him in the ribs three times before Hanson gives in and lays back on the floor, writhing in pain.

Matt kicks the broken dishes out of the way, grabs Avery's hand, and picks Vera up from her highchair while younger me stoops to check on Hanson. I'm still dumbfounded now, as much as I was then, at how in the world things had gotten so heated so quickly. Seeing it now, though, all the tell-tale signs were there. Like usual, I chose to bury my head in the sand and ignore them. Hanson goes from gasping for breath from the punch to sobs that wrack his entire body.

"Calm down, baby. Calm down. Where's it hurting?"

"My side," he says past his tears.

"Can you stand? We need to get you to the hospital." Younger me grabs his arm to try to pull him up.

After several attempts, he is finally able to stand, and we slowly make our way to the car. Hanson slumps into the back seat, and former me drives as quickly as I can to the hospital. I wish I could be carried away now, back to the funeral home. But, no. I'm stuck here to re-live this nightmare.

I know that my younger self's thoughts are spiraling out of control, trying to figure out what to do because I couldn't subject my son to any further abuse from Matt. But I was consumed with thoughts of the girls and wondering if I could really take them from their father.

"Yes, you can!" I shout, hoping former me can hear me on some level. "Take the kids and get the hell away from him. He'll destroy you all."

My alive self's hands shake on the steering wheel as waves of crushing anxiety consume me, wondering how in the hell I will support myself and the kids if I leave him. I hadn't worked since Avery was born, eight years earlier. Even though I knew I could get another job, it would never pay enough to support us.

"You will figure it out!" I shout. "Just leave!"

Once Hanson is settled into a room, the staff is quick about running their battery of tests and completing x-rays. Hanson calms a bit thanks to the cocktail of meds they give him to help ease the pain.

"So, what happened today? What set you off?" former me asks.

"I'm sick of his shit, Mom. I wish he'd just leave me the hell alone." I wrap my arms around Hanson, something I should've done then.

"First of all, language. Second of all, he's my husband, Hanson. He's done his best to be a good father to you."

"Shut up!" I yell at my former self. "Stop making excuses for him!"

Hanson lets out a sarcastic laugh, wincing in pain. "Seriously, Mom? I love you, but are you really that blind?"

"Blind? I know he's not perfect, but he does try."

Seeing myself through Hanson's eyes, I want to cower in a corner and cover my face in embarrassment. Why did I constantly try to skew Hanson's perception of reality? He obviously saw things more clearly than I did.

"I'm used to his shit. His fake trying and lies. But the way he treats you. That's another story." Hanson breaks eye contact before continuing. "You have to know how many times he's screwed around on you, right?"

Former me recoils, stumbling a few steps backward.

"Wh…what are you talking about?" My younger self can barely spit the words out.

"Have you ever checked his phone or his computer history, Mom? If not, you should. Do you realize how many of my friends have told me about his latest flings?" He laughs again, but there is no joy in it. "Hell, do you realize how many of my friends' moms he's screwed around with?"

My former self raises my hands to my chest. "Hanson, I know

you're mad at him, and I am, too. But this is uncalled for. You're just being vindictive, trying to hurt him like he's hurt you."

"Wake up, Mom. I'm not being vindictive. I'm sick of seeing him make a fool out of you!" Hanson shouts. "Okay, you don't believe me. Keith caught Matt in bed with his mom. His assistant, Cheri—yeah, they've had quite a few romps in the hay. Jake's step-mom and Matt like to do it out in the open, in the woods behind the school. Layla, the waitress…"

"Hanson, stop it. Shut up. You're lying." My younger self shouts, trying to wrap my mind around his words. "There's no way. I'd have heard or seen something."

"You'd have to look for the truth first. Which obviously you don't want to see. Matt is a cruel, narcissistic, lying, cheating whore."

"Hanson…" Former me is cut off by the doctor entering the room.

I'm sickened at how solid my wall of denial was. Even as Hanson was clearly spelling out the truth for me, I'd closed my ears and heart to the truth. Always wanting to believe the best about Matt, even though reality was right in front of me, being dished out to me by my son. Why did I trust Matt over my own flesh and blood?

Three of Hanson's ribs were broken, and we were sent away with a prescription for painkillers. But, not before a caseworker from Children's Services interviewed us both. She instructed us not to return to the house until their investigation and recommendations were complete. Thank God because this enabled me to make the decision I should've made a long time ago…to leave Matt. I'm stuck in the car as we drive to the only place I knew to go. My mother's house.

I'm thankful for the sea of color and thundering whoosh that carries me away.

CHAPTER THIRTEEN
NOW

The now-familiar ambiance of the funeral parlor is a much-needed relief from the trauma of reliving the moment Matt literally broke my son. I snort as the funeral director helps my mom up from her faint. It's insane that I'm actually glad to be back among grief and my own dead body over reliving my past.

Mom quickly "comes to" with the help of the funeral director and several of Matt's friends. They take her to the back office to lie down for a bit on the couch. She's in heaven, loving every bit of the attention she's getting. Someone rushes to get her a cup of water while Caleb, Matt's best friend, checks her pulse. Outside the door, a gaggle of mom's friends awaits news on how she's doing. Finally, Mr. Pearson, the funeral director, exits and says that someone should go sit with Mom to make sure she's okay. No less than six women volunteer to do so, all seeming to delight in being able to get the inside scoop to share with all their friends later. Since they can't decide amongst themselves, Mr. Pearson points to Becca and elects her for the position. She smiles from ear to ear like she's won a fabulous prize.

I step into the room seconds before Becca enters. Once the door opens, her smile disappears, and concern works its way into place. She shuts the door behind her. "Oh, Linda. Are you okay, honey?"

The tears start to fall on cue. "Oh, my Lord. It was just awful."

"What happened?"

"I don't know. I went outside and found Matt and Hanson both covered in blood. And my poor sweet Avery! Her daddy punched her," Mom says as she fidgets with her bracelets.

"How awful, Linda!" Becca rubs Mom's back, giving her a moment before she continues. "Well, what were they fighting about?"

"Who knows! Probably something Hanson started. That boy sure knows how to get under Matt's skin. Don't repeat this, but Hanson has tried to break up their marriage so many times," Mom whispers knowing full well that the information will be repeated to anyone willing to listen.

"That's terrible. Why would he do such a thing? Does he have mental problems or something?" Linda asks, digging for more gossip to share.

"Well, you do know about his real father, right?"

Becca shakes her head as her eyes go wide with the revelation she's about to get to the good stuff. I want to slap my mother. How dare she use my pain of Hanson's story for attention! This shouldn't surprise me after all she's done throughout the years.

"Mackenzie was starting her junior year of college, and she didn't always make the best choices. She'd dress trashy with too much skin showing. I was always telling her to dress more lady-like, but she never listened to a word I said. Anyway, she went to a party and probably had way too much to drink." Mom leans forward and drops her voice to a whisper. "You can't repeat a word of this, because it's embarrassing for Hanson. Someone raped her, or so she says. She doesn't even know who the father is. She didn't even tell me herself; I had to find out from my sister. I'd never tell her this, but I bet she was just sleeping around, got knocked up, and doesn't even know who the daddy is."

I lunge towards my mother. She shivers as I pass right through her. I'd give anything to be able to wrap my hands around her neck and squeeze until that stupid, shit-eating grin disappears. How dare she? First of all, that woman has absolutely no right to comment on anything to do with my past or sexuality. She's used more men to get her way than I can count. Secondly, she knows nothing about my life then as I saw her as little as possible. The only detail she knows is that I was raped; the rest of the story she made up. As usual, she's tried to turn it into the tastiest morsel of gossip she can, while also painting it as being my fault.

"Linda, that is just awful. Why didn't she get an abortion?"

"I have no idea. I would've tried to talk her into it but, by the time I found out, it was too late. She was too far along."

"No wonder that boy's such a mess," Becca says, a slight smile pulling at her lips.

"If you ask me, she would've been better getting an abortion or giving him up for adoption. It's hard enough to be a mother, let alone to a child a part of you hates."

Her implication makes me want to vomit. I hate my child? That's ridiculous. Sure, on occasion throughout the years, I remembered the rape when I looked at Hanson, but from the moment I felt him move inside of me, I loved him. I never told my mother this, nor would I ever, but I did consider an abortion and was ready to go through with it. That is until Aunt Lill told me about my mother's multiple abortions throughout the years. I'm fairly certain she told me to help comfort me, but, instead, it made my decision clear. I didn't want to be anything like darling Linda, so abortion was out of the question.

So, instead, I decided adoption was the next best choice since I wasn't ready to raise a child. I was sure of my choice until I held him for the first time. Gazing into his eyes, I knew I'd figure it out. I'd do whatever I had to do to make sure he was taken care of. That he'd have a better life than I did. I'd make sure he never went through the same hell.

Now, I'm left reliving all my mistakes and the thousands of ways I fell short.

I walk through the door, back into the foyer, to get away from my mother and her vile words. The world starts to sway; people meld into a swirl of color and voices into a thunderous whoosh!

CHAPTER FOURTEEN
THEN

In the moments I'm being sucked away from now, I'm almost certain about where and when I'm about to land. Before I even open my eyes and regain my balance, chemical smells burn my nose, telling me I'm right. It's September twenty-third of my junior year of college, and I'm in the darkroom. The day my life changed forever. The day my sense of security completely vanished.

I was an art major, focusing on my true passion, which was photography. That semester I had a full course load and was scrambling to keep up with it all. Sleeping and eating were luxuries that I usually couldn't afford. I had a full day of classes and had been in the darkroom developing prints since midnight. I open my eyes and see my former self pouring yet another cup of coffee and reaching for the boombox to turn up the music. I had hoped the hard rock would wake me enough to finish developing two more prints so I could go home and grab a couple of hours of sleep before my nine-a.m. class.

I lunge toward the boombox to try to force the volume down, so my former self will hear what's coming. Or rather who's coming. I fail to make a difference.

He sneaks in the darkened room without my former self noticing.

He wraps his arm around younger me from behind and covers my mouth with his hand.

"Leave me alone! Get away!" I punch him and scream, which doesn't deter him.

My younger self tries to break free, but he's too strong. He smells of smoke and garlic. He shouts at my younger self to be quiet, or he'll kill me. There is an evil in his eyes that I've never seen before or since. The animalistic growl he elicits as he shouts out his threats convinced me he was telling the truth. I remember praying that someone, anyone, would help me. Would stop him. But the music is so loud, and it is the middle of the night. No one is going to rescue me. My former self stares at the picture hanging above his head while he rapes me. It was always one of my favorite shots of a girl sitting underneath the biggest maple tree on campus, a sunbeam illuminating the area above her head, so it looked like she had a halo. For the next ten minutes, she is an angel for my former self, distracting me from my pain. My horror. My hell.

Tears burn my cheeks along with those that trail down the face of my former self. His hot breath burns my neck. Pain rips me apart as he penetrates me. My hands tremble as I'm forced to watch, unable to look away, even though I desperately want to. I don't want to relive this nightmare. I had buried it long ago so that I could move on.

He wears a mask, so the only thing visible are his eyes. I have never forgotten those eyes as black as the depths of hell itself. Sometimes when I look at Hanson, I see his eyes staring back at me. He calls me by name as he walks out the door of the darkroom, saying that if I tell anyone, he'll find me. He'll kill me. Back then, I believed every word. I comfort my former self as I cry on the floor for hours before younger me is able to fight past the pain to pull my pants back on and walk home. The whole time I beg for God, or whoever has me trapped here, to please take me away. To take me anywhere but here. Those prayers go unanswered.

While I sit with my broken, younger self, I remember all that followed this dreadful night. I tried my best to put it out of my mind, but he visited me in my dreams, having his way with me over and over again. I failed my photography class that semester because I couldn't force myself to go back in the darkroom. The first two months I missed my period, I convinced myself it was because of the trauma and accompanying stress along with my inability to eat. I was convinced the nausea was from the constant state of anxiety I lived in after the rape. I would study the eyes of every man I walked by, searching for those black holes of horror. Terrified I'd find them but wanting so desperately to know who to fear so that I could stop fearing everyone. But I only found them in my nightmares.

Finally, as my former self rises to leave the darkroom, I'm transported away from this hell.

INSTEAD OF GOING BACK to now, though, I'm stuck in the past, outside of Aunt Lillian's house. I remember how relieved I was to go home to Aunt Lill's for Thanksgiving—to get away from all the people, from my fear, from my failures. I knew that Aunt Lill would keep me safe so that maybe, just maybe, he'd stop tormenting me each night in my sleep.

Younger me lifts my skinny legs while climbing the stairs. Not enough food and too much stress dropped my weight at the time to a dangerous low. Alive me swallows hard, runs shaking hands over the dark circles beneath my eyes, but manages to plaster on a smile when Aunt Lillian answers the door.

"Baby girl, what happened to you? Are you okay?" Aunt Lillian wraps me in her arms.

My younger self collapses into tears as Aunt Lill leads me to the couch. I'm filled with a longing for my aunt. For her to be able to comfort me now like she always has in the past.

Aunt Lillian wraps a blanket snugly around my younger self to help ease the tremors. Younger me tries to spit out the story, but the words won't come—only tears and sobs letting pieces of the horrors out.

"It's okay. You're okay. You're safe now," Aunt Lillian whispers over and over again as younger me rocks back and forth, back and forth. Her arms always had a way of soothing the worst hurts.

I'm stuck here with Aunt Lill and my former shattered self for three long days. In some ways, it's a relief because safety and comfort surround me just by being in my aunt's presence. But it's also torment because I see how broken I really was. Somehow, I'd blocked out most of that pain throughout the years.

On day three, my younger self finally manages to get out most of the wretched truth, along with the declaration of wanting to die. How everything is screwed up. Younger me admits to failing my classes and being unable to eat or sleep.

It was after these confessions that I was shipped off to spend most of the next month in a psychiatric facility trying to get stabilized, trying to find the point in carrying on. It was exactly where I needed to be. If I hadn't stayed, I have no doubt I would've killed myself, especially after finding out the news that changed my life. I was pregnant. After doing the math in my head, I knew he had to be the father. Not only had the devil raped me, stolen my plans and future, but he'd also impregnated me. Ensuring that I'd never recover from the damage he'd done.

ONE MINUTE, my former self is spilling my guts to Aunt Lill about the rape, my depression, and the next moment I'm with a healthier-looking me, back at Aunt Lill's. She had convinced me to take the rest of the year off school and stay with her to decide what to do, to get healthier. I could barely take care of myself, let alone raise a child. Through my therapy and talks with Aunt Lillian, I decided to get an abortion. I felt like it was really the only choice.

It only takes me a moment to realize what day I've been transported back to this time. It's a Tuesday—the day before I am scheduled to have an abortion. Younger me is distraught and crying during my admission to Aunt Lill about being terrified to go through with the procedure. My younger self rattles on about all the horror stories of women not being able to have children after an abortion and how I wanted to be a mom more than anything. Aunt Lill tries to offer comfort by ensuring younger me that I'd be okay. That I'd still be able to have children one day. As proof and consolation, she speaks the words that sealed my fate. I listen as she tells my former self of my mother's past and how she had two abortions before having me. At the time, I knew it was supposed to make me feel better, to show me that I'd still be able to get pregnant since my mom was able to. Instead, it sickened me then, and now, that I was considering doing anything even remotely similar to what my mother had done. I've never wanted to be anything like that woman.

I sit in the bed with my former self, who tosses and turns all night. It's almost as if I'm trapped inside of my own mind back then. My thoughts go back and forth between those black eyes boring into my soul and my mother. Indecision keeps me from sleep. I try to comfort younger me by saying it will all work out; it will all be okay. But, is that a lie? Obviously, it didn't all work out because I'm dead. How did I end up dead? Did I kill myself as my mother suspects? Did Matt murder me? He wouldn't do that to his girls—steal their mother away. Would he? Could he?

As soon as the sun rises, former me knocks on Aunt Lillian's bedroom door. My younger self lies next to her and cries for the longest time. Finally, my former self tells her my decision not to go through with the abortion. I would give the baby up for adoption, confident that this was the best choice for me.

Aunt Lillian wraps her arms around my younger self as I plead with her not to tell my mother. I didn't care what she had to say about the situation. I hoped that I would be able to go my entire pregnancy without seeing her so that she'd never know. She knew I was staying with Lillian after being released from the hospital and taking the rest of the year off. Thankfully, she was distracted by her newest romance, so she stayed away from the hospital, her focus lying solely on her new man. We told her it was so I could adjust to my medications and get a little more stabilized. She, of course, threw a fit, saying I should be staying at home with her. That it was a mother's job to care for her child. Like she'd ever done anything the way a mother should.

As Aunt Lillian promises to keep my pregnancy from my mother, the whooshing sound drowns out her voice, and the bursts of color carry me away.

ONCE I GET MY BEARINGS, I see that I'm back in my old bedroom at Aunt Lill's. My younger self lies on the bed with a stomach so swollen that I may burst at any moment. My due date was June twenty-third, so it must be sometime around then. My mother's shrill voice rings out from down the hallway, and butterflies rise into my chest—this is the date my secret was revealed. My former self springs to attention and tries to bunch the covers so that it conceals my stomach. Younger me whispers a prayer. Please, dear God, let Aunt Lill tell her I'm sick. Please don't let her come back here. I can't deal with her now.

Footsteps echo down the hallway as my former self's body trembles.

"Now, Linda. Let her rest. She's not feeling well, and she may be contagious. You don't want to get sick, do…"

Mom throws the door open, cutting Aunt Lill off mid-sentence. Younger me squeezes my eyes shut with the blankets bunched to cover my swollen belly as much as possible, hoping she'd just peek in on me and leave, returning to her newest fling.

"Oh, dear God, Mackenzie. What have you done?" she gasps.

My younger self's eyes fly open just in time to see Mom burst into tears and push Aunt Lill out of the way so she can barrel down the hall, back into the comforting arms of her man.

Before she leaves, she shouts loud enough for all the neighbors and us to hear. "How dare you keep this from me? I'm done with both of you! I have a right to know I'm about to be a grandma!" She wails as though she's been punched, before slamming the front door.

Younger me gasps and presses a hand to my swollen belly. Ah, right, the baby had kicked hard at the exact moment my mother yelled. It seemed like the little one was as disturbed by my mother as the rest of us. Alive me laughs despite the pain and murmurs to my belly—the first time I ever spoke to the unborn baby.

CHAPTER FIFTEEN
NOW

Red, yellow, blue, purple, and green swirls are everywhere. Carrying me away from my pregnant belly and my obnoxious mother. In only an instant, I'm back outside the funeral home where Avery stands with Hanson, trying to calm him down after the fight with Matt. Matt's nowhere to be seen and must've gone inside to clean himself up. Avery studies her hands while Hanson smokes another cigarette. Finally, the words tumble out before she can stop them.

"What is going on? What happened?"

"Just drop it, Avery. Okay? Everything's crazy enough," Hanson says angrily, but there's weariness in his face. "Are you okay? You got hit pretty hard."

Avery's cheeks redden, and she shouts, "Physically, I'm fine. But, no Hanson. Everything else is not okay! I need someone to tell me what the hell is going on. First, Grandma and Aunt Lill fighting. Then you and Dad." Tears stream down her face, but she doesn't bother to wipe them. "I'm not a baby. I need someone to tell me what's going on. It's bad enough Mom's dead, but with all this fighting, I'm lost."

Sobs overtake her, and Hanson encircles her in his arms, holding her tightly. It warms me to see him comforting her. They need to be there for each other in my absence.

"Okay, you win. You're right. You deserve the truth," he says. "Let's take a walk."

They head down the sidewalk, away from the funeral home, and I follow along.

"First off, Chloe. Do you really not know?" he asks, and she shakes her head. "Well, your father and Chloe have been sleeping together for years."

Avery stops and stares at him with her mouth gaping open. "No way. She and mom were friends. Dad wouldn't do that. Neither would Chloe."

"He would do that, and he did. Didn't you ever wonder why Mom and Chloe stopped hanging out? Why Vera wasn't allowed to go to their house anymore?"

The truth finally sinks in, and Avery's eyes go wide. "Wow! I never put it together. What the hell? Aunt Lill knew?"

He nods. "Along with half the town. That's why Aunt Lill lost it back there."

"What else don't I know?"

They continue to walk and talk, Hanson filling Avery in on all of Matt's indiscretions along the way. Avery listens even though I can tell it's painful for her. She stays quiet until they've looped around the block and are almost back to the funeral home.

"Do you think that's why…" she pauses, unable to get the words out. "Mom killed herself?"

I gasp. Did I? Things had gotten bad, but were they so horrible that I didn't see any other way? Did I really choose to end my life and leave my kids behind? After my history with my mom and always feeling unimportant and like such a small factor in any decision she made, I always tried to do the opposite. I cannot imagine a scenario that would ever make me willingly leave my children.

Hanson stops and grabs Avery by the arm, forcing her to make eye contact. "Mom didn't kill herself."

I breathe a sigh of relief before the questions have a chance to form in my mind.

"What? What do you think happened?" Avery asks, but then it hits her, and she doubles over as though she's been punched. "Do you think Dad killed her? Or Chloe?"

I study Hanson closely, needing the answers as badly as Avery does. Did I kill myself, or was my death at Matt's hand? I dismiss Chloe as an option almost immediately because she wouldn't go to the trouble of killing me—she already had exactly what she wanted from Matt. Hanson doesn't answer right away, rather he lights another cigarette and takes a few drags before responding.

"I wouldn't put it past either of them, honestly."

"I hate him. I don't want anything to do with him. How could he have done all of that to Mom?"

"He's your dad, Ave. It doesn't matter how I feel about him or how he feels about me. He loves you. You don't hate him."

"I do. And I'm pissed that no one told me any of this. Our mom had to die for me to find out the truth. God, I'm such an idiot. A blind idiot!"

I ache for her. What she sees as being an idiot, I see as her innocence. Her ability to find the good in everyone and to focus on that instead of the negative. It's a quality I wish she could hold onto as she gets older instead of being forced to deal with all these awful facts about life.

"It's not exactly great dinner time conversation now, is it? 'So, Matt, who'd you screw today? Any of my friends' moms?'" Hanson says with a smile and, despite her best efforts, Avery chuckles.

"I guess you're right. It's not something either one of them was proud of, I'm sure. I just can't understand why she didn't leave him before now," Avery says.

"She tried. Several times, but that's a story for another time because look who's headed this way." He points to Matt barreling toward them.

Avery's entire body goes stiff, and she turns to Hanson as if to ask what she should do. He mouths just act normal.

"Where the hell were you guys? I've been looking everywhere. Avery, baby, you okay?" Matt says, pulling Avery into his arms and glaring at Hanson over her head. Avery doesn't return the hug.

She pushes away. "We just went for a walk, Dad. We both needed to get away from this place."

"Well, we all need to get back in there. They're about to close the room to everyone except family so we can say our goodbyes before the service."

"You two go ahead. I'll come in a minute," Hanson says.

Avery looks at him with raised eyebrows, as though she's asking for permission to go inside with her father. Hanson gives a slight nod and a smile. Avery wraps her arms around him and whispers, "I love you," before heading inside with Matt.

Hanson paces back and forth, running his hands through his hair. All his tension had dissipated when he and Avery were walking. But, now it's back full force. I wish I could take him in my arms and tell him it's okay, that he will be alright. I wish he could see me and know that I'm still here, watching out for him, protecting him the best I can. I want him to hear me as I tell him I love him, no matter what.

As much as I want to stay and comfort my son, I'm drawn back into the funeral home. Perhaps hearing what people say during their goodbyes will help me figure out what happened to me. I leave Hanson outside and head into the funeral home, wishing he'd come in. Saying goodbye must be a pain he isn't yet willing to face.

CHAPTER SIXTEEN
THEN

B y now, the whooshing sound and swirl of colors don't take me by surprise as much as fill me with dread at wondering what painful part of my past I'll be forced to relive. This time I come to in the kitchen of one of my mom's houses. I look around, trying to ascertain which one. Wayne's—where Hanson and I lived for a while. Initially, Hanson and I lived with Aunt Lillian until he was six months old, which was a good thing because post-partum depression hit me hard. Or perhaps it was a touch of that and post-traumatic stress from the rape. Aunt Lillian really should've had her own kids as she was a natural with children. She mothered us both those first crucial months. The only drawback to living with her was how much room all the baby supplies took up in her small bungalow.

Then, my grandmother got sick and needed someone to care for her. Mom, of course, suggested that she be put in a nursing home, but Aunt Lill refused to do so. Grandma lived about two hours away, so Aunt Lillian was forced to choose between finding someone else to run her business while she cared for Grandma or bring her to live in the bungalow. There was no way she could afford to hire someone to take care of all the daily tasks with the store, so Grandma needed to come to stay.

I overheard Aunt Lillian's end of many conversations with my mother, even though she tried to shield me from them, begging for Mom to let Grandma stay at her house. I couldn't hear Mom's responses, but I had no trouble imagining the list of excuses she came up with for why it wouldn't work. Deep down, I knew that the biggest reason was because she wanted Hanson and me to be forced to live under her roof. She wanted control over me but, more so, she didn't want me to be with Aunt Lill.

Aunt Lillian moved Grandma in on Christmas Eve, and I moved in with Mom and Wayne, her latest fling. Wayne owned a house right outside of town, and it was huge, complete with an inground pool, large yard, and five bedrooms. Wayne traveled a lot for work, so he wasn't home often. Mom was always there, other than her lunch dates and hair appointments.

Out of all the men who Mom had paraded in and out of my life, I liked Wayne the most. He was a bit older than Mom and had four grown children and three grandchildren. He was a successful business-man, as well as caring and gentle. How Mom nabbed him, I've never understood. When he was home, Mom was a completely different woman. She cooked. She cleaned. She interacted with Hanson and me. When he was out of town, Mom was her usual self—she'd have nothing to do with Hanson or me for days on end. There were no family meals or time spent chatting. She was in her world; we were in ours.

It was quite a shock to go from always having Aunt Lill around to help out to getting zero help from my mother. It was a constant emotional struggle adjusting to motherhood and trying to plan for my future. Mom made sure to insert her constant reminders about Hanson's conception whenever she could.

When Hanson would cry, Mom would look at him with disdain and say, "It's no wonder he's so unhappy; his father obviously wasn't a stable person."

Or Hanson would giggle at something, and Mom would stare at him like he'd grown another head and ask, "I don't know where in the world those dark eyes came from! Do you suppose they're from his father?"

Out of nowhere, she'd often announce, "I don't know why you didn't have an abortion or give him up for adoption. It must be impossible to really love him."

I'd do my best to keep my mouth shut and not show any reaction to her statements because a response would further fuel her cruelty. She was like a predator—show her your weakness, and you would easily become her prey. But each statement was like a punch in the gut, raising my anxieties, reminding me of my rape. I can recall less than five times that she helped with Hanson when Wayne wasn't around, and those times were only after I'd begged, cried, and pleaded because I was sick or tired or just needed five minutes alone to take a shower.

Then Wayne would come home, and her other personality would come out—the one that was the doting mother and grandmother. She'd get upset because Hanson would cry every time she held him. He knew what a fraud she was, even as a baby. I didn't really trust her with him when Wayne wasn't around anyway, so it was a relief when I could leave Hanson in Wayne's care, knowing he'd make sure he was okay.

We didn't get to see much of Aunt Lillian during that time because between work and taking care of Grandma, her hands were full. I didn't have access to my own vehicle, so I was completely dependent upon Mom to take me places. God forbid I ever asked though because, no matter when it was or what she had going on, it was always a major inconvenience. Mom rarely even went to see her mother, even when Aunt Lill begged for help, forcing her to hire caretakers to take care of Grandma during the day while she worked. I offered to do it, but, in reality, there was no way I could take care of a baby and her at the same time with my lingering depression.

My mother's voice snaps me from my memories of that time and back to Wayne's kitchen.

"Dinner!" she shouts up the stairs.

I move to the bottom of the stairs as younger me descends with a chubby, nine-month-old Hanson. Given his age, it means we'd been living with Mom for about three months.

Younger me goes into the kitchen and puts Hanson in his highchair with some puff snacks to eat. Wayne isn't home, but Mom made dinner anyway. My favorite—tacos. My younger self takes the first bite of my taco when Mom starts in. I know what conversation is coming.

"So, dear. What are you going to tell him about his father?"

Younger me finishes chewing my bite before answering. "Well, I don't know yet. I figure I have some time before deciding."

Hanson squeals and bangs his toys against the tray of his highchair. Younger me blows him a kiss before taking another bite. I can't help but smile—this was one of my favorite ages with Hanson. He was so joyful and carefree.

"You need to come up with something because he's going to ask as soon as he starts playing with other kids, meeting their fathers. Unless you find a man, and soon, to be his daddy."

Former me pushes my plate away, having hardly eaten anything. Nothing like my mother to spoil an appetite. There were so many things I wanted to say in that moment, but I bit my tongue because it was pointless. It'd all been said before and never made a difference.

"Well, what is your plan? You certainly can't tell him his daddy is a rapist."

"Shut up, Mother!" I shout to no avail. She could barely hear me when I was alive because she never cared to listen.

Younger me takes a deep breath. "Mom, I said I don't know. I will come up with something. I'm not going to go out and find a man to avoid having a hard conversation with my child."

Mom's hand flies to her chest, and she gasps as though she's been attacked. Tears fill her eyes, and her hands shake. "How dare you!"

Younger me slumps back against the chair. "How dare I what, Mom? What did I do?"

I know how frustrated I was back when this conversation happened. But now, I can't help but laugh at my mother's dramatics. I shout, "Not everything is about you, Linda!"

Through gritted teeth, Mom says, "You think you're so smart and that I can't tell when you're getting in a dig at me. But I can. You act like you're a better person than I am and always find a way to fit that into every conversation."

Oh boy, here we go! The old me doesn't say a word. Perhaps part of her is right; maybe I did, and still do, think I was a better person than she was because I made better choices. She'd forbidden me to have any contact with my father throughout the years, acting like he was the spawn of Satan. Whichever man was in her life at the time became daddy to me. It didn't matter if I couldn't stand her current plaything, I still had to call them Daddy. I had asked so many questions about my father throughout the years, and she'd tell me that he was a no good, son of a bitch, that wanted nothing to do with her or me. Talk about devastating to a child. Her lies crushed my self-esteem. So, yes, there was some truth in her statement. I wasn't about to parade men in and out of my child's life or make up lies to crush my son. I drape my arm around my younger self, trying to give the comfort my mother should be providing.

Mom screams as tears build in the corners of her eyes. "You're so much better than me, right? Is that it? I did the best I could with you. I wanted you to have a good life and did what I had to do to make sure you were taken care of. Guess what? You're no better than me. You may not have a boyfriend taking care of you, but here you are. Wayne and I providing for you! How's that any better? Maybe I should've had an abortion like I'd planned to."

She storms to the sink and drops her full plate in, shattering it. Hanson begins to cry because of the commotion. Younger me picks him up from his highchair and turns to leave the room. I'd learned through the years that when she was this wound up, it was best to walk away. I follow behind my younger self, wanting to spend a little more time with Hanson as a nine-month-old.

"I can't. You have to clean up. I've got to lie down." She grabs her head. "I don't feel well. All of this stress isn't good for me." She throws the towel on the counter and sulks off, leaving me with a crying baby and a mess to clean up.

Once she is gone, Hanson instantly calms. Younger me settles him on the floor with some toys and begins the kitchen clean-up. I gained clarity as I did the dishes. One thing was crystal clear to me. I couldn't become my mother. I decided that night that no matter what it took, I was going to get the hell out of her house. I would go to school again, and I would get a job. I also decided that, when the time came, I would come up with a story of the most loving, caring man to tell Hanson about his father. I would never make my child believe he wasn't wanted.

I'm allowed to stay here with Hanson and my younger self through the kitchen clean up. I swear Hanson can see me. I sit on the blanket with him, and every time he looks my way, he giggles or smiles. For a short while, I am content. Then, the swirls of color and whooshing noise return to carry me away.

CHAPTER SEVENTEEN
NOW

M r. Pearson makes an announcement in his soothing voice, asking all visitors to exit the room to allow the family some time to spend final moments in reflection. It's as though he's reminded everyone why they're here. They'd forgotten in the midst of their conversations, the drama among my family members, the laughter. Everyone wears sullen expressions as they leave the room.

Once only family members remain, Mr. Pearson pulls the heavy wooden doors closed behind him, and a hush falls over the room. Everyone takes a seat as Mr. Pearson moves into place next to my casket.

"Please take this time to spend with Mackenzie and offer your private goodbyes prior to the start of the service. We will re-open the doors to guests in one hour. I will be in the back of the room, so don't hesitate to ask for anything you need," he pauses, and his eyes move from person to person. "Again, I am sorry for your loss."

Mr. Pearson walks soundlessly to stand guard next to the doors. There are several moments of silence other than the occasional sniffle. Even Vera sits quietly on her father's lap, which is completely unlike her. People shift in their seats, attempting to add some noise to break up the quiet. No one steps forward for the longest time. I look from person to person, trying to figure out what's going on in each of their minds.

Vera starts to squirm on Matt's lap. Even though he whispers, the sound carries, bouncing off every wall.

"Sit still, Vera. Shh."

Vera attempts a whisper, but it's not an art she's mastered too well yet. Finally, she pushes with all her might and shouts, "I want to say goodbye to Mommy!"

Matt rises as though to walk with her, but she turns to him and says, "No, me alone."

Someone has attempted to fix her hair—it's a bit less unkempt than earlier. She dashes toward the casket where I stand waiting for her, even though she can't see me.

She reaches out and puts her hand on my lifeless one.

I say, "Hi, baby girl!" hoping and praying that even though the words don't reach her ears, they reach her soul. "I love you so, so much. I don't want to leave you."

"Mommy, are you in there?" she whispers.

"No, but I'm right here."

It's as though she's heard my voice. She glances toward me for a moment and then back at my lifeless body. "Well, I hope you can hear me. I love you and miss you. You were the best mommy in the whole big, wide world." She sighs a shuddering breath as tears fall down her cheeks. "I miss your smile and your hugs and your goodnight stories and your cookies. I miss sitting on your lap. Daddy says you're in heaven. And, I hope you are with Bullet. I bet if you are, he's wagging his tail and licking you all over. That makes me happy."

She pauses and wipes her nose on her sleeve, something I would've scolded her for when I was alive. Now, I see how unimportant and trivial it really is. The pain is overwhelming. I want to scoop her up in my arms and never let her go. I want to see her grow into the strong, independent woman I know she'll become. I want to be there each day to listen to her silly stories and watch her prance around from room to room with her dolls. I don't want to leave my baby. She still needs me so much.

"Mommy, everyone says how pretty you look, but I have a secret. You don't look like Mommy at all. I like you much better with your hair all messy and no make-up on." She cocks her head to the side as if everyone has lost their minds, which makes me laugh.

She stands quietly for a moment, her hand on my cold, lifeless one, with tears streaming down her little cheeks. I wrap my arm around her and stroke her soft hair and cheeks, trying to wipe away her tears. Finally, she removes her hand and blows me a kiss. "I love you forever and ever and always and always."

She runs back to Matt, who scoops her up. She buries her head against his chest, and her cries quickly turn to sobs. Every eye in the room glistens with tears. Matt carries her to the restroom, a blanket of silence again falling over the room.

Part of me wants to go with them to try to comfort my little girl. But my mother makes her way toward the casket, and I can't bear to walk away. I need to hear what she has to say.

Before she makes it to the casket, the world around me sways, and the thundering noise fills my head. I'm being carried away again. To relive yet another moment full of regrets.

CHAPTER EIGHTEEN
THEN

This time, when I return, I'm in our bedroom. Matt and my former self are still sleeping, tangled up in the sheets. The clock on the bedside table reads seven. Even on the weekends, Matt usually woke up by six, regardless of how late he'd worked the night before. I squint to see the clock—it's a Thursday, and we must have missed our alarms. Younger me sits up and grabs the clock.

"Matt," my younger self says while shaking his arm. "It's seven."

He kicks the blankets off. "Shit! I have a meeting. Shit, shit, shit…" He tromps off toward the bathroom as my younger self rushes down the stairs.

After making his lunch, younger me gathers his briefcase, his lunch box, a coffee to go, and his cell phone and carries them out to his car. My chest fills with lead, certain of what day this is. Former me carries his stuff to the car so that he can just hop in and leave as soon as he's ready. My younger self opens the passenger door and puts his items on the seat and his cell phone in its holder on the dashboard. His phone rings. I don't have to look to remember that it's a number with no contact information attached. My former self pauses, in a debate about answering because it's his work cell phone. I justified my decision to answer it since it could be important, and he normally would be at work by this time.

"Hello, Matt Bartholomew's office. May I help you?" former me says in a professional sounding voice.

I lean close to hear, even though this conversation is unforgettable, ingrained in my heart. After a brief pause, a woman's sleepy voice says. "Ummm, yes, is Matt available, please?"

"I'm afraid he's not, can I take a message?"

"Ummm, sure. This is Yvonne. We had a late meeting last night, and he left some important papers in my… umm… in my possession. I believe he needs them for a meeting this morning."

My stomach jumps into my throat, as it did the first time this happened. Shock courses through me because Matt told me he was at the office all evening, working alone. I'd called several times that night, and he'd taken each call, sounding like his usual self.

Former me takes a few shuddering breaths. "I will certainly tell him. Where can I have him return your call?"

"He knows how to reach me, but I have a meeting this morning and won't be available. Tell him I'll leave the papers at the front desk of the Windmere Hotel under my name," she says.

"I certainly will," my younger self says as tears pool. I remember clearly the thoughts that are racing through my younger self's mind. The Windmere Hotel? That is nowhere near his work. "Can I get your last name, Yvonne?"

There is a slight pause before she hangs up without giving me her last name. Former me sits there holding the phone for a moment, trying to make sense of the conversation and its meaning.

"You'll be okay!" I say to my younger self. "Put the phone back before Matt comes out. You'll be okay."

My former self responds by putting the phone back in the holder. I had forgotten this next part. How in the world had I let this memory slip away? As my younger self rises to get out of the car, I reach down and grab something between the seats. My heart sinks now, as it did then, when I realize what I've discovered. A red lacey thong. My younger self shoves the discovery in the pocket of my robe and heads inside.

I had suspected Matt of infidelity many times throughout the years. I think in my gut, I always knew. I went through phases where I searched for proof and, other than hushed phone conversations or late nights at the office or strange phone numbers showing up on slips of paper from time to time, I could never find anything concrete. I confronted him with my suspicions many times. It didn't matter if I cried, screamed, yelled, begged, pleaded, Matt would remain calm and adamantly deny that he had ever been unfaithful. He always had a reason for every single thing I brought up. Hushed phone conversations were because of a surprise getaway he was planning for us. Late nights at work were because he was busy, or they were short-staffed or preparing for trial. Random scribbled phone numbers were explained as a colleague's number he scratched down during a meeting and forgot to put in his desk. There was always a reason. Always an excuse. And Matt never got rattled by my concerns.

But, for weeks after I'd raised one, he would get jabs in toward me in other ways. In casual conversations with the kids, he'd mention my "crazy ideas." Or talk to me about my "wild imagination." Always comments to make me seem or feel crazy. The sad part is that they often worked. I did feel crazy most of the time. I never knew why my gut was screaming at me that something was off, but it was, and I could find no proof of why. What I saw, what I thought, and what I felt never lined up. Just like how I'd spent most of my life.

All those mixed emotions and questioning my sanity continued until the moment I found proof—the phone call and the red, lacey thong. During that time, Matt had been working late most evenings for several weeks, not coming home until one or two in the morning some nights. A couple of times, the scent of alcohol actually pulled me from sleep. I convinced myself that, once again, I was being insecure, crazy, irrational. I applied all the labels Matt had given me over the years to myself. I was in a constant battle within myself those weeks because my gut was screaming at me that something was off. Matt was more distant than usual, but I tried to convince myself it was because he was working so hard. He was tired. He was overwhelmed. Instead of being crazy, today was the day I found the proof. The proof was in the pocket of my robe and in the phone call I just took.

Former me goes back into the kitchen.

"I put all of your things and some coffee in the car," younger me says in as even a voice as possible.

He pulls younger me into a hug and kisses me gently on the lips. "Thanks, hon. I love you. I'll call later, but it's going to be another late night."

"You sick, sick bastard!" I shout and punch him in the back. He breaks his embrace and turns slightly to look behind him. "I hope you can hear me, asshole! How dare you try to convince me that I was crazy!"

He shudders and walks to the door. His hand is on the knob when former me speaks. "Oh. Yvonne called and said that you left some papers with her last night. She's leaving them at the front desk of the Windmere Hotel for you. She said you might need them for this morning's meeting."

I can't help but smile. He knows that I know. He pauses with his hand on the doorknob for a moment. I study my younger self and remember how my heart pounded as I waited on his reaction, knowing I'd caught him in a lie.

He glances over his shoulder and smiles, "Oh, great, thanks. I must have left them in the conference room or something, and she picked them up. But, yes, I do need them for my meeting. Love you. Gotta run!"

This moment imprinted on my soul because the million little lies he'd told me over the years finally came perfectly into view. I finally knew that I wasn't crazy. I wasn't imagining things. I finally had clarity that he was a liar. He could look me dead in the eye and lie to me, without missing a beat.

I am with my younger self the rest of that day into the next morning. Younger me drives to the bank and opens an account in my name only, emptying half of our savings into it. That afternoon former me finds an apartment for Hanson, Avery, and me and makes an appointment to sign a lease the next afternoon. I had finally decided I was done with him. With his lies. With his moods. With his treatment of Hanson. This was the first time in forever, I could see it all so clearly. I had a solid plan to leave. I would go to my doctor's appointment in the morning, sign the lease in the afternoon, pick the kids up from school, and take them to our new place. I knew it'd be hard, especially for them, but we'd make it work. I didn't need a man, like my mother did, to survive. I would figure it out. I would make it work.

The next morning, my younger self gets the news from the doctor that changed everything. Made me realize I was stuck—at least for a while, anyway. I was pregnant. Once the doctor utters the words, and before the first tear can fall down my younger self's cheek, I'm yanked away from the past, back to the funeral home.

CHAPTER NINETEEN
NOW

When my mother rises, Elliot, her newest man who I only met twice in person, grabs her hand as if to ask whether he should accompany her to say goodbye. Without breaking her stride, she pulls away and ambles toward the front of the room. Everyone holds a collective breath, waiting to see what's about to unfold. My mother's tendency toward dramatics is well known among everyone in the room.

When she first reaches the casket, she just stands there, looking my body up and down, finally settling her gaze on my face. Her expression is blank, as lifeless as the one worn by my corpse.

Finally, she speaks in a whisper so soft that I must lean in closer to hear. "Oh, baby girl. What happened to you? Did you do this to yourself?"

I answer, even though she can't hear me. "I'd never leave my kids. I'm not you." My last sentence is filled with venom, and I hope that I'm speaking the truth. I didn't kill myself, did I? Why can't I remember how I died? It's as though I can remember all these other details about my life but draw a blank whenever I try to recall my final moments here on earth. Would I have committed suicide? I shake my head, trying to clear the thoughts. No way would I do such a thing. As I told my mother, I'd never leave my kids.

"I don't even know what to say. I'm not sure how to say goodbye to my child." Tears begin to slip past the corners of her eyes.

My questions are replaced by anger bubbling in my chest. "Really, Mom? You can't say goodbye? You've always been the master at leaving me behind. It seems like it'd be second nature to you by now." I'm flooded with memories of the hundreds of times she's done just that, leaving me crying, begging for her to come back, questioning why my mother doesn't love me. I want her to hurt. I want her to realize all the ways she screwed up throughout the years. What a terrible mother she's been.

She wipes her eyes as shuddered breaths escape her. "I know I've made a lot of mistakes, but I did the best I could. I've always loved you."

I know on some level that's true. In her own sick, twisted way, she has always loved me. It's never been healthy, or enough, but she's loved me more than anyone else. Besides herself, that is. She's always been number one.

It's as if her admission makes her remember who she really is, and that's not someone who takes the blame for anything. "But you weren't perfect either. You always made sure to let me know, loud and clear, that I wasn't good enough for you. That I was always second fiddle to Lillian. You always judged me for my choices, but you didn't make the best ones yourself."

I'm stunned. Even with my death, she has to try to make me out to be the bad guy by pointing out my failures and faults. She doesn't even know I can hear her, yet here she stands spewing accusations at my dead body. What a sick, crazy woman!

"Regardless of what you thought of me, I made sure you had a good life. That you were provided for and taken care of. Everything I did, I did for you," she says, no longer whispering.

I brace myself for what's coming. She's been so restrained up until now but, that's about to change. The tone of her voice, the reddened face, the tears building are all signs of the show to come. She's got a full room, a captive audience, with all eyes on her performance.

My attention gets pulled across the room as Matt and Vera come back from the bathroom. She walks next to him, eyes downcast, and holding his hand. Both she and Matt have been crying, their eyes swollen and red. Matt takes a seat at the edge of the room and pulls Vera onto his lap. She buries her face in his chest and plops her thumb in her mouth, something she hasn't done for years. My baby girl. I will never again be the one to comfort her or help dry her tears.

The wailing from my mother snaps my attention, and everyone else's in the room, back to her. "I did the best I could. Why wasn't it ever enough for you? Why wasn't I ever good enough in your eyes? I tried. I tried and tried and tried." She reaches forward and strokes my cheek. I laugh. I can't ever remember my mother touching me so tenderly. Affection was saved for her men, not me.

Sobs wrack her body. Tears flow down her cheeks, dripping onto me in the casket. Her wails grow louder. Elliot slowly makes his way toward her, rubbing his chin as though he has no idea what to do. Like most of the people in my mother's life.

He's almost to her when she screams, "Oh God! Why didn't you ever love me?" She throws herself over my body, clutching it in her arms.

Elliot quickens his pace and tries to pull her away, but she clings harder to me. I laugh, imagining her tipping the casket over and spilling my body onto the floor. But then I remember Vera and Avery. That would be awful for them to see. My laughter becomes a prayer that she pulls herself together, if for no other reason than my children.

Elliot tries to get her to hear him past her wails. "Linda, sweetheart. Let's sit, okay?" He tries again to pull her away from me. When that doesn't work, he rubs her back. "It's okay, honey. It's okay."

Every eye in the room is glued to the theatrics. It wouldn't be as entertaining if everyone in the room didn't know the truth. Her history. Our story. But seeing as how everyone here is family, they see right through her broken-hearted act.

After what feels like a lifetime, my mom lifts herself off my corpse and clutches onto Elliot for dear life. Her hands shake, and knees tremble. He takes her by the arm to guide her away. She pulls away one more time.

"My baby. My baby. I can't say goodbye. I can't let her go."

As if on cue, her legs give out, and she falls to the floor before Elliot can catch her. She curls into a fetal position, which is quite impressive for a woman of her age, and sobs. Mr. Pearson walks determinedly toward her. Matt puts Vera on the chair next to him, where she starts to cry again and makes his way toward my mother. Aunt Lill sighs loudly and leaves the room. Avery frowns and bites her lip, confused about whether she should follow Lillian or step forward to offer help with my mother. She's stuck to her seat in indecision. I sit next to her to distance myself as much as possible from the drama.

After several attempts, the three men finally get my mother to her feet and have to practically hold her up. They make their way to the front row of chairs, where they slowly ease her down. Elliot sits next to her and pulls her into an embrace. Matt returns to Vera, who promptly resumes her thumb-sucking, which quiets her cries. Mr. Pearson kneels to talk to my mother and Elliot.

"What can I do to help you, ma'am?"

Elliot raises his eyebrows and turns to Mom, not daring to speak on her behalf.

"I need to lie down again. I can't do this. I feel like I'm going to vomit. Or pass out."

"Of course, ma'am. Let's get you to my office." He rises and holds his hand out to her.

Elliot and Mr. Pearson spend the next several minutes slowly making their way toward the back of the room with my mother. She stops every few feet to steady herself and sob. Everyone tries not to stare, but it's impossible. Finally, they exit the doors at the back of the room, and again, quiet falls like a blanket.

My mother was never abusive, physically, at least. Mentally and emotionally was another story entirely. Of course, I didn't realize the full extent of it or recognize her treatment of me as abuse until I was an adult. Until some of the same patterns with her repeated in my marriage. As a child, though, I accepted her behavior as normal for the most part.

Mom has always been one of the most manipulative people I've ever met. She is skilled at twisting any situation with me, her men, her friends, into her being the victim and the other person being the bad guy. I don't think I've ever heard her offer a genuine apology. Her "I'm sorry's" are always surrounded by hundreds of excuses as to why she acted the way she did or said the things she said. And, someone else is always, always to blame. Nothing is ever her fault.

As a child, I constantly felt guilty. Like it was my fault Mom's relationships didn't last. Or that she was sad. Or that she didn't love me or want to spend time with me. She constantly reminded me what a burden I was to her. If she couldn't go out with friends, it was my fault because I "needed" her. She couldn't work and needed all her relationships to provide for me. Everything, from the mundane, like being tired, to the extraordinary, like needing to move again or me needing to stay with Aunt Lill, was somehow my fault.

When she'd get angry, I knew to stay out of her way, because that's when the venomous words and name-calling would spew out of her mouth. Usually, she was restrained, but not when she was pissed. Then, I'd be called every name in the book from whore to little bitch to good-for-nothing brat. I had no idea how much all of this affected my perception of myself until I started dating. I found myself being drawn to man after man who had the exact same view of me as my mother. Which is probably why Matt was so easily able to sweep me off my feet.

In the beginning, he seemed so different than anyone I'd ever been in a relationship with. He was witty, charming, and affectionate. Any time he'd spontaneously touch me, my entire body would tense. I wasn't even aware of it until he pointed it out. I'd had so little affection in my life that it felt unnatural, foreign. He was also so complimentary, which I desperately craved. He'd always take the time to tell me I was beautiful and smart. And he'd apologize quickly if he ever hurt my feelings or we had an argument. He was like a breath of fresh air. Until him, I didn't realize how messed up my childhood had been.

I'm pulled out of my memories and back to the funeral home when Aunt Lill storms back in the room and sits next to Avery again. Matt rises, carrying Vera in his arms, and walks toward them. After only a little resistance from Vera, he places her on Aunt Lill's lap and makes his way toward the front of the room.

This ought to be good. Disappointment floods me along with the swirl of colors and the whooshing sound in my mind. I hope I don't miss hearing what Matt has to say.

CHAPTER TWENTY
THEN

W hen I come to, I'm confused as to where I am. I'm sitting in a car next to my former self, driving on unfamiliar roads. I look around the car, trying to figure out where and when I am. It's not until my younger self speaks that I grasp where we're headed.

"Hi! I'm Mackenzie. Your daughter," younger me says with a shaky voice. "No! No! No! Get it together, Mack! We're almost there."

We're on the way to my father's house. I was two the last time I saw him and have zero memory of him. I finally coaxed his name out of my mom when I was sixteen, but she had filled my head with so many horrible things by then that I had no desire to meet him. Although I often fantasized about who he was and that he'd come whisk me away to a new life. One where I mattered. One where I was wanted.

Matt encouraged me to try to find him early in our marriage, so I did some internet searches. I was finally able to track him down via social media. I became almost obsessed with piecing together details of his life. He was married to a beautiful woman, and they had four kids, aged sixteen to four. Two girls. Two boys. When I first learned that I had half-siblings, I wanted to find them immediately and get to know them. I'd always wanted a sister or brother. But then reality hit me. I'd be a stranger to them. My father didn't want me as a part of his life. Trying to connect with any of them was only likely to cause me more heartbreak, more pain.

So, instead, I observed from afar, although Matt referred to it as stalking. My father and his perfect little family lived about three hours north of where I'd lived my entire life. Three hours! And he never bothered to have contact with me. At first, this realization crushed me. Then, it pissed me off.

This time I'm re-visiting is the day I decided to heed Matt's advice. While he was at work, I loaded Hanson in the car and decided I was going to pay dear old dad and his new little family a visit. I found his address and employer thanks to his wife's oversharing on social media. I, of course, didn't tell Matt of my plans. He would've made fun of me or tried to talk me out of it. There was no need for him to know.

The drive goes so quickly because former me is fueled by anger and nervousness. Hanson has fallen asleep in the backseat. Younger me clenches my jaw, imagining all the possible scenarios for meeting the family. My younger self mutters quietly, trying to sort out the best option for introductions—something I always used to do when I was stressed.

"Walk to the front door, ring the bell, and when he opens the door, I'll throw myself into his arms and tell him I'm his daughter. He'll hug me back and welcome me into his home and life. Or, he'll push me away and tell me to get the hell off his property. Or his wife will open the door and stare at me with shock and confusion as I explain who I am. She'll welcome me in to meet my siblings, saying she wished she'd known about me sooner. Or she'll slam the door in my face and tell me never to come back again." Younger me slams my fist onto the steering wheel a few times.

"Think, Mack! Think!" younger me shouts. "Okay, how about this? I'll show up at my father's engineering firm. His secretary will call him, saying only that Ms. Bartholomew is outside to see him. He'll have no idea who I am because my last name is different now that I'm married. He'll walk out of his office, instantly recognize me and invite me in, closing the door behind him. He'll sit behind his desk and ask me how I've been. He'll tell me how much he's missed me and how he's wondered for years what my life has been like. It will be like talking to an old friend, and the conversation will come easy for both of us. He'll invite me to come to dinner with his family and meet my siblings. Or, as soon as he realizes who I am, he'll call security to escort me from the building. Damn it! None of this will work. What do I do?" younger me shouts and runs a hand through my hair.

"Calm down, Mackenzie! You're wasting precious energy on something that doesn't even matter. Stop getting so worked up." I say to my younger self, and, for a moment, I wonder if the words penetrated as younger me sits quietly studying the road ahead.

"Okay, I got it. I'll wait outside of his house until he comes home from work and walk up to his car as he's getting out and slap him across the face. I'll question him about all the things I've wondered over the years, like how dare you walk out of my life! Why didn't you ever come see me? Why don't you care that I exist? You're a bastard! I hate you! Then, I'll get back in my car and drive home. I'll never tell Matt." My younger self takes a deep, shuddering breath.

"That's not going to happen. And, if it did, it wouldn't help. Mother's a liar. Don't believe a word she's told you about him."

The car pulls onto Larkin Way, his street, and, even though I know the outcome, butterflies creep into my throat from my belly. I pat my younger self on the arm, hoping to help quell some of the anxiety. Younger me slows down to search for his house, 7725. Hanson's soft snores ring out a nice melody that I'm not sure I took the time to appreciate back when this happened the first time. Now, the sound soothes me.

"Wow!" younger me says, taking in the neighborhood.

My father and his new family live in an extremely nice development with huge homes and nicely manicured lawns. His house is one of the biggest on the street. The car slows to a crawl as younger me approaches. His three younger kids are playing a game of tag in the front yard with some neighbor kids. Tiffany stands talking animatedly with a woman with bleach blonde hair, each holding a coffee mug in their hands. The kids' laughter sneaks in through the closed car windows. Tiffany glances away from her friend and meets my younger self's eyes. She breaks into a huge smile and waves. Younger me gives a half-wave, trying to decide what to do—stop and meet my father and siblings or drive away without any answers.

Younger me glances in the rearview at Hanson sleeping and slows the car, deciding to stop because my son deserves to know his family. I remembered all of this so clearly that I can't believe I'd forgotten what happens next. As soon as I see my younger self's eyes leave the road, though, it all comes back.

"Stop! Stop now!" I scream with all my might.

Younger me must've somehow heard at least a whisper of my voice from this alternate dimension I'm stuck in. My former self's eyes shift back towards the front of the car right as a flash of red flies in front of it. Tiffany's scream fills the air, and she runs towards me as everyone else stands frozen, looking on in horror. Younger me slams on the brakes just in time to miss hitting my eight-year-old little brother, Cameron, who ran into the street after his ball.

Reliving all of this now, I wonder if my younger self did, in fact, hear my voice. It played out almost exactly the same when it happened the first time around. What made me stop if it wasn't my own voice screaming at me?

Cameron picks up the ball and waves, oblivious to the fact that he was inches away from being hit. Tiffany continues running until she grabs him in her arms, crying and yelling at him at the same time. She rushes to the window, and younger me lowers it.

"Thank you so much for stopping. I thought for sure you weren't going to…" Tiffany clutches a hand to her chest as tears spill past her eyelids. She pulls Cameron close again and kisses him on the top of the head. "Anyway, Cam, tell the nice lady thank you."

"Uh, thanks!" he says, but his brow scrunches in confusion as to why he is thanking someone for not running over him.

"Thank God you were going so slowly. Are you trying to find a certain house number? If so, I can help you," she asks, smiling. Cameron pulls away from her, back into the yard, to resume his game.

It takes a moment for younger me to speak. "Ummm, no. I was just admiring the beautiful neighborhood and houses. My husband and I are thinking of moving to the area, and this seems like the perfect place."

"Tell her who you are. Give them a chance to accept you," I say, knowing that younger me won't listen, but figuring it's worth a shot.

"Oh, it is. You'd love it here. And so would your little boy." She leans in to get a closer look at him. "I'm Tiffany Sanders." She extends her hand.

"I'm Kenzie." Younger me takes her hand. It was soft and warm, like a mother's should be.

"C'mon Mack! Just tell her the truth!"

"Well, nice to meet you, Kenzie. If you and your husband end up settling here, please do come by. I'd love to get to know you."

Tears fill my younger self's eyes because I knew in that moment that I couldn't wreck this nice woman's life. Hurt her kids. Disrupt everything. "I sure will. I'm so sorry about everything."

"No need to be sorry. Thank you!"

"I've got to go," younger me says, needing to leave before the tears spill past my eyelids.

"This is your last chance. Don't go. Open the door and tell her who you are." Passion fills my voice as tears burn my eyes. I wish my younger self would listen and give Tiffany and my father a chance.

Tiffany steps back and waves as the car pulls away. I felt more alone than I'd ever felt before as I made the drive back to my life with no father. A mother that didn't want me. No siblings and my own little family with Matt. I never told him about my visit to my father, Calvin Sanders. That same sense of isolation and despair fills me now. Why didn't I stop? I could've had a whole different life if I'd just been brave enough to stop.

Some things can apparently never be undone. I'll never have that chance now. This journey back and forth in time is a stark reminder of all my missed opportunities and times where I should've made a different choice.

There's no time to ponder this, though, because the lights and noise return before we're even out of my father's neighborhood. My visit to this time and place is over.

CHAPTER TWENTY-ONE
NOW

Back at the funeral home, Matt makes his way forward as Vera tries to relax against Aunt Lillian. It's amazing that, after everything that's happened, I still find him incredibly handsome. He has thick, wavy light brown hair and the bluest, dreamiest eyes. Although I realized over the years that they tended to change color with his moods. When they turned gray, I knew to steer clear of him. I wish Hanson would've been astute enough to do the same.

He stands by the head of the casket and stares at my body. Is he glad I'm gone? Does he feel like he can finally move on with his life, without me, without Hanson? Just him and the girls—his perfect little world. We were, of course, going our separate ways anyway, but death is more final. It gives him absolute and complete control—something he craves. Had I lived, we would've had to share custody of the girls and, thus, still communicate with each other. Death provides a clean break. Sure, the girls will have some emotional stuff to work through, but he'll make sure they get the help they need.

Did he want control badly enough to have killed me? He's full of rage and more than capable of doing so, but did he?

There's a hint of relief in his face, but there's also something else lingering there. I can't quite tell what it is. Perhaps a question. He clears his throat a couple of times as though he's about to say something but stops short of allowing the words to come out. Aunt Lill loudly sighs, and I turn to her. She's studying Matt closely, surely for any sign of guilt he might display. Or anything he may do to alleviate her suspicions.

At first, like the rest of us, she was totally enamored with Matt. But, over time, she grew wary of him, even before I opened up to her about the truth of our marriage. His indiscretions. His treatment of Hanson. Of me. Toward the end, I think she would've gladly killed him with her own two hands, seeing how much pain and devastation he'd caused. She would be happy to see him locked up for a very long time for his "crimes," his cruelty.

Finally, Matt leans down close like he's telling me a secret. Perhaps he'll apologize for everything, tell me how sorry he is that things turned out this way. Him taking a morsel of ownership would be a bit of a relief. But, only a bit.

"You know, it didn't have to end like this," he whispers. "Thank you for my daughters. They'll miss you, but we'll be fine."

God, how can he be so callous? What a narcissistic, self-consumed bastard! The only good he can see in our sixteen years of marriage is the fact that I gave him two daughters? No thanks given for putting up with his shit throughout the years? For standing by his side as he built a successful career, made a name for himself while he screwed every woman he could get his hands on? No acknowledgment that I stayed much longer than I should have. Zero mention of any love he once held for me. Maybe he did kill me. That seems far more likely than me killing myself.

He takes a step back, then stops. He leans down close again and says with a smirk, "Just so you know, I'm done with Hanson. After today, I hope I never have to see that little shit again. He will not get one penny of my money; that's for damn sure."

"You bastard!" I shout and hit him in the chest. His hand flies to the spot where the punch landed. He grips his chest a moment while I continue to pound. "You're a sick, cruel man. How did I ever love you?"

With his hand still resting where my punches landed, he begins blinking rapidly. It takes me only a second to realize what he's doing. He's trying to make it look like he has tears in his eyes. How many times had he done that with me when I thought he was displaying genuine emotion? How did it take me so long to see what a chameleon he has always been?

"You're a damn liar!" I shout and punch him once more in the chest.

After he's satisfied that he appears sad enough, he walks back to Aunt Lill to get Vera who has fallen asleep, with her thumb still in her mouth. He leans down as though to take her away from Lillian's arms, but she shakes her head firmly and mouths the word "sleeping" to him while shooing her hand. His posture goes rigid, and he stands there for a moment as if contemplating putting up a fight. He must decide it wouldn't go too well with his role of "grieving husband" though and goes to sit at the other end of the row, alone.

I wish he could feel the full extent of my punches. That I could hurt him as much as he's hurt me over the years. Make him feel the same pain he's caused Hanson. Thank God, I was smart enough to take out a separate life insurance policy in Hanson's name only. I always knew that if something happened to me, he wouldn't provide for my son. I chuckle, remembering when I believed that Matt thought of Hanson as our son. How gullible and desperate I was.

Matt lowers his gaze to the ground to give the appearance that's he's distraught, broken, crying. But, it's all bullshit, just like most of our marriage. He's ecstatic, relieved to be done with both of us.

The flowers, the people, the sounds all meld together in my mind. It's time for me to go back again.

CHAPTER TWENTY-TWO
THEN

Avery and younger me are in Dr. Flanders' office for one of her yearly check-ups. I wrack my brain to figure out why I would be brought back here. Did anything tragic or impactful happen at a doctor's appointment with Avery that I need to revisit? I can't come up with anything. The doctor finishes his check-up and leaves the room. While Avery is getting dressed, former me pulls out the phone. I peer over my younger self's shoulder to see who the text is going to. It's to Matt, asking him to throw the lasagna in the oven. What a strange place and time to come back to. Although it is a bit refreshing to be able to visit a normal day in my past rather than one with heartbreak and heated emotions.

I enjoy listening to the chatter between Avery and my former self on the ride home. My chest tightens—I'm never going to be able to have a heart to heart with my daughter again. God, I'm going to miss her. For now, I watch her every move, cherishing each one. Perhaps coming back to today is a gift—a bit of pleasantness amidst the chaos. The only break in the conversation is when former me calls Matt to make sure he put the lasagna in the oven. His voice fills the car.

"Sure did and set the timer for an hour. It smells delicious."

Too quickly, we arrive back at the house. I was enjoying the time with just Avery. I could do with never being around Matt again. The funeral home is more than enough. As former me heads straight to the kitchen, I remember what day this is. One of the many times that I was slapped in the face with Matt's dishonesty over the smallest, most insignificant things. I breathe deeply. There's no smell of lasagna cooking, just the normal household smells. Younger me opens the oven, then the refrigerator.

Former me calls Matt into the kitchen. "I thought you said you started dinner," pointing to the pan sitting in the fridge.

He looks at it and then back at younger me. With a straight face and a shrug, he says matter-of-factly, "I did."

My former self's jaw drops open in surprise. "Ummm, no. You didn't. It's still in the refrigerator. Right there. Not in the oven."

"I put it in the oven," he says and turns to walk out of the room.

Younger me reaches in and touches the pan to see if it is warm. It's not—it's ice cold. "What the hell, Matt? Why are you lying to me? I can see with my own eyes that you didn't put it in the oven. Why won't you just admit it? Why this big act?" younger me shouts with hands shaking in anger.

He raises his right hand. "I swear to God, I put it in the oven. I don't know why you're screaming at me and acting like a crazy person. Your accusations are hurtful."

With that, he leaves the room. Younger me puts the lasagna in the oven and stews in anger while it cooks. I remember the questions that bombarded me. I chuckle. No wonder I remember them so clearly— they are ones that played on repeat in my mind for years over so many scenarios. How dare he lie to me and then twist it around to make me feel like I did something wrong? And why in the hell would he lie about something so incredibly stupid, to begin with? And he accuses me of acting like a crazy person? Only a crazy person would lie about something so trivial, something I could see with my own two eyes was a lie. I stay in the kitchen with younger me while the lasagna cooks and reflect back. Things are so much clearer now. I wish I could've seen then what I know to be the truth now.

My relationship with Matt deteriorated slowly, so much so that it was hard to pinpoint an exact time or instance in which I knew our marriage was bad. When did he go from charming, witty, and engaging to manipulative, condescending, and arrogant? At first, I noticed small things like him acting like a completely different person at home than in his office. If I went to work to meet him for lunch or attended an office function with him, I felt like I was with a stranger. He became someone I didn't know. If I said anything to him about it, he'd laughingly tell me I was crazy or imagining things. At some unknown point in time, I must've decided that he was right. Over time, I made sure to avoid any interaction with him in his work environment because it left me in a state of confusion and just feeling yucky afterward.

The lying started in the same manner. Lies about things that didn't even matter, like putting the lasagna in the oven. Lies that made me question his sanity at first and then eventually my own. The sound of dishes being slammed onto the table snap me back to the kitchen.

"Guys, dinner," younger me yells once the lasagna is on the table. Hanson and Avery come, but no Matt. He told the kids to tell me he wasn't hungry. At the time, I was still so pissed off that I didn't care. Now, I'm grateful that he didn't come. I get to sit at the table and enjoy a dinner with two of my children, even though they can't see me. I love listening to their laughter and seeing the joy in my younger self's eyes when I'm with them. I hope they know how much I loved them. How much I still do, even though I'm gone. I'm glad to see that I had moments of happiness despite everything with Matt.

Once the meal is finished, the kids scurry off, and younger me slowly clears the table and does the dishes. For some reason, I'm still here.

After this night, I received the silent treatment from Matt that lasted for over a week. He wouldn't speak to me. He wouldn't stay in the same room with me. He slept on the couch. He didn't interact with me again until I apologized for our misunderstanding. He made sure to let me know how deeply hurt he had been by my anger, never taking ownership of his lie or his behavior afterward.

The same scenario repeated itself hundreds of times throughout the years. He'd tell a little lie that I'd catch him red-handed in. He'd pretend like he'd done nothing wrong and that it was me who was imagining things. If I got upset, he'd pout and ignore me then, over time, the kids, too. Until I'd apologize so that our lives could return to normal. Now, I realize how crazy the whole cycle was, but, at the time, I started to actually question my sanity. I was convinced that perhaps I wasn't seeing things correctly. Or maybe he hadn't lied at all, it was just my mind inventing these whole scenarios.

And then there were the big lies. The ones that hurt the most. His other women. Yvonne was the first woman with which I had proof, but I'd had my suspicions for years. And then, of course, Chloe. At least when he was caught cheating on me, he expressed remorse. Although it never felt genuine. His words never matched his reactions. No matter how well he said the right words in his apologies, I never truly felt like he was sorry or that he had any regrets. He was only sorry that he got caught.

He was never able to keep up the act for long, either. The first couple of weeks after he'd get caught, he would send flowers, take me out to dinner, cry, and tell me how much he loved and needed me. Tell me how wrong he was. But usually, after about the third week, it'd get twisted around to somehow be my fault that he'd cheated. If I hadn't "been so frigid" or I had paid him more attention, he wouldn't have had to seek out affection elsewhere. If I'd made our marriage a priority, then he wouldn't have to find other women for companionship. I learned, over time, that unless I wanted to be berated, insulted, and verbally assaulted by him, I shouldn't bring the affairs up once that three-week mark passed. Did I forgive him? No. But, the only way I could keep from feeling crazy, wondering if it was somehow my fault, was to not discuss it with him. I figured that if I was dumb enough to stay, then I shouldn't dwell in the past.

"Why did you stay? " I shout as anger pulses through me. Why couldn't I see how sick this all was when it mattered?

We tried marriage counseling a couple of times over the years, but, again, it was like the work scenario with Matt. We'd get into the room with the counselor and a different man, one I had never even met, would emerge painting an entirely false picture of himself, our marriage, our life. I'd try to discuss the realities of our life, but he'd look at me like I was delusional, inventing problems out of nowhere. Again, I'd leave the sessions more confused than when I'd walked in the door, questioning who in the hell Matt really was. Was he the man I knew as my husband? Was he the person he was at work? Was he the man that showed up in our counseling sessions? Was he none of them? Was he all of them? Honestly, it scared me. How little of the real him I felt like I knew. How little of the real him he even knew. Now, I'm certain that he was all of those people and none of them at the same time. He's a chameleon, becoming who he needs to be in any given situation. There is no real Matt. Only a version of him that best suits his needs.

The few times I tried to leave, I saw the side of him that was full of rage and vengeance. Like the time after he and Hanson got into the physical altercation when Hanson was twelve. I wanted our marriage to be over. I'd been through enough, as had Hanson. His emotional abuse was one thing, but when he laid hands on my son, something in me snapped, and I was just done. Then, adding to that was the fact that Children's Services got involved and was investigating our family. I would not lose any of my children for his crazy behavior. Not to mention all of the affairs that Hanson brought to my attention—some I'd suspected, but others caught me completely off guard.

Hanson and I went to stay with my mother because she lived closer to Hanson's school than Aunt Lillian, even though I hated going back there. I had to get out of our house immediately and try to come up with logical next steps. Somehow, through the course of the two months that we were with my mother and children's services was investigating, Matt convinced the caseworkers and my mother that I was mentally unstable and needed help. That the fight between him and Hanson was because of lies I'd told, that I'd somehow provoked them. He expressed remorse to the caseworker about the whole situation and agreed to attend anger management classes but insisted that I get help for my "depression" and "drinking," both of which played a huge role in the chaos in our family. Convincing the caseworker of this was one thing, but my mother believing it, too, was the ultimate betrayal. Yes, I'd had bouts of depression throughout the years, but no more than many people. I had taken anti-depressants for years that stabilized me. Other than a bad day now and again, I was okay. Well, at least until the whole investigation. As far as drinking, I would have an occasional glass of wine in the evenings or a drink with dinner when we went out, but I hadn't been drunk in years. Matt made it sound like I was a daily drinker who couldn't function without alcohol.

As he was convincing everyone around me that I was an insane drunk, he'd threaten me that if I left him, I'd never see Avery or Vera again. He wouldn't let me see them or talk to them the entire two months I lived with my mother. He held them as ransom for me to come home. I begged him time and time again to let me talk to them, see them, but it was as if he believed his own lies. That I was a danger to my children.

It was the darkest two months of my life. Thank God I had Hanson, who knew the truth. I tried to shield him from Matt's deception, but he was astute enough to pick up on the implications when he was questioned by the caseworker. He realized that Matt had fed them a line of bullshit. Hanson tried his best to set the record straight, but it was written off as him having an unhealthy, enabling relationship with me.

In the middle of the memories, the kitchen begins to fade away— my signal that I'm going to a different time again. I expect to be back in the funeral home, but instead, I'm at my mother's house. Younger me is lying in bed, in the dark, with tears waterfalling. It's as though remembering this time brought me back here. I sit on the bed next to my younger self.

"You're okay. You need to get healthy so you can go home. Your girls need you." I whisper the words I needed to hear back then. I was unable to eat or sleep during those dreadful months.

The door creaks open, and Hanson tiptoes across the room.

He sits on the bed and pats my younger self's arm. "Mom?"

Younger me tries to answer in a normal voice but fails miserably. "Yes, hon?"

"Let's go home," he says.

"Hanson, he hurt you. I can't subject you to that."

"I'm okay, Mom. I'll be alright. But I miss home and the girls. You need the girls, and they need you. Let's just go home," he says and laughs. "Plus, Grandma is going to drive both of us nuts."

Younger me laughs despite the tears. "No doubt about that. But are you sure?"

"I'm sure, Mom."

Younger me sits and pulls him close—my boy in a man's body. I know now what a huge sacrifice this was for Hanson. I'm filled with rage at myself that I let him sacrifice himself for me.

Alive me called the caseworker the next day to tell her our plans. I was ordered to undergo treatment for alcoholism and depression as part of the condition for me to be allowed to be around my children again. Matt had already attended a three-day anger management course and was supposedly deemed stable.

Matt welcomed me back with open arms, saying he was glad I was going to get the help I needed. I don't think I was crazy before that situation, but, afterward, perhaps I was. Seeing how well he manipulated everyone around him, including me, confused me. More than anything, it chilled me to the core. Now, it just fills me with rage. At Matt. At the situation. At myself.

I'm carried away from my conversation with Hanson, this time back to the funeral home.

CHAPTER TWENTY-THREE
NOW

E veryone fidgets in their seats, and no one steps forward after
Matt's visit. Avery twirls her hair around and around her finger
as she always does when she's nervous. Poor thing is twirling so fast,
I'm afraid she's going to wind it into a knot. Finally, she pulls her hand
free and walks to the casket. She glances at her father as she passes by
him, her lips drawing down into a frown. He's so consumed by playing
the part of grieving husband, he doesn't seem to notice.

She stands by the casket and bends to kiss my cold cheek. My
sweet, sweet Avery. My death is going to hit her the hardest. She's
already at such a tender age where life is overwhelming and confusing;
this is only going to make it worse. Thank God, she's so close to Matt
—perhaps that will help her get through all of this okay. But, the
cutting. How will he get her the help she needs if he isn't aware that
she's been hurting herself? If she was able to keep it hidden from me,
he'll never find out unless she confesses to him.

"Mom, I miss you so, so much already. I kind of feel like you can
still hear me, even though that sounds crazy," she laughs, but there's no
happiness in it. Tears fill her eyes.

"I can hear you, baby girl; I'm right here." I put my arm around
her, hoping, somehow, she hears me in her soul. She edges slightly

closer to me and, maybe it's wishful thinking, but I must believe she knows I'm here.

"Hanson told me everything. I know what happened."

What is she talking about? Did he tell her more after their walk, or is she talking about the infidelity? I search the room for Hanson, hoping to be able to read his expression and figure out what exactly he told Avery. He's not in the room, as I expected. Avery's voice draws me back to her.

"I'm so sorry that I didn't know what was going on. I feel so bad, like I chose Dad over you every time he did something, and I didn't see the truth." Tears waterfall down her cheeks. She sniffles and continues. "I hate him for hurting you."

"Oh, Ave. It's not your fault. He's your dad. You're supposed to love him. He loves you."

"Mostly, though, I just hate myself. For being so blind. So trusting. So gullible. I've been going along, living life in my own little world, blind to everything else. I mean, I knew things weren't good between you guys. But I had no idea how bad they were even after everything there at the end. I'm so stupid."

She tightens her grip on the side of the casket and sobs.

"Don't say that, Avery. You're not stupid. You are so kind and loving that you only see the best in people. Don't ever change."

She removes her hands and leans in close to me to whisper, "I think he killed you."

What? He couldn't have. Could he? My dead body lies only a few feet away. Of course, he could have—I died somehow. That makes more sense than me killing myself.

"Oh, Avery!" I wrap my arm tightly around her.

Her sobs only grow louder. Despite my desire for her to hear my voice, sense my presence, it seems she can't or, if she can, she finds no comfort from it. I can tell she feels broken and very alone. Finally, Matt's pulled from his acting role enough to notice his daughter falling apart at the front of the room. He rushes towards her and pulls her into his arms.

"It's okay, Ave. I'm right here," he says.

She pushes away. "Get the hell away from me. I hate you. I hate you for what you did to Mom."

Matt's brow wrinkles with worry. It is not like Avery to have an outburst, cuss, or to throw phrases like "I hate you" around.

"What are you talking about?"

"Just leave me alone. It's your fault Mom's dead."

Every eye in the room is on the two of them. The room is silent, except for the ticking of the clock.

"What?" Matt flinches like he's been slapped.

"I. Know. What. You. Did. All. of it." Avery puts her hands on her hips, her face reddening with rage. "It's. Your. Fault. Mom's. Dead."

Before he has a chance to respond, she pushes past him and bursts out the doors into the front hallway of the funeral home.

Matt doesn't become speechless too often. He usually can turn everything into a joke and lighten a heavy situation with his charm. But, now, he's left standing with his mouth hanging open and no words to make the situation better. He scans the crowd and sees everyone staring at him. He shrugs his shoulders and fakes a laugh. He hesitates, seeming to ponder whether or not to take his seat or go after Avery. Aunt Lillian makes the decision for him. She rises and hands him Vera.

"I'll go after her. You stay here." There's no humor, no love, no lightness in Aunt Lill's tone.

I hate that there's now a rift between Avery and Matt, but how could I expect any different? That's part of the cost of the choices I made. There was no way anyone could come out of such a toxic relationship unscathed. But she's going to need her father to get through this pain. I don't want my death to make her crumble into a million tiny pieces.

I start to follow after Ave and Aunt Lill when the world beneath my feet sways. I'm going elsewhere. Again.

CHAPTER TWENTY-FOUR
THEN

This time, I'm transported back to our house. Younger me stands outside of Avery's door and knocks softly before nudging it open a crack. Avery lies on the bed, her cheeks blotchy from crying and her nose so stuffy that her voice is an octave lower than normal. Mounds of wadded up tissues surround her. Younger me throws a handful in the trash before sitting next to her on the bed.

"I wanted to come check on you. You need to eat."

"I can't." Her voice trembles.

"Talk to me, please. What's going through that pretty little head of yours?"

Sobs overtake her body. "I just don't understand. Why did Daddy leave? What's going on?"

Younger me struggles to find the right words that would hold some truth, yet not crush her view of Matt. "I don't think I can explain it so that it makes sense but, we're going through some things and need some time apart."

She sits quietly and spins her hair round and round her finger. "What things?" she finally asks quietly.

"Just grown-up stuff, hon. Not anything you need to worry about. I still love you with all my heart. So does your dad. Nothing could ever change that," former me says and pulls her hand from her hair. "I know this is hard. But I promise you that everything will be okay."

She pulls her hand away and resumes her twirling. "It's not okay. How can you say that? Okay means we're all here as a family."

While Avery and I have always had a close relationship, she was a big daddy's girl as well. She made sure to always spend time with both of us. If she and I went out for a day of fun, that evening, she would curl up on the couch with Matt to watch a sci-fi film. It was as though she wanted to make sure to share herself equally between the two of us. And Matt had been wrapped around her little finger from the moment she was born. He'd do anything she wanted if she looked at him with her big blue eyes. Not that she was a manipulator—that was a trait that wasn't in her nature.

As the middle child, she'd fully embraced the role of peacemaker. When problems were too big for her to fix, she collapsed into herself. My normally even-keeled, smiling daughter turned into an anxiety-ridden, crying, nervous child. She'd stop eating, not for attention, but because she simply couldn't enjoy food when life was falling apart. It broke my heart that she'd try to play therapist to me, and I can only assume also to Matt.

I tried so hard to keep her shielded from the truth because I didn't want to tarnish her sweet, optimistic, and loving attitude. I wanted her to still think of Matt as perfect, even though he was far from it. Although my feelings about Matt had changed over the years, I still loved the relationship he had with the girls. It was the type I'd always dreamed about having for myself as a child. One I never got the chance to have. I also didn't want her to have to face the ugly truths about life any sooner than necessary.

Perhaps I should've been more honest with her. This moment I'm witnessing would have been the perfect chance to do so, but again I failed. Another regret to carry with me to the grave. If I ever make it there and out of this hell hole of revisiting all my mistakes.

Former me stalls, struggling to find the right words. Younger me smooths the comforter as though it holds a magic formula to make Avery understand.

"I know it's confusing, and I wish I could tell you more. But it's all so complicated. I just want you to be a thirteen-year-old girl and hang out with your friends, enjoy cheer and not worry about your dad and me."

She slams her fist on the bed. "How can you say that? I can't just go on with my life, pretending like everything's not falling apart! I hate you and Dad being separated. I want our family to be okay. It doesn't make any sense."

Avery breaks down into sobs and allows younger me to pull her into a hug. I rub her back as younger me strokes her hair. My heart breaks as badly now as it did the first time. I wished then, as I do now, that I could make it okay for her. The only way I knew to do it back then was to forgive Matt, yet again, and sacrifice myself, my happiness.

"Tell her the truth. It will hurt, but she deserves to know. She's going to find out anyway," I say, wishing it weren't true.

The door opens, and Hanson walks in.

"What's wrong, Ave?"

Younger me tries to shoo him away. But, typical of Hanson, he refuses to leave.

Avery pulls away from me and turns to Hanson. "I just want Dad home. I don't know what's going on. None of this makes sense."

"Mom, you need to tell her the truth. Tell her why he's gone." He crosses his arms.

"Hanson, please," younger me begs.

"You're not being fair. She deserves the truth," he says, standing his ground.

I see now how correct he was. I should have listened.

"I explained that we're having some issues and need time apart," former me says, glaring at him to just leave it alone. Let it drop.

"Hanson, what's going on? Please tell me," Avery cries.

"Hanson…" younger me says firmly.

"This is bullshit! The secrets. The lies. The cover-ups that happen in this family. It makes me sick," he shouts. "Sorry, Ave. I guess you're too young to know the truth. My lips are sealed."

"Hanson, language," younger me says as Avery pushes out of bed and throws her pillows to the ground.

"For God's sake, he's right. Listen to Hanson!"

"I'm not a baby. I'm sick of you treating me like one. This is my family, too." She storms into the bathroom, slamming the door behind her.

"What the hell, Mom? Why do you keep this stuff from her? She's right about not being a baby. She needs to know the truth about her precious daddy. He's an asshole."

"You aren't helping anything right now. We all know how you feel about Matt. That's no big secret. But Avery adores her father. I can't destroy that for her."

"You aren't destroying anything. He does that on his own. All you do is enable his bullshit by keeping his secrets!" Hanson shouts.

Out of the mouths of babes. Why didn't I listen to what he said? Or see that he was speaking the truth?

"You don't understand, Hanson. You're not a parent. Things aren't always so black and white," younger me says as tears pool in my eyes. "My job is to protect all of you. Sometimes that means keeping the truth from you."

Hanson slowly shakes his head in disgust. "Something you do quite well."

"What does that mean? Please clarify."

His words hit like a punch to the gut. Now, I don't need any clarification. I know exactly what he meant. He was speaking the truth that I was too ignorant to accept.

"Never mind. It's not worth it. I'm going for a walk. I can't deal with this house of lies and secrets right now." He turns to walk away.

"Don't you dare. Get back here."

He doesn't even stop to say a word, just stomps off. A few moments later, the front door slams.

Younger me knocks on the bathroom door. "Ave, please come out and eat some dinner. Please."

"Just go away. I don't want to talk," she shouts.

"Leave them both alone. Give them space!" I shout, but younger me lingers outside the bathroom door.

"Mommy! Daddy's on the phone. He wants to talk to you," Vera's voice rings out from downstairs.

Younger me slowly descends the stairs, in no hurry to take his call. I shouldn't have gone to the phone because I'd already let him wreak enough havoc for one lifetime. But I did. I remember having my reasons, like not wanting him to show up at the house if I refused his call, along with a litany of others. But now, they all just seem like lame excuses made by a woman too weak to do what she needed to do to protect herself and her family.

I don't get to stick around long enough to witness the rest of this scenario play out, though. My house fades away as I wish my regrets and mistakes would.

CHAPTER TWENTY-FIVE
NOW

Everyone sits quietly after Avery's emotional outburst. I head out to see what's going on with her and make sure Aunt Lill found her. Although, what am I going to do about any of it? Nothing. Because I can't. I'm powerless to change anything now. In some ways, it feels as though I always have been.

Avery sits crying on a bench outside with Hanson on one side of her and Aunt Lillian on the other. Hanson has his arm wrapped protectively around her.

"What happened, Avery?" Aunt Lillian leans in close. Avery has her head buried in her hands, muffling her sobs.

She shakes her head but doesn't answer.

"Hanson. What's going on?"

"I'm not sure. I didn't see what happened," he mutters.

Aunt Lill's eyes narrow. "Come to think of it, I haven't seen you in the room at all. Where have you been?"

"Out here. I can't stand being in there with all that fake bs," he says with anger heavy in his voice.

"It's your mother for God's sake. You need to suck it up and get in there. This is one of your last chances to say goodbye." She uses the tone that always made me snap to attention and listen.

But Hanson isn't me. "Aunt Lill, don't start, or I'll leave. I already said my goodbyes. I'll come in for the funeral. But, otherwise, I'm good out here."

I've never seen her back down easily before, but this time, she does. She keeps her gaze on him for a moment before turning her attention back to Avery.

"Talk to me, please," she says and rubs her back like she used to do to me when I was young.

"I feel like I've lost everyone. Mom died, and I just can't even with Dad," she spits out between sobs.

"What happened with your dad?" Hanson clears his throat and averts his gaze, which doesn't escape Aunt Lill. "Hanson, do you know what's going on?"

Avery pushes up and crosses her arms across herself. "Leave him alone. It's not his fault. All he did is tell me what's been going on. Treated me like an adult. Something no one else bothers to do," she shouts loud enough to draw the attention of everyone standing outside.

"I'm sorry. Sit back down, honey. Let's talk." Aunt Lill pats the seat beside her, and Avery complies.

They sit quietly for a few minutes until finally, Hanson speaks. "I'm sorry, Ave. I shouldn't have told you that stuff today."

"You're right. Someone should've told me what my father is really like before today. But, since no one bothered, you absolutely should've told me," she says defiantly, an attitude that doesn't suit her well.

"Everyone was just trying to protect you, honey. He's your daddy, and you love him. No one wanted to take that away from you," Aunt Lill says.

"I'm not a baby. I don't need to be protected from the truth." She wipes the tears away. "He may be my dad, but that's my mom in there. Dead. And, I think it's his fault that she is."

Aunt Lill sucks in a breath. "What do you mean, Ave? Do you think he hurt her?"

Hanson goes rigid.

"I honestly don't know. I wouldn't be surprised if he killed her. If he didn't, it's still his fault for hurting her so badly that she killed herself. Either way, it's his fault. I can't ever forgive him."

"I don't know for sure what happened, but the police are looking into everything. They'll get to the bottom of this and figure it out. I know that your mother didn't kill herself. She wouldn't do that to you."

Hanson stands and lights another cigarette. I want to snatch it from his mouth and throw it to the ground. But, of course, I can't.

"Well, if she didn't kill herself, then someone killed her. Who does that leave? Dad. No one else would have a reason to hurt her. He probably wanted to get rid of her so he could screw whoever he wanted without a fight." She gags as soon as the words are out.

"Like a fight ever stopped him!" Hanson says.

"Hanson!" Aunt Lill snaps with a scowl to let him know he's not helping the situation one bit.

He raises his hands as if to say he'll stop.

"How about we trust the police to do their job and figure this out? They're smart. They know what to look for. When they talk to you again, be honest. But for now, try to keep the peace with your dad. You don't want to do or say something you'll live to regret."

"I hate him. I hate him for hurting her."

"I understand," Aunt Lill whispers. "Me, too."

Hanson holds out his hand for Avery. "C'mon, sis. I'll go back in there with you. You can sit with me."

I'm shocked by his offer. It was apparent that he was trying to avoid this at all cost. Perhaps there's hope for him yet.

Avery pauses a moment before taking his hand. Once she's on her feet, he pulls her into a hug. "I love you, sis. I'm sorry about all of this." Tears glisten in his eyes. It's the first time I've seen him cry since I've been awakened from the dead.

"I love you, too. It's not your fault."

Hanson squeezes her tighter. I'm not sure if he's there to comfort her or if she's helping hold him together at this point.

Aunt Lillian stands. "C'mon kids. Let's do this. I still need to say my goodbyes."

The three of them walk back inside and into the room. They take their seats in the back row. Matt turns when they enter and starts to rise, but Hanson shoots him a death stare that tells him to stay where he is. For once, Matt backs down and sits, turning back toward the front of the room.

I hate that my kids are hurting so badly. What kind of a mother puts her kids through such hell? A million moments flash before me of times I should've made different, better choices. My bad decisions have irreparably harmed my children. I plead with God to protect them all. From harm. From more loss. From the truth—whatever that may be.

I don't have time to finish my prayers when the room around me swirls into the vortex that's carrying me away. Transporting me back to another time I'm sure I'd rather forget.

CHAPTER TWENTY-SIX
THEN

Younger me stands, wringing my hands outside of Aunt Lill's store as if I'm debating about whether or not to enter. Finally, younger me takes a deep breath and opens the door. Aunt Lill looks up from the counter and breaks into a grin.

"Mack, hi!" Her face drops, realizing this isn't a time for smiles. "Sarah," she calls out toward the back room.

After only a moment, Sarah's head peeks out from behind the door. Aunt Lillian quickly makes her way over and whispers something in her ear, then rushes over to pull younger me into an embrace. Former me tries to fight back the tears threatening to fall. The struggle is lost as soon as Aunt Lill wraps her arms around me. She grabs my hand and guides younger me toward her office, now that Sarah has taken her place behind the register. Younger me slumps into the sofa next to her desk, and the waterfall begins before she even has time to shut the door.

Lillian sits next to my younger self and extends her arms to cradle me. How I wish I could be wrapped in the safety of her arms now. I need a hug from Aunt Lill to make me believe all of this may turn out okay.

After a few moments, she finally speaks. "What's up, Mack? You're worrying me."

Younger me struggles to force the words out. "I'm…pregnant."

"Isn't that good news? I always thought you and Matt wanted more children."

OH SHIT! This is the day of my doctor's appointment, where I found out I was pregnant with Vera. The same day that I got confirmation of Matt's affair with Yvonne. I had kept the truth of my marriage hidden so well that no one could see past the façade. I had never spoken about my insecurities, my fears, or my suspicions with anyone.

"I just found out Matt is having an affair. I think he's been having them for years. He's awful to Hanson. I was going to leave him today, but now I'm stuck. Oh God, I'm stuck," younger me manages to spit out before sobs take over.

I vividly recall the complete and utter despair I felt in this moment I'm being forced to witness again. It was bad enough the first time around.

Aunt Lill pulls younger me closer and rubs circles on my back. "Shhh. Just take some deep breaths, Mack. Try to calm down so we can talk this through." She reaches for a box of tissues on the end table and hands over several.

I wanted to disappear because I felt like such a failure for staying in a miserable marriage for so long. Like such a fraud for pretending everything was fine when it was so far from it. My shame weighed me down like a blanket—as it still does, even in death.

"I'm so ashamed," younger me whispers.

"Of what?"

"Of staying so long. Of turning my head the other way when I knew things weren't right. Of letting Matt treat Hanson like shit and pretending it would all just work itself out. I feel like my mother," younger me sobs.

"Oh, Mack. First of all, you are nothing like her. You are such a good mom to Hanson and Avery. You'll be a great mother to this new baby, too…if you decide to have it. You stayed in your marriage because that's what people are supposed to do. If you were like your mom, you would've moved through about four more men by now," she pauses, and I laugh right along with my younger self at the truth of her statement. "We all have been blinded to the truth at some point in our lives. Or denied reality."

Now, I can acknowledge some truth in what she is saying but, back then, not all of it sank in. "Aunt Lill, you're just trying to make me feel better. You're such a straight shooter and honest. You never would've lived a lie like this for so long. Let everyone believe you were something that you weren't."

Lillian sits back, dropping her arm from around my younger self, with a faraway look in her eyes. She wrings her hands in her lap. "You're wrong. I'm not the person you think I am."

"Oh, Aunt Lill!" I wrap my arm around her, knowing what she's about to reveal. Understanding how hard this conversation was for her.

Younger me looks at her, waiting for more. "Okay…"

"Mack, have you ever wondered why I never got married? Had kids of my own?"

Younger me nods even though I really never have wondered this. Aunt Lillian always seemed content to be single. Before this conversation, the thought of her in a relationship was foreign to me.

"Truth is, I've been in a relationship for the past ten years."

My former self's eyes go wide and mouth drops open. "What? With who? Why didn't you tell me?"

"Mack, I've been in a relationship with a woman named Monique for the past ten years. You are the first person in our family that I've ever told."

The room is silent for a minute as younger me tries to wrap my mind around the fact that Aunt Lillian is a lesbian. Before this day, I'd always thought of her as my asexual mother figure. "Oh, Aunt Lill. Why didn't you tell me? I never would've judged you or cared. I want to know the person you love."

"I know you wouldn't, Mackenzie. But I was raised in a different time and with very strict, religious parents. If I'd have ever told them, I would've been cut off and no longer considered family."

"That's crazy! Look at my mother and all the shit she's done in her life. How could they judge you when they have her to compare you to?"

"I didn't say it made sense, but it's the reality I grew up with. And because your mother is the way she is, I knew she'd never take care of our parents as they got older. I had to live a lie so that they'd be okay. Maybe I didn't have to, but I felt like I did." A single tear falls down Aunt Lillian's cheek. I try to wipe it away, to no avail.

I experience the same heartache for Aunt Lillian now, as I did then, realizing how awful it must've been for her to have to keep such a large part of herself hidden from the world out of fear of judgment. My younger self's eyes go wide, and I remember what revelation hit me at that moment. I'd been doing the exact same thing.

"First of all, I want to meet Monique. I'll always consider anyone you love to be a part of our family. Secondly, I see your reasons for telling me now."

She nods, and her entire body relaxes like a heavy burden has been lifted from her. "Monique knows all about you. That you're like a daughter to me. Nothing would make me happier than the two of you meeting. But please don't tell your mother. I cannot deal with her drama about this. I can see it now, we'd go somewhere together, and she'd introduce me as her lesbian sister, Lillian, just to get some attention."

Younger me laughs because she would totally do something like that. Mom would love the supposed scandal around having a gay sister and take pride in revealing it to everyone. "Oh, please. Do you think I tell her anything of significance? Why do you think I'm here instead of with her?"

"I know," she pauses. "Now, back to you. I will support you, regardless of what you decide. If you don't want the baby, I understand. If you do and want to leave Matt, I'll support you however I can —financially, emotionally, whatever. If you decide to stay with Matt, that's your choice as well. I love you, no matter what. But I am worried about you."

"I'm worried about me, too. And the kids. I just don't know what to do."

"Can I tell you a little secret?"

Younger me nods.

"I've never liked Matt. He's a pompous ass if you ask me. But I will respect him as your husband."

My younger self's head jerks back along with widened eyes and a gasp, completely surprised by this revelation. My reaction makes me chuckle now. I always thought Aunt Lill had bought into his nice guy act hook, line, and sinker. She'd never acted in a way to make me think any differently. Perhaps that's what unconditional love looks like. Hopefully, my children learned the same thing about love from me.

My former self laughs. "You're absolutely right. He's such a pompous ass. But he'd fight me for Avery and this new baby if I tried to leave."

"You're right. He would. I have no doubts about that. That's why you need to think for a while about what you want to do," she says. "Is Hanson okay?"

"I don't know." Former me spills out all the details about their physical altercation, the tension between the two of them, how I must always walk on eggshells, and put myself in the middle.

Aunt Lillian listens without speaking until finally, younger me stops talking.

"There's no easy answer. Any choice you make is going to come with a cost. You have to decide what price you're willing to pay. You'll make the right choice."

How I wished I felt as sure as she did. My bad choices had gotten me in this situation and kept me stuck here—for the rest of my life, it seems. Younger me agrees to take some time to consider my options and to be honest with her from this point forward. She agrees to do the same.

Before younger me leaves, we schedule a date for the following Sunday to go out to lunch with her and Monique. I was so excited that she was going to let me into that part of her life. The thought of Aunt Lillian in love brought me joy then, as it still does.

Over the next week, younger me will play through every possible scenario, making mental pros and cons lists. My ultimate decision was to leave Matt but not until after the baby was born or after I had a miscarriage, which was my preference. I would come up with a plan to stash money away before trying to do this single parenting thing, especially with three kids. At that point, I had been living a lie for so long already that another few months wouldn't hurt anything. I would put on my happy face and act as if everything was okay, like I was an expert at doing. I said so many prayers that Hanson would be okay and vowed to do my best to protect him from any further physical or emotional damage from Matt.

My PREGNANCY with Vera was even harder on me than with Hanson. I had convinced myself back then that I was going to give him up, that there was an end in sight, which made it a bit easier to accept the pregnancy and try to enjoy some of the moments. But with Vera, I knew that there was no escape. Her existence was a noose around my neck, keeping me trapped further within the misery of my marriage.

I briefly considered an abortion with her but then would look at Hanson and Avery, and there was no way I could go through with it. I prayed daily for a miscarriage and held off telling Matt as long as I possibly could. I don't regret keeping her, my little bundle of joy and energy. I do regret not leaving Matt as I'd planned.

For now, I'm returned to the funeral home. The consequence of all my bad decisions.

CHAPTER TWENTY-SEVEN
NOW

After Hanson and Avery get settled in the back row, Aunt Lill makes her way forward. Matt turns around several times, trying to catch Avery's eye, but she stares at her feet, refusing to look in his direction. Vera is awake and, upon seeing that her brother and sister have returned, she runs back and climbs on Hanson's lap. The scowl leaves Hanson's face, seemingly thankful for the distraction she provides.

Aunt Lill runs her hand along the pearly white casket and stops to admire the beautiful spread of red and white roses resting on top of it with the tag that reads, "Mother, Wife, Daughter." It should include "Niece" since she's the one that made the purchase, no doubt. No one else would've thought to do it otherwise.

Finally, Aunt Lill stills by the head of the casket. She clears her throat several times before attempting to speak; her eyes glisten with tears. I have only seen Aunt Lillian cry a few times in my life, and my heart aches for her.

"Well, Mack. I guess this is our official goodbye. I'm gonna miss you, lady. You know this, but you always felt like my daughter. I couldn't have loved you more if you came from my body."

"I know, Aunt Lill," I whisper. "You're the most real mother I've ever had." I rest my head on her shoulder.

"I know you didn't kill yourself despite what Matt and your mother are trying to convince everyone of. You wouldn't do that. I know right here." She places a hand over her heart. "I promise you that I will not rest until the truth is known. Whoever did this to you is going to pay."

Relief floods me. Since I can't remember what happened that final day, I was starting to believe that maybe I did kill myself. But I'm convinced that Aunt Lill knows me better than I know myself. She glances over her shoulder at Matt with a scowl. She thinks Matt killed me. Did he? I shudder as memories of his violent side bombard my mind. Was he angry enough to just end me?

I'm absolutely certain Aunt Lill means every word—she will make sure that someone pays for my death. I know beyond the shadow of a doubt that she's not going to just write it off as a suicide. She's spent too much of her life hiding from the truth to let the cause of my death be another secret.

"I feel so guilty, Mack. Like there was something I should've done. Something that could've saved you. I keep going over our conversations again and again in my mind. Did I encourage you to stay with Matt? Did I not take your concerns seriously enough? I wish more than anything I could go back in time and get you and the kids away from him. Take you all somewhere where you'd be safe." A few tears escape and trickle down her cheek. She quickly wipes them away.

"Aunt Lill, there's nothing you could've done differently. I promise. Please don't feel guilty. You were everything I needed in a mother and a friend. Please. None of this is your fault."

"I promise I'll look after the kids. All of them. I know Hanson's an adult now, but he's still hurting. I'll make sure they're okay. You have my word."

"I know you will. Knowing they'll still have you is the one thing that gives me any consolation or hope."

Aunt Lillian grabs a tissue and dabs her eyes, wipes her reddened nose. "I love you, Mack. Thank you for being the daughter I never had. And for being my friend. I will miss you until I take my last breath."

She kisses her hand and puts it to my lips like she used to do when I was younger.

I reach out and touch her hand, imagining its warmth, before she pulls away. I'm filled with the comfort her touch has always provided. As she makes her way toward the back row, she glares at Matt, whose gaze is glued to her. She touches Hanson on the cheek, pats Vera on the head, and sits, pulling Avery close.

She leans forward and pats Hanson on the leg. "It's almost time for the service. Why don't you go and say goodbye?" she whispers.

"I'm good." He refuses to make eye contact.

"Hanson. You'll regret it one day if you don't say goodbye."

He clenches and unclenches his jaw several times before answering. "I'm good. Really. I already said goodbye."

Aunt Lill's eyes plead with him. I wish he'd do it for her. To help ease her pain. But I understand why he won't. It's too much for him to bear. He's stayed as far away from my body as possible the entire time he's been here. I know that being in the room is almost too much for him to stand.

Mr. Pearson quietly shuffles toward the front of the room. "We will re-open the doors to guests in ten minutes and begin the service shortly thereafter. This would be a good time for you to visit the lavatory or get a drink."

It's as though everyone in the room releases their breath at the same time, finally able to relax a few moments. As if on cue, the back door opens, and my mother walks in. Well, not really walks, stumbles would be more accurate. She has black circles under her eyes from her mascara and runs in her foundation. I almost feel sorry for her. I wonder if she really is hurting or if this is all for show. Yes, she has her issues, but is she really so callous that she could lose her only child and not feel pain?

Mom sits next to Lillian, whose posture immediately goes rigid. It's sad that there's such a rift between them. I wish Mom could just be normal so that Aunt Lill wasn't so alone. But, that's not likely to happen anytime soon. It seems she gets worse as she ages.

Matt walks to the back row. Hanson sees him coming and dashes out the door before he gets there. "Avery, can we talk before the service, please?" Matt asks.

Avery is still cuddled up with Aunt Lill and refuses to look at Matt.

"Avery!" he says more sternly.

"Matt, leave her the hell alone, okay? She obviously needs some space. And time," Aunt Lill says, and Mom gasps.

"I wasn't speaking to you, Lillian. I was speaking to my daughter."

"And your daughter has made it clear that she does not want to talk right now."

Vera walks over to her dad, wrapping her arms around his waist. "Please, Matt. Let it go. Just walk away." I beg, knowing that his ego probably won't allow such a peaceful resolution.

He stands speechless for a few moments. "Fine, I'll go. But Avery, you're going to have to talk to me sometime. I don't appreciate your attitude, young lady," he says in the voice he normally reserves for Hanson. He takes a few steps and then turns around with a sneer. "Oh, Lillian. Your girlfriend, Monique, is out in the vestibule. I thought you'd like to know."

My mother's jaw drops, and her wide-eyed gaze goes back and forth between Matt and Lillian with her brow furrowed. Lillian goes rigid. Matt chuckles and walks away.

I attempt to slug him for his callousness at outing Aunt Lill when I'm swept away again, back to the past.

CHAPTER TWENTY-EIGHT
THEN

My bedroom is as dark as a cave, and my younger self is snuggled under the blankets even though it's noon, according to the clock on the bedside table. I move closer and notice my huge, protruding belly. If I had to guess, I'd say I am in about my seventh month. That dark time rushes back over me like a wave of despair as former me sleeps.

I waited as long as possible to tell Matt about my pregnancy, just in case I changed my mind about keeping the baby or had a miscarriage. Once the three-month mark passed, I knew I had to tell him. Matt was thrilled, of course. Avery was excited to be a big sister, and Hanson didn't have much to say. I could tell that he knew it meant we were stuck with Matt for at least a while longer. I tried to talk to him several times about everything, but he'd tell me he didn't want to talk about it and sulk off to his room, locking himself behind closed doors.

I sunk into a deep depression due to the combination of hormones and our situation. I tried for all those months to put on a happy face for the kids and act like everything was fine, but inside I was dying. Matt took full advantage of my weakened state by being crueler than ever and "working" many late nights. I didn't care though. The more time he spent away from home, the better—I could hardly stand to be in the same room with him. Every time he was around, he'd make cruel remarks about my appearance, saying I was getting fat with this baby, which I wasn't because I could barely eat. Or that I looked like shit, which I did because caring about my appearance took way too much wasted energy. And for what? To catch the attention of the man I called my husband but that I couldn't stand? There was none of the doting on me like when I was pregnant with Avery. The only tenderness he showed me at all is when he'd touch my belly and talk to his child.

Matt also became more controlling during that time, something that hadn't been much of an issue before my pregnancy. He sold our second car, saying we needed to save money now that we were having another child. To be cruel, he'd phrase it, "now that we're having a second child. Oops, I guess it's your third." He threw this one in as often as he could, especially if Hanson was around. Without a car, I was trapped at home. He cut our home phone service, citing the same concerns about saving money, and reduced our cell plan to the bare minimum, which put a cap on the number of calls and texts I could make each month. He also cut up all my credit cards.

I had been involved in our finances over the years, and I knew for a fact that we weren't struggling. Matt made more than enough to support ten children; an extra baby wasn't going to add any undue financial stress. I believe he knew deep down how miserable I was and figured out that I wanted to leave him after the baby was born. Essentially his plan ensured that there was no way for me to squirrel away money for my escape plan. Every penny was accounted for, monitored by Matt.

I had suffered with bouts of depression before, but this time was much different. This time, I wanted to die. I couldn't see any hope, any way out. If it weren't for the kids, I would've killed myself. I couldn't leave Hanson, especially. Not with Matt. Every time I felt the baby move, it was a reminder of my misery. I wouldn't ever say it aloud, but I hated the baby growing inside of me. I blamed it for making me stay with Matt.

Avery was my little shadow during this time, obviously able to sense my despair. Every waking hour that she was home, she was

glued to my side. Telling me how much she loved me. Offering to help
with housework or dinner. Hugging me. The deeper my despair grew,
the more Hanson withdrew. I saw him slipping into his own depression, but I couldn't find the strength to pull him from his pit when I
was getting buried in my own.

During this time, I had very little contact with Aunt Lill, even
though she had called, left messages, and texted. I couldn't make
myself respond because I knew she'd see right through any act I tried
to put on. She always had.

My despair is evident on every surface of my former bedroom.
From the piles of dirty laundry littering the floor to the dusty furniture
to the laundry baskets of clean clothes piled chest-high that I hadn't
bothered to put away. Hopelessness and emptiness cover the room like
a blanket, a weight too heavy to lift.

The doorbell rings and younger me rouses, starting to get up but
then plopping back against the bed, not having the strength to bother
seeing who is at the door. Again, the doorbell chimes repeatedly, as the
kids used to do when they were younger, thinking it was hilarious.
Finally, former me kicks back the covers and puts on a robe.

Monique and Aunt Lill are at the door. As soon as younger me sees
them, the tears flow. Aunt Lill guides younger me to the couch while
Monique goes to the kitchen to make tea.

"Mack, I'm worried about you," Aunt Lill says.

Former me isn't even able to find the energy to respond and just
sits there, leaning against her, as the tears stream down my cheeks.

"What's going on? Please talk to me," she pleads. Monique stays
in the kitchen, probably cleaning up since the house is such a
disaster.

"I'm okay," former me whispers.

"No, you're not. Tell her the truth!" I shout.

"No, you are not okay. I haven't talked to you in a month. You
don't return my calls. You look awful. What's wrong?"

I'd already told her about Matt's changes to our budget, but, of
course, I hadn't been completely honest about my suspicions of him
doing all of it as a means to control me.

"I'm sorry. I'm just so tired. All the time. Taking care of the kids is too much most days."

"Have you told your doctor how you're feeling?" Former me shakes my head. "What can I do to help?"

A chuckle escapes my former self. "Take the kids and me far, far away from here."

"I wish I could. I'd do it in a heartbeat. Is Matt hurting you?"

"Physically? No. In some ways, I'd prefer that. He's meaner than ever. Staying here is destroying me."

Monique comes in and hands over cups of tea. It smells delicious— I wish I could enjoy one, too. "Do you mind if Monique stays in the room?"

"No, that's fine. Thank you for the tea." Former me gives her a slight smile. She sits on the couch next to Aunt Lill but reaches forward and pats younger me on the arm. Monique is such a loving, kind, and gentle woman. I see why Aunt Lill loves her so much.

"Honey, we've both been worried about you. We want to help," Monique says with her southern drawl.

"I appreciate it. I really do. I don't know how you can."

"Well, for starters, how about we visit every Monday and help you get this house cleaned up?" Aunt Lill says.

I glance around the living room, as my former self does the same. She's right—the house is a disaster.

Younger me nods. "I appreciate that."

"And, darling, if you ever need us, you know where to find us. You call anytime, day or night," Monique says. Aunt Lill pulls her close and kisses her on top of the head.

They are in an embrace when the front door opens, and Matt walks in. They quickly pull apart, but not fast enough.

"Oh, hi! I didn't realize you had visitors, Kenzie." He flashes a smile at us and walks to the couch with his hand extended. "I'm Matt, and you are?"

"Pleased to meet you. I'm Monique, Lillian's friend." Monique rises and takes his hand. There's none of the usual warmth in her voice.

"Friend, huh?" he says and chuckles.

He needed to make it known that he'd seen their embrace. Their secret would become just another thing for him to hold over my head. To torture me with.

"We were here offering Mackenzie some help for the rest of her pregnancy with the house, grocery shopping, taking care of the kids. Since you're so busy all the time," Aunt Lill says with heavy sarcasm.

"Oh, we don't need that. Do we, Kenzie?"

Younger me pauses a moment, not sure what to say. "Actually, I do need some help. They'd just come once a week."

"Lillian, that's nice of you. But, you're a busy lady with the store and all. We can manage." His tone is firm.

"Shut up, you asshole!" I scream. "Why the hell do you care?"

"I've made arrangements to be out of the store every Monday so that I can come help my niece," she says through gritted teeth.

"Mondays? That's ironic. I made arrangements with the office to take each Monday off from now on so that I can be here more. That's why I'm home today."

My heart sunk, wondering the same thing I do now—why is he doing this? Why does he care? Younger me tries to hold back the tears burning my eyes. There was no way in hell I wanted him to see that he was hurting me.

"I can arrange for a different day," Lill sneers. Her face goes beet red, and her hands shake as her fury builds.

"Actually, it's okay. We're fine," former me whispers.

"What'd you say, darling?" Matt leans closer to me.

"Back off, asshole! Can't you see that you're destroying me? Does it make you happy to see that I'm an empty shell of a woman?"

"I said we're fine. We don't need the help."

Aunt Lillian shakes her head and starts to speak, but former me interrupts. "Really, Aunt Lill. It's okay. Especially if Matt is taking Mondays off. That will be a big help." Younger me forces a smile.

"Actually, I made some plans for Kenzie and me this afternoon, so if you don't mind," Matt says, pointing toward the front door.

Aunt Lillian looks at former me, her eyes asking what to do. Matt stands, hovering. "Thanks so much to both of you for stopping by. Aunt Lill, I'll call you next week, okay?"

"Don't go! Don't leave me with him." I shout.

Perhaps she hears me because she hesitates a moment, glancing back and forth between Matt and younger me. But I already know how this plays out.

"Okay, hon. I love you. If you need anything, call me. Okay?"

Former me stands and lets Aunt Lill pull me into an embrace. I didn't want her to leave, but Matt made it clear they needed to go. "I love you, too."

Monique gives younger me a hug, and they leave.

The weight of despair crushes me, along with my younger self, as they drive away. This was one of the many times Matt had, once again, stolen my hope.

I wrap my arm around my younger self, trying to provide even an ounce of comfort. Instead, the furniture, walls, and my former self all swirl together into an unrecognizable place, rushing me back to the funeral home.

CHAPTER TWENTY-NINE
NOW

Mr. Pearson opens the doors to the vestibule at three-fifteen, forty-five minutes before the start of the service. Many people must've hung around in between the viewing hours and the service because people file in to find seats as soon as the doors open.

There are so many people. Some I haven't seen for years; others I've never met. I suppose I should feel touched that so many people took the time to come say their goodbyes and celebrate my life, but instead, I'm angry. Where were all these people when my life was falling apart? When I needed support and help as a single mother with Hanson? When someone needed to speak up to tell me what a philanderer my husband was? Or even just to be a friend and meet me for lunch once in a while?

Jeanette, my best friend from high school, comes in, her eyes scanning the room for someone familiar. She sees my mother and heads towards her with her arms open for an embrace. I haven't had any contact with Jeanette since high school. She is just an older version of the perky, somewhat ditzy girl I used to know.

A few of my former co-workers from Victoria's come in. I'd kept in touch with a couple of them over the years, at least via social media. I think back to the person I used to be, and a profound sense of loss floods me. How did the determined young woman I once was, with distinct goals and a bright future, manage to get so lost? I guess that person died years ago. If only Matt wouldn't have come in the restaurant that day. If only I would've had the strength to stand my ground and say no when he asked me out on that first date. If only…there are so many ways I could finish that thought. It's the phrase that's plagued me most throughout the years. I hate that it's still able to do so in death.

A pang of guilt stabs me at the thought, though. If I'd never met Matt, I wouldn't have Avery and Vera. I don't regret their existence for a moment. I just wish things could've been different. I wish we would've provided the family for them that I thought we were going to. I wish Matt was even half the man he pretended to be in the early days of our relationship.

Matt is surrounded by groups of his colleagues at the law firm. I wonder, as I watch them talk with him and express their condolences, who they think he is. What mask does he put on for them? I know he comes across as determined, hard-working, and cutthroat when it comes to his work but, do these people believe he was a loving husband? Do they think he's heart-broken and distraught that I'm gone? Or do they all know about the countless women he's slept with through the years?

Emily, Avery's best friend, comes in and quickly rushes to Avery's side. When did the two of them become young women? It seems like just yesterday that I was the room mother for their kindergarten class. Now, here they are with their high heels, too short skirts, and shirts revealing the slightest bit of cleavage. They're no longer the little girls of my memories. Emily embraces Avery before they head off to chairs in the corner to chat.

Various teachers and school faculty from the elementary, middle, and high schools are here. I'd done more than my fair share of volunteer work at the schools throughout the years, so I got to know most of the staff quite well. Vera is delighted to see her second-grade teacher, Ms. Monahan. She pulls free from Matt's hand and rushes over to give Ms. Monahan a hug. The teacher speaks so tenderly to Vera that it warms my heart. Hopefully, she'll be able to help her cope with my death and all the emotions that are sure to follow.

Quite a few of my mother's friends have arrived so far. Of course, Mom is putting on one heck of a show for them. The tears flow one minute; the next, she talks way too loudly about how full of despair she is for her grandbabies. She scans the room for them and points each of the kids out to her ogling group of old lady friends. This seems like even too much for my mom. She's having trouble picking an angle to go with for her audience. It's as if she's seeing which response gets the biggest reaction. Some things will never change.

I search the room, trying to find Aunt Lillian but don't see her anywhere. I peek out into the vestibule where she's standing off to the side, talking quietly with Monique. I'm relieved that Monique came to be a support to Aunt Lill, but I'm pissed that Matt outed her to my mother. Tact is not a word in my mother's vocabulary, so I have no doubt that she is going to say something to Monique that will mortify Aunt Lill. Perhaps if she stays out of the room long enough, Mom will be too distracted to keep from cornering the two of them. Aunt Lill has already had enough stress today—I hate that this even has to be a concern on her radar.

A gentleman I don't recognize walks over to Aunt Lill and Monique. Aunt Lill shakes his hand and leans in to hear him talk. I move closer, trying to figure out who he is. After only a few words, I realize it's a detective from the police department. My head swarms. I understand they're investigating my death, but why is a detective here? He points across the room to a young woman and an older gentleman leaning against the front windows who must also be with the police department. A mixture of relief and panic consumes me. Perhaps, I'll soon have my answers about what happened to me. How I died.

I go back in the room and search the crowds. Matt is still surrounded by his colleagues. I can't find Hanson anywhere. I move through the room, quickly trying to locate him. Avery is still in the corner. Vera's still with her teacher. Where is Hanson? God, I wish I had a voice that others could hear so I could call out his name. Once I'm confident he's not in the room, I make my way outside. He's standing with CJ, his best friend, smoking a cigarette. I calm a little, realizing he's still here, and he's okay. The young female and older gentleman stand inside, peering out the windows at Hanson. A thought from out of nowhere rushes through my mind—If ever there was a time for Hanson to pull one of his vanishing acts, this would be it. Why does Hanson need to disappear? Why am I filled with fear for him right now?

Aunt Lill and Monique walk outside with the detective. She calls Hanson over. He puts his cigarette out and slowly makes his way to them, clenching and unclenching his jaw with each step.

"Hanson, this is Detective Andover. He wanted me to introduce the two of you," Aunt Lill says.

Hanson reaches his trembling hand forward. "Nice to meet you." He says the right words, but his narrowed eyes, shaking hands, and clenched jaw tell a different story. He's not happy to meet the detective at all.

"Nice to meet you as well. A few detectives are here today. Me, Detective Collier," he says and points in the window. "And, Detective Jacobs. I think you've talked with Detective Jacobs before. We may have some additional questions later for you."

Hanson clears his throat several times, as he always does when he's nervous. "Okay. Yeah. Sure."

"Thank you. I'll find you later, okay?" Detective Andover says as he walks away. He stops and turns back towards Hanson. "I'm very sorry about your mother. I promise we'll get to the bottom of this."

Hanson nods and lowers his gaze to the ground. Aunt Lill pats him on the arm, and, once the detective is out of earshot, she whispers. "Are you okay?"

"Yeah. Why are the cops here, though?"

"I guess it's part of their investigation. They want to be here to observe," she says and smiles. "It's a good thing. It means they realize that she didn't kill herself like I've been trying to tell them."

"I guess so. It's just weird. It seems like they should let this day be about Mom, ya know?"

"I, for one, am glad they're here. They know what to look for and, hopefully, they will see clearly what we already know. That Matt killed her."

Hanson sighs deeply. "Let's hope so. I hope he rots behind bars."

"We all do, honey. He'll pay for the hell he put you and your mom through. I have no doubts about that."

She pulls Hanson into a hug and pats him on the back. She seems so small wrapped in his arms.

"Okay, Monique and I are going back inside. I'll save a seat for you."

"Thanks, Aunt Lill. I'll be in soon."

Lillian and Monique head back inside, and Hanson lights another cigarette, staring off into the distance. I wish I knew what's going through his mind. And that I could make this all okay. For now, the only thing I can do is travel back in time again. For what purpose, I have no idea.

CHAPTER THIRTY
THEN

I squeeze my eyes shut, dread bubbling in my chest at where I'll end up this time. This all hurts too damn much. It's as though I'm stuck in a movie watching all the horrible parts of my life play out in front of me, and I'm unable to change a thing. Maybe I'm in hell.

Before opening my eyes, I sense the motion and know I'm in a car. I slowly open them and am sitting next to my younger self almost to the elementary school. Within moments, Hanson runs up to the car and jumps in. He's missing his front teeth and is adorable. He must be about seven. Since I'm not bound by natural laws, I move to the backseat to sit next to my son. He briefly turns his head in my direction, then wipes his eyes. He's not his normal chatty self, rather he stares at his shoes, kicking back and forth against the seat. His normal smile is replaced by a scowl.

"Hey, bud! What's wrong?" former me asks.

"Nothing," he says, shifting his gaze from his feet to outside the car window.

"Well, it certainly looks like you're upset about something. What's going on? Did something happen at school?"

He sits silently for a few seconds and then says, barely louder than a whisper, "Yeah." He wipes his eyes in an attempt to hide his tears.

Younger me pulls over alongside the road and puts the car in park. My younger self reaches into the backseat and softly touches his leg, bringing back a flood of memories from this day.

"Please tell me what's wrong, bud."

"Who's my real dad?"

My heart leaps into my throat, exactly as it did when this happened the first time. I had always known this day would come at some point, but I definitely didn't expect it so soon. I remember how it felt like it came with no warning, seemingly out of nowhere. I'm sure I thought I was hiding my shock and panic, but my bulging eyes and reddened cheeks tell a different story.

"Wh…what?" younger me spits out even though my mind races.

"Jackson said that Matt's not my real daddy. Who is my real daddy?"

The same thoughts swirl through me now as they did back then. I was, and still am, so pissed at myself. I'd confided in Jackson's mother, Heidi, over lunch one day that Matt wasn't Hanson's biological father. How stupid could she be to tell her child? Did she not understand how cruel kids could be? Thank God, I didn't tell her any more details even though she tried to pry them out of me.

"Why were you guys even talking about that?"

"We read a book and were talking about our dad's jobs. I told everyone that my dad was a lawyer, and Jackson yelled real loud so everyone could hear that Matt wasn't my real daddy." Hanson's bottom lip quivers.

"C'mere, bud!" Younger me pulls him into the front seat. Both versions of myself wrap our arms around him. "That was very mean of Jackson, and I'm sorry."

"Is it true?"

My former self's brow furrows as I scramble to come up with the right words to help him understand. "Matt is your real dad because he loves you, takes care of you, and would do anything in the world for you. He's the only daddy you've ever had."

I want to slap myself. "Just tell him the truth. He will find out anyway, and it will destroy him."

"So, why did Jackson say that?"

I had no idea how to explain the situation to someone so young without going into the whole discussion of the birds and the bees. "First of all, he shouldn't have said it. It wasn't nice of him to do that. But, when mommies get pregnant, a man has to help make the baby. A man, someone other than Matt, helped give me the best gift of all. You. I didn't know Matt when you were made, so someone else helped make you. Isn't that wonderful?"

Younger me smiles, but there's no joy in it, only pain. Bile rises in my throat now, as it did when this happened the first time, with the memory of the man's eyes who helped "make" Hanson. The feel of his hands on my body. The way he defiled and violated me.

Hanson scrunches his eyes like he always does when he's deep in thought. "So, someone else helped make me but then gave me to Matt as a present?"

Younger me kisses him on top of the head as I stroke his back. "Yes! Exactly. He helped make you so that you, me, sissy, and Matt could all be a family."

"Did someone else make Avery, too?"

"Since Matt and I already knew each other, he got to help make Avery," former me says, hoping it will be enough.

Again, Hanson sits quietly. After a few moments, he asks, "Why didn't Matt give her to someone else as a present like the man who helped make me?"

"Because we needed to keep her as part of our family so that you could have a sissy!"

Hanson nods and sighs. "Okay. I'm glad we kept her! Even though she is annoying sometimes."

"Me, too, buddy! And I'm glad that Matt got to have you as a present." He wraps his arms around younger me, and I lean forward to give him a butterfly kiss on the cheek.

Hanson laughs. "That tickles, Mommy!"

My former self's brow furrows. "What tickles? My hug?"

"No, silly. That butterfly kiss on my cheek!" His giggles fill the car.

Relief washes over me. He felt me here with him. He may not be able to see me, but he knows I'm here.

My younger self's eyebrows scrunch in confusion. Younger me clears my throat and says, "Okay, bud. Let's get going! Crawl back in your seat and buckle in so we can go home to get a snack!"

I move in the back with Hanson again, wanting to be close to my boy. My younger self's hands tremble the entire drive home, as my thoughts race. This conversation was so hard for me because I didn't know how long the explanation would suffice for him. This was the day that I decided I'd come up with a story to tell him when he was old enough to understand. I decided on this car ride home that I'd tell him his father was someone I went to college with that died so that there'd be no chance of him wanting to reconnect. I'd tell him what a good, kind, and caring gentleman his father was and how he passed away before I found out I was pregnant. That way, Hanson would never think that his father didn't want him like I did with my own father throughout the years. I was adamant that there was no way in hell I would ever tell him the truth. That his father was a cruel, sick, and twisted rapist. I'd never burden my child with that truth.

I told Matt the truth early in our relationship, and he agreed whole-heartedly that Hanson should never learn the details. He agreed that he would be Daddy to Hanson. I'd been naïve enough to believe that would be enough for my boy, that he'd never really need to find out that Matt wasn't his father. I didn't expect the questions to start so early.

This first conversation went relatively well, even though it almost destroyed me at the time, and Hanson seemed satisfied with the answers.

I'm aware now that his satisfaction only lasted a few years until he was old enough to understand a bit more about where babies came from. The next time he brought it up was when he was eleven. I whisper a prayer that I don't have to go back to that day as well. But, since I'm perhaps stuck in hell, I don't think anyone is listening to my prayers.

As we pull in the driveway of our house, the world swirls together —it's time for me to leave again. I squeeze Hanson's hand as I'm being ripped away, wishing I could stay just a little bit longer.

CHAPTER THIRTY-ONE
NOW

The pianist begins playing some melancholy music, the cue for people to lower their voices to a whisper and find their seats before the start of the service. The front two rows are reserved for family. Mom and Elliot sit on one side of the aisle while Matt firmly plants himself and Vera at the end of the other row. Avery makes her way over to find a seat with her arm linked with Emily's. She sees Matt and turns the other way, finally choosing a seat next to my mother. Emily gives her a hug and leaves to sit next to her parents. Avery must be really pissed to choose my mother over Matt. While she's always kind and cordial to her grandmother, Mom drives her crazy with her theatrics. Surprisingly, Mom wraps her arm around Avery's shoulder, nuzzling her close. It's so unlike her to offer comfort or support to anyone—she's usually the one seeking it.

The pianist plays Amazing Grace, my favorite hymn. I'm sure Aunt Lill played a huge part in the planning of my service as neither Mom nor Matt would've known what songs I would want to be played.

The song must've been Aunt Lillian's cue that the service is about to begin. She slowly makes her way forward, leaving Monique in the vestibule. Monique deserves more of a seat in the front row than Elliot for God's sake, who I've only spoken to twice in my life. Aunt Lill looks back and forth, trying to decide where to sit. She finally plants herself in the seat next to Matt and Vera, probably so that Hanson would have a choice of where to sit, both options being separated from Matt.

Monique waits to enter the room until Hanson walks in. She pulls him into a hug before taking a seat in the back row. Hanson slowly makes his way forward, eyes lowered to the ground, avoiding looking at the casket. Without hesitation, he moves to the seat beside Avery. Avery lets out a huge breath as though she can relax now that Hanson's there to rescue her from my mother.

Most of the seats are filled, and the detectives scatter. One stands by the doors at the back of the room. One stands on the side to the right. The female detective stands on the side to the left. Matt takes notice of the female almost immediately. His eyes scan her up and down. How did I never notice what a perverted asshole he was? Or did I notice, but chose to live in denial because it hurt less and was easier? The detective must feel the weight of his gaze because she locks eyes with him, crosses her arms, and pulls back her suit jacket just enough to reveal her holstered gun. His cheeks redden, and he shifts in his seat, turning away from her. I chuckle, seeing her put him in his place as few others have been able to do so quickly. Her smirk is the icing on the cake.

The pianist moves onto It Is Well With My Soul, and Mr. Pearson moves to the back of the room to pull the doors closed. The service must be beginning. How weird this will be to witness my own funeral. The room falls completely silent as a woman I've never met walks slowly toward the podium.

She waits until the song ends before speaking. "Good afternoon, and thank you all for coming to celebrate the life of Mackenzie Bartholomew. I am Reverend Gwendolyn Callahan from Pleasant Valley United Methodist Church. While I didn't have the pleasure of knowing Mackenzie personally, I feel like I've come to know her through her aunt, Lillian Sumner. Mackenzie was taken too soon from her children, Hanson, Avery, and Vera, as well as her mother, Linda, and her Aunt Lillian."

I'm so glad she didn't mention Matt's name. I'm sure that was Aunt Lill's doing. Matt scowls, realizing that his name wasn't on the list.

"Mackenzie was a wonderful mother and a loyal wife," the reverend says as the back doors to the room open.

I see the man first and don't recognize him, but then, when the woman comes into view, I gasp. It's my father and Tiffany. A million questions swarm through my mind as they quietly make their way to stand along the back wall. Why are they here? How the hell did he know I died? Why did he bother to come to my funeral when we had absolutely no relationship?

I recall that day so many years ago when I talked to Tiffany outside their house. Is she going to see me and make the connection? Realize it was me and that I'd lied to her?

The questions spin round and round, muddling everything in my mind so much that I don't hear anything the Reverend says. Her voice is simply background noise to the questions clanging together like cymbals in my brain. I move over closer to them, wanting to study my father.

He's gotten so old. His thick head of hair has gone white. Wrinkles line his face, and he's thinner than in the pictures I've seen of him. His eyes are locked on my body in the casket. I wonder what he's thinking. Is he filled with regret? Does he wish he would've tried a bit harder to have a relationship with me? Do any fond memories come to mind?

It seems that Tiffany hasn't aged at all since the time I saw her outside of the house. She holds Dad's hand, tenderly caressing his fingers. It's apparent that she adores him.

I wish I could be happy that he found a woman that loves him and cares for him in a way that I truly believe my mother isn't capable of. But I can't be because I'm pissed off. How dare he leave me alone with my mom, never bothering to check on me or make sure I was okay? He just left and never looked back. He really has no right to be here now.

I'm so lost in my thoughts and anger about my father being here that I fail to realize the service has progressed until I hear Matt's voice. He stands behind the podium and is doing his best to look contrite, his mouth downturned into a frown and tears glistening in his eyes. If I didn't know better, I'd think he was sad. That's not a feeling he's capable of, though.

"I'd like to thank all of you for coming today to grieve with us the loss of my beloved wife, Mackenzie." He pauses for a moment and dabs his eyes with his handkerchief. The man truly deserves a standing ovation for this performance. "On behalf of our children, I want to express sincere gratitude. Our lives will never be the same without her joy, her smile, her love, and..."

Hanson interrupts Matt's eloquent speech by standing up and kicking his chair out of the way. He storms out into the vestibule with Avery on his heels. The outburst catches Matt off guard, and he stumbles over his words trying to regain some composure.

My mother turns around to watch the children flee the room. Her eyes scan the crowd and land on the one place I was hoping they wouldn't. On my father and Tiffany. Instead of handling the situation with any sense of decorum, she continues to stare and pats Elliot on the arm, causing him to twist in his chair. She "whispers" loud enough for everyone in the first three rows to hear,

"That's Mackenzie's fa...sperm donor back there. How dare he!"

Everyone ignores Matt's speech and instead focuses their attention on the back of the room, toward Dad and Tiffany. They seem oblivious to the stares and whispers at first, clinging to every word coming out of Matt's mouth. Perhaps trying to gain some sense of understanding of who I was as a person since they never took the time to get to know me in real life. Finally, my dad must feel the weight of all the stares because he breaks his gaze from Matt and clutches Tiffany's hand.

He gives a slightly uncomfortable smile until he sees my mother. They lock eyes as if they are in a staring contest like children. The anger in Mom's grimace is nothing compared to the pure hatred on my father's face. There's obviously much more to the story of him not having contact with me than my mother ever told me. I'd always suspected it, but this exchange confirms it. I haven't heard his voice since I was two, but I have no doubts left in my mind that he tried to stay involved in my life. He wanted to be my father. But that didn't serve my mom's agenda. It's apparent, witnessing their stare-down, that she robbed him of the chance to get to have a relationship with me.

I'm filled with a hatred towards her that I've never felt before. Sure, she's let me down, embarrassed me, never loved me well or enough, but this is something altogether different. She stole my chance to have a relationship with my father. She tainted my view of him. She made me feel unwanted, unloved. The blame for my unhealthy marriage and the emotional abuse I've endured doesn't rest on his shoulders, where I'd long ago placed it. It sits squarely on hers. That devious, deceitful bitch.

Why didn't I try to reach out to him? Why didn't I stop and tell Tiffany who I really was that day? Why did I accept my mother's version of reality even though I know how crazy she is? I want to run into my father's arms and tell him I'm sorry. I want the chance to get to know him, his wife, and my siblings. I want him to have the chance to be a grandfather to my children. But it's too late. All of it is too late.

My mother is the first to break the stare and turn back toward the front of the room, her cheeks flaming red. I hope she's embarrassed. I'm glad he stood his ground, at least in this little game. Whatever intimidation and lies she's used in the past have no hold over him anymore. Eventually, everyone loses interest in the spectacle at the back of the room and turns again toward Matt, as he's finishing his eulogy. At least the lack of interest made his fake tears and sadness go away, both replaced by a scowl.

"Anyway, in closing, thank you all for coming. We hope you'll join us at the graveside ceremony as well as the reception afterward, which is generously being hosted by Pleasant Valley United Methodist Church."

He gathers his notes from the podium. Each of the detectives watches him closely. Can they tell how full of shit he is? Could they tell from his body language that this was a performance from him and not heartfelt in the least? I believe the female detective can. The firm set of her jaw, along with her narrowed eyes, tells me she can see right through him. I'm sure his little once-over earlier helped make it even more clear.

I wish I could be in three places at once. I want to go out to check on Hanson and Avery. I want to be in my dad's presence. I want to be in the front of the room, scrutinizing my mom and Matt. More than anything, I'd love to see the detectives slap some handcuffs on Matt and drag him away. Will I be stuck here, somewhere in between life and death, until that happens?

Instead of being in any of those places, I'm again sucked away to the past.

CHAPTER THIRTY-TWO
THEN

When I come to, I'm in one of the houses that mom and I rented during one of her phases with no men. It was the little house on Shanley Street. I always hated this house, and a shiver works its way up my spine at being forced to return here. The house is dark, as it always seemed to be, with all the blinds and curtains closed tightly. The only sound comes from the tiny TV in the living room. I make my way in there and find my younger self sitting on the couch with a bowl of popcorn, zoned out in front of an episode of Oprah. I must be about fifteen or sixteen. This was my daily routine around that time.

I sit and study younger me. I was such a pretty girl at this age, but I felt so insecure and ugly back then. Younger me gasps, and I turn my attention to the television. As was the norm, a woman is on the show talking about memories of her abuse surfacing every time her husband touches her. The guest claims she's on the brink of losing her marriage because she can't work through her issues. This episode is so clear in my mind as if I saw it only yesterday. A slew of emotions and questions cross my younger self's face.

I'd always had so many questions about my father and tried to get the answers from my mother. She never had anything nice to say about any of her exes because, of course, everything that had gone wrong in the relationship was their fault. Never hers. But when it came to my father, she was particularly brutal and filled with anger. Venom dripped from her tongue every time she uttered his name or the words your father.

I spent years in desperation, wanting to know what happened between the two of them. Why he left when I was so young. Why he didn't maintain contact with me throughout the years. I knew better than to trust my mom's account of their marriage and who he was as a person, but I picked up enough through the years to form an image in my mind of what he was like.

According to all the things that Mom told me, he never wanted children and encouraged her to get an abortion when she announced her pregnancy. Depending on the day, and her mood toward me, sometimes she'd declare she wished she would've listened to his request. Also, he was supposedly abusive to her and me. When I'd ask her for more information about how he was abusive toward me, she'd whisper that he hurt me "in ways we don't talk about." As I got older, I understood that meant he'd supposedly sexually abused me.

After I figured out what she meant, I hounded her for more details. I'd learned enough to know that sexual abuse was traumatic for children, even those too young to remember it happening. I'd seen the talk shows like younger me is watching now where women had uncovered repressed memories of their abuse once they had their own kids. I didn't want that to happen to me. I longed for the details so that it didn't catch me by surprise later in life, leaving me a broken mess.

Clearly remembering what's about to happen once the show ends, dread fills me. I wish I didn't have to live through this again. I chuckle when I realize my faux pas with my thinking. Technically, I'm not living through it—just being forced to watch it. This is the day I finally managed to coax my father's name from my mom. Teenage me leaps up the stairs to my mother's room, where she is lying in the dark with an ice pack on her head, suffering from another stress headache.

Younger me flips on the overhead light, which makes her throw her arm over her eyes. "What the hell are you doing? My head is pounding. Turn it off."

Usually, I left her alone when she was like this, but that day, I wanted answers. I desperately needed them. Younger me doesn't turn the light off, rather sits on the edge of her bed.

Finally, she uncovers her eyes and glares at younger me. "The light is still on."

"Mom, you need to tell me about my dad. I have the right to know about him."

"You know everything you need to about that bastard."

"No, not really, Mom. I don't know much at all. Like what's his name? How did he abuse me?" younger me asks, leaving off all the other questions. The ones that broke my heart.

"I don't want to talk about him. My head hurts," she whines, throwing her arm back over her eyes.

"I know, I know. There's always something wrong or a reason you can't talk to me about him. Well, I'm sick of it. I'm not leaving until you give me some answers."

She sighs and props herself up against the pillows. "Fine, his name is Calvin Sanders. He was an asshole. We had only been married a few months when I found out I was pregnant with you. He didn't want a baby and wanted me to have an abortion. Which, obviously, I didn't."

I remember how I repeated his name over and over in my mind Calvin Sanders, Calvin Sanders, Calvin Sanders, hoping and praying I wouldn't forget. "Okay, what about the abuse? You said he abused both of us. How?"

"He'd push me around whenever he drank, which was a lot. Drinkin' made him meaner than a skunk. I just stayed away from him when he was drunk, until the night I caught him...ummm...touching you where he shouldn'ta been."

My younger self's mind is being bombarded by a million questions thanks to her declaration. They echo through my mind now, too. Why did she leave me alone with him if he couldn't be trusted when he was drunk? What exactly was he doing to me? Was it the only time something had happened? Wouldn't I have some memory of this even though I was so young?

Finally, my younger self spits out, "Why did you let him near me when he was drunk?"

"How dare you blame me for that sicko's behavior! Of course, it's my fault. Everything is according to you!" she yells. "For your information, he sneaked into your room after I fell asleep. I woke up to pee and found him there, touching you. I threw that sick bastard out that night and didn't see him again until court."

My younger self closes my eyes, trying to slow the questions swirling round and round. The same questions I carried for so many years. Did he really hurt me? How much of what she's saying is really true? Would she have thrown him out as a way to protect me? Why didn't she call the police? Perhaps that's why he never tried to contact me again – he knew he could get in legal trouble.

"Are you satisfied? I don't know why you needed to know all of this. I kept this from you to protect you. Now, can you leave me be and turn off the light?"

Tears pool in my teenage self's eyes. Younger me nods and rises quickly to turn off the light and leave her room. I never liked my mother seeing my tears because showing her any sign of weakness just gave her ammunition to use against me later. I'd learned at a young age to hide my feelings from her so they wouldn't be thrown back in my face.

Younger me goes into my bedroom and lies on the bed, trying to make sense of everything my mother just said. The confusion is legitimate because so little of what she said jived with the things Aunt Lill had told me through the years about my father. Lillian always used words like loving, kind, and generous when it came to him. I'd pressed her over the years for more details on him, like his name, why my mom hated him so much, et cetera. She'd always say the same thing. "I have to respect your mother's wishes about not giving you his name, whether I agree or not. And, you know how your mom is. Take it all with a grain of salt."

Finally, the dam breaks and younger me lets the tears fall. I rub my teenage self on the back, something I wish someone had done for me at the time. Comfort was something I rarely got from anyone other than Aunt Lill.

"Call Aunt Lill. She'll make you feel better."

My younger self picks up the phone as though perhaps my voice came through.

"Aunt Lill," younger me says with a shaky voice. I scoot closer to hear Aunt Lill's responses.

"Mack, what's wrong? You okay?"

"I'm okay. I just needed to hear your voice."

"Do you need me to come get you? Did something happen?"

Younger me puts my hand over the mouthpiece to block out the sob that escapes despite my best efforts to keep it away. "I talked to Mom about my dad. She finally told me his name."

"It's about damn time. But why are you crying, hon?"

Younger me chews on my bottom lip, unsure whether to repeat the things Mom had said. Finally, my younger self spits out the truth. "She said he abused me. Umm, touched me where he shouldn't have, and that's why she kicked him out. Is that true?"

Aunt Lill stays quiet for so long that teenage me finally asks if she's still there. "I'm here, hon. I was just figuring out how to answer your question."

"With the truth, please. That's all I want. The truth."

"You know I don't like to talk badly about your mother because, well, she's your mother. But you really can't trust everything she says. You know that."

"So, are you saying he didn't hurt me?"

Seconds tick by with nothing but silence. Even though what she's going to say is clear in my mind, my heart flutters, as it did back then, with anxiety while waiting. "I'm saying I don't believe the man I knew as your father would ever have done that to you. Your mother sometimes spins things in a way that aren't true."

"So, she lied to me? Why would she do that?" The tears are back, waterfalling down my teenage self's cheeks.

"Only the two of them know the absolute truth, but when you're older, perhaps you should try to find the court documents and see for yourself what they say."

Rage boils in me now, as it did then, at just wanting her to tell me the damn truth. Something I don't understand to this day is why she was always so protective of my mother and her games. She was the only person in the world I trusted, why wouldn't she come out and say what needed to be said?

"Mack, you there?"

"Yeah."

"Are you upset with me?" she asks.

"I just want the truth."

"I know, sweetheart. And you deserve the truth. I can't come between you and your mother more than I already have because I love you. Your mom wouldn't hesitate to cut me out of your life if she knew I'd contradicted anything she's told you."

That makes sense to me now, but it certainly didn't back then. Perhaps Lillian wasn't protecting Mom at all through the years. Rather, she was protecting me.

"I will tell you that your daddy loved you. When you're older, promise me you'll figure out the truth," she says.

"I will. I love you!"

And I always meant to. But, somehow, as the years passed, my mom got further and further into my head, convincing me that all she'd said about him was true. Once I became a parent, there was no excuse for him not to have kept in contact with me. Nothing or no one should've been able to keep him away. With that realization, my hatred for him grew to the point where the truth no longer mattered. All that mattered was that he didn't want me in his life. Regardless of the reasons behind that decision, his actions were the only important thing.

My old bedroom spirals into a tunnel of color, and the whooshing sound throbs inside my head. Once again, I'm carried away.

CHAPTER THIRTY-THREE
NOW

After the closing prayer, Mr. Pearson quietly makes his way back to the podium. "Thank you for coming. Please remain seated until an usher comes to release your aisle. We hope you can join us at Greenwood Cemetery for the internment," he says. His voice is so mellow that he could easily put everyone in the room to sleep if he read them a story. And, I've never heard someone be able to move about so quietly, as though he's gliding instead of walking. Perhaps he's a ghost!

Matt, Elliot, Keith, Caleb, and Lance, another of Matt's colleagues, step forward to serve as pallbearers. Matt searches the room for Hanson, who was supposed to help. He clenches and unclenches his jaw while his eyes scan the sea of faces, devoid of Hanson.

"Where the hell is Hanson?" he whispers to Elliot.

Elliot shrugs.

Mr. Pearson senses the confusion and meanders over.

"Is there a problem?" he whispers.

"Uh, yeah. A big one. Hanson is supposed to help us. We can't do this with only five people." Matt was never good at whispering, especially when he was angry. Now, he's pissed, and his voice reverberates through the quiet room.

Mr. Pearson touches him on the arm in an attempt to calm him. "I can go outside and look for him if you can wait a moment."

Matt jerks his arm away. "No, never mind. I don't want him here. Brian? Can you help?" he asks, pointing to a man I've never met.

My dad clears his throat and pulls away from Tiffany's arm, slowly making his way toward the front of the room. Matt's eyes narrow as he rubs his chin.

About halfway up the aisle, my father declares, "I'll help."

Matt waits to speak until Dad has reached the group gathered by my casket. "Thank you. But who are you?"

My dad recoils as though he's been punched in the stomach, forcing all his air out. He puts his hand in his pocket, jingling some change around for a few seconds before he answers. "I'm Calvin. Mackenzie's father."

The look on Matt's face is priceless. He stands there with his mouth gaping open, and, for once, he seems to be at a loss for words. "Oh, okay. Thanks."

I'm surprised it took this long, but my mom screeches, "You have no right, Calvin. No right to be here. No right to touch my baby's casket." Tears stream down her reddened cheeks, leaving trails through her foundation.

"Linda, please," Dad says calmly. She jumps to her feet and lunges toward him. He steps back, causing her to crash into one of the floral bouquet stands, making a waterfall of flowers and dirt.

Aunt Lill rushes to the front of the room and grabs my mother by the arm. "Linda, stop it. You're making a spectacle of yourself."

Mom tries to jerk her arm away, but Lillian refuses to let go. "Let me go, dammit. He has no right to be here!"

Tiffany marches toward the front of the room, her eyes fixed on my mother, and her hands balled into fists. Oh my Lord, what a fiasco! She plants herself next to my father before she speaks. "He has every right to be here. You did everything you could to keep them apart when she was alive. Let him at least do this for her," Tiffany shouts.

"Who the hell are you? Another one of his children?" Mom spews.

"I'm his wife. And you are making a fool of yourself."

"C'mon Linda. Sit down. Let's just get through this. For Mack," Aunt Lill whispers.

Mom looks back and forth between Tiffany and my dad, refusing to budge. Tiffany's hands are balled into fists, and her feet are planted firmly as if she's ready to punch my mom square in the nose. Dad remains standing calmly at attention. If this whole spectacle has him rattled in the least, it surely doesn't show.

Mr. Pearson inserts himself between Tiffany and my mom. He turns to Mom and says, "Mrs. Williams, I know this is extremely stressful, but please allow the men to carry the casket to the hearse."

"But that man! He shouldn't be here. He shouldn't be near my daughter. You don't understand what an awful man he is. She wouldn't want him anywhere near her," Mom shouts and starts wailing.

Tiffany has had enough and pushes past Mr. Pearson. She grabs Mom by the front of her dress and gets within inches of her face. "You bitch! You don't know what your daughter would want if she knew the truth. You filled her head with lies all these years, made her think her father hurt her. All he wanted to do was be her dad. But you wouldn't allow it. You tried to destroy him. But, no more!" Tiffany releases Mom with a push backward, and she crumples to the ground.

Typical Mom, she doesn't even put her hands out to try to break her fall. It wouldn't be nearly as dramatic that way. Mom screams in pain, and Elliot rushes to her side, kneeling on the floor next to her.

Mr. Pearson faces the group. "I'm afraid things have gotten a bit heated here. I'm going to ask everyone to depart out the back doors and wait in the vestibule for further instructions." At his announcement, several ushers move forward to start corralling the guests to the back door. Mr. Pearson runs his hands through his perfectly styled hair, the stress of this fiasco even getting to him. I'm sure he's never experienced the likes of this madness before.

As the guests exit the room, he speaks sternly to the group remaining by the casket. "Everyone needs to take a seat. Linda, you over there," he points to the right side of the aisle. "Mrs., I'm sorry I didn't catch your last name, you and your husband over there." He points to the left side of the aisle.

My father reaches forward to grab Tiffany by the elbow, guiding her towards a seat. Elliot helps my mother to her feet and settles her into a chair. She moans and cries as though she's been beaten. Everyone else finds a seat as the last of the guests, other than the detectives who are still standing at attention, straggle out the doors.

Once the doors close, Mr. Pearson crosses his arms in front of him and says, "What is going on here? This is unacceptable."

"Him. He's the problem," my mom shouts and points at my father with a shaking finger.

My dad lowers his gaze and studies the carpet.

"Linda. He stepped forward to help carry your daughter's casket because we needed an extra set of hands. It seems to me that he was trying to be helpful," Mr. Pearson says.

"Helpful? That man destroyed our lives. He's an abuser and a child molester!" she shouts, spittle flying everywhere.

Dad jerks his gaze up from the carpet and directly to my mother. "You are a liar. I never laid a finger on you or my daughter," he says calmly through gritted teeth, the only indication that he's seething on the inside.

"How dare you! You liar!" Mom shouts and tries to stand, but her legs "give out," and she falls back to her chair with all of the dramatic flair she can muster.

Tiffany rises to her feet. "You bitch! Calvin, do something. Don't let her say all of this about you. Do something!" she shouts at my father.

Mr. Pearson holds up a hand to Tiffany, trying to stop her from moving any closer to my mom and looks to Detective Andover, who finally steps forward.

"Ma'am, I'm going to need to ask you to sit down," he says in a deep, gravelly, commanding-of-respect type of voice.

Tiffany's eyes go to his hand, resting on the gun at his hip, and she sits without another word. Her face flames with anger.

Detective Andover holds out his hand to indicate that Mr. Pearson should continue.

"What happened here today is a disgrace. We need to lay

Mackenzie to rest peacefully. We've had enough outbursts, yelling, and chaos for one day. Can we all agree to just get through the next hour peacefully?"

Slowly everyone nods, with my mother being the last one to give in to the pressure.

"Thank you. Seeing as how the normal order of things got completely disrupted, I am going to step out into the vestibule to ask the guests to stand to the side in silence so that Mackenzie's casket can be carried to the hearse," he instructs. "I would like everyone who is not a pallbearer to come out into the vestibule with me."

He walks to the back of the room, and when he sees no one but Aunt Lill has followed, he says, "Ladies, this way, please."

Elliot helps Mom to her feet where she sways a bit for dramatic effect, I'm sure, and leads her to the back of the room where Mr. Pearson takes her by the arm. Finally, Tiffany rises to her feet, kisses my father on the cheek, and joins them in the back of the room.

Before he opens the doors, he looks from Mom to Tiffany. "Please. Control yourselves. For Mackenzie. For the children."

Tiffany nods, and Mom wipes tears from her eyes, never giving any type of agreement but not speaking out in disapproval either, which is an improvement.

"Gentleman, I will be back in a moment to instruct you," Mr. Pearson says and pushes the doors open.

Once he and the women are out of the room, Matt chuckles. "Well, that was something!"

Nervous laughter fills the room, and all the men seem to relax a bit. My father rises and goes to Matt with his hand outstretched.

"Since we didn't get properly introduced, I'm Calvin. And I promise you, I never laid a finger on my daughter or that raving madwoman," he says as Matt shakes his hand.

"I'm Matt, and that's good to know." Matt laughs.

"I'm so sorry about all of this. You losing her. Me not getting to know her. All of it," Calvin says, and tears fill his eyes. There's genuine regret lurking there. "What happened if I may ask? How did she die?"

Matt lowers his gaze to the floor and says quietly, "Suicide."

No one has noticed, including me, that Hanson has returned until his voice echoes from the back of the room. "You liar! You killed her!"

My body goes rigid. Does Hanson know what really happened? Matt must have killed me, or he wouldn't have stormed in here with this announcement. I turn to study Matt when everything in the room melds together. Shit! I'm being taken elsewhere...again.

CHAPTER THIRTY-FOUR
THEN

The three kids and my former self are sitting at the dinner table, chatting and laughing, as was the norm when Matt wasn't home. He must be away on business—something I grew to appreciate more and more throughout the years.

Former me says, "Okay, I've got a fun game! What name would you pick for yourself if you could choose a new one?"

This must've been around the time when things started to really go downhill in our marriage. To escape the reality of my hell, I'd often daydream about running far away from Baysville and starting over somewhere new. Even though I'd moved around so much as a child because of my mom's many failed relationships, we always stayed within the same twenty square miles. My address had never been outside of this area. I'd imagine packing all of us up and just driving until the car ran out of gas. Wherever that was is where we'd stay. I could work to support us.

I never thought about trying to find another relationship. If I ever was bold enough to leave Matt, I knew I'd be done with men. I hated the person I'd become with him. I used to be so confident, so independent, so full of life. The longer I stayed with him, the less of me there was. I started slowly disappearing many years before my death.

I wanted to paint, take pictures, laugh with my kids, go on adventures with them to discover new things. But with Matt, none of that was possible. I always felt heavy, weighted down by our marriage, by him. I got to the point where I could no longer distinguish truth from fiction. Even when I was absolutely certain of something, he'd wear me down, insisting that I saw things incorrectly, so that I'd end up questioning my sanity. I don't know how he did it, but he could convince me the sky was green and the grass was blue. I'd have moments of clarity, particularly those times when he'd go away on business for a few days. The longer he stayed away, the more of me returned. I felt like a different person during those times. Even the kids noticed and would tell me that I was a nicer Mommy when Daddy wasn't around.

I knew though that Matt would hunt us down if I left. He would never allow me to move away with the girls, and I couldn't leave them behind. That was the one hurdle I could never get over in my mind. I had dreamed up a plan that perhaps I could find someone to help me get new birth certificates and social security cards for the kids and me. If we changed our identities and broke off all contact with family and friends, perhaps he'd never find us.

Avery's voice snaps me back to the kitchen, out of my memories. Her eyes sparkle, and a smile spreads across her face at the mention of it. "I know what I'd pick, Mommy. Try to guess."

"I have no idea, sweetie. Give us clues and Hanson and I will try to guess."

"She's a beautiful princess," Avery says and pauses.

"Cinderella?" Hanson asks.

Avery shakes her head. "That'd be a silly name. She lives in a castle."

"Duh, Avery. All princesses live in a castle," Hanson says.

"Aurora, like Sleeping Beauty?" younger me guesses.

Again, Avery shakes her head and giggles. "She talks to dishes and lives with a beast."

"Belle!" Hanson shouts.

"You got it! Belle!" Avery smiles from ear to ear.

"That's a beautiful name, Ave. Great choice! What about you, Hanson?"

"I dunno. I like my name," he shrugs.

"Me, too, but if you had to choose a new one, what would you pick?"

"Like if we wanted to run away and hide?" he asks with raised eyebrows. He always was smarter than his own good.

"Well, I guess that could be one scenario. Let's say that's it, what would you choose?"

He drums his fingers on the table and stares across the room, trying to think of something. Finally, he speaks, "I'd choose Arthur."

"Arthur, that's interesting. Why Arthur?"

"Well, you could call me Art for short. But I think Arthur sounds like a strong man's name. Like King Arthur and the Knights of the round table. I could protect us all, keep us safe and hidden."

Tears spring to my eyes both now and then. At that moment, I knew Hanson saw me disappearing. He saw past all my attempts to plaster on a smile and act like everything was okay. My heart shatters all over again, as it did the first time this happened, at the realization that I'd done a terrible job at hiding my misery. It seems I became a ghost long before I actually died.

"I like it, buddy. Art. Arthur!" younger me says. "You're right, it sounds like a strong name."

"What about you, Mommy? What would you choose?" Avery asks.

"I like the name Dana. When I was a little girl, one of my best friends was named Dana, and I was so jealous. I hated my long name and thought it sounded weird. But I thought Dana was beautiful."

Hanson nods. "It's a good name. But, could we still call you Mom?"

"Of course, buddy!" Former me ruffles his hair. "I'll always be your mom, no matter what."

"What about Vera? What could we call her?" Hanson asks.

Vera bangs her spoon against the tray of the high-chair and babbles. All of us laugh.

"Let's pick a name for her since that didn't make much sense," former me says and boops her on the nose. "I'll pick Gwendolyn for her, and we can call her Gwen!"

"That's pretty. Can we pick a last name, too?" Vera asks excitedly. "If so, I want mine to be Rose. Belle Rose."

"Well, if we pick a last name, we'd all have to choose the same one since we're a family!" my former self says. "So, what's one we could all agree on?"

They both shout out possibilities, most of them pretty far out there. Finally, younger me interrupts. "It would need to be something easy, that we'd all remember. Like Stone. Belle, Arthur, Gwen, and Dana Stone."

Hanson nods his affirmation. A frown replaces Avery's smile.

"Don't you like it, Avery?" younger me asks.

She nods. "What about Daddy? You didn't say Daddy?"

At the time, her words felt like a knife piercing my heart, shattering my dream. How could I ever justify taking the girls away from their father? Just like my mother took me away from mine. Would they ever forgive me if I did? Panic rises in my younger self, through flushed cheeks and wide eyes. My younger self realizes that no one can ever mention this game to Matt because he'll see right through it.

"It's just a game, Avery. A pretend game for just us. Let's not tell Daddy. It will be our secret game we play only when he's not around, okay?"

If there was anything Avery loved, it was thinking she was keeping a secret. She finally nods, her smile returning. "Okay, Mommy, Dana Stone and brother, Arthur Stone! Oh, and baby, Gwen Stone." She giggles.

Hanson smiles, but a sadness fills his eyes.

"Look at your son!" I shout at my former self. "Can't you see that your marriage is killing him? Look at him!"

I couldn't see it then, but now it's crystal clear what the sadness in his eyes means. He knows the impact of Avery's question. With one innocent, small question, our dream of escape was shattered. It was a game we played throughout the years, whenever Matt would go out of town for an extended stay. It was the only time I felt like I could breathe—when I was dreaming of a life in which Matt didn't exist, and I was far away from home. Perhaps though, playing that game and giving Hanson even that tiny bit of hope was essentially like twisting a knife in his back. He was always smart enough to know that I was too weak or scared to follow through. Or perhaps, in his mind, he thought the girls' happiness was more important than his.

"I'm so sorry, Hanson. I should've left. I see you now. Your pain. Your sadness." I wrap my arms around him and put my lips to his cheek. He leans his head into my embrace right as I'm carried back to the present.

CHAPTER THIRTY-FIVE
NOW

I'm back in the funeral home right at the moment the accusations toward Matt have left Hanson's mouth. A hush falls over the room for a moment before all hell breaks loose.

Matt lunges toward Hanson, screaming, "What the hell did you say, you little punk?"

Detective Andover rushes toward Matt, pulling him into a bear hug before he can reach Hanson, who had decided to meet Matt's challenge head-on, so he was also barreling towards Matt. Detective Jacobs pulls Hanson into a similar hold, and Detective Collier plants herself between the two.

Everyone else stands with their mouths hanging open, not sure what to say or do. Matt and Hanson continue to wrestle against the officers, trying to break away to get to each other. Both of their eyes are full of hatred and venom.

"That's enough!" Detective Collier shouts in a voice that could scare the toughest of men. Both Matt and Hanson freeze.

Detective Andover gives Matt a little push and points, saying, "You, sit there."

Detective Jacobs points to a seat on the opposite side of the room and lets Hanson go. Both men follow their orders.

"I'm going to ask that everyone else clear the room. We need to speak to these gentlemen alone," Detective Collier directs.

Mr. Pearson runs his hands through his perfectly styled hair and paces back and forth while everyone else exits the room.

"That includes you, Sir," Detective Collier says a bit gentler this time, obviously sensing his distress.

"Yes, okay. Umm, but what do I do with all the guests? We're supposed to be heading to the gravesite. Everyone is waiting. I'm not sure what to do," he says, continuing to pace, his normal calm and cool demeanor gone.

"I would suggest that you direct the guests to leave at this time and reschedule the rest of the service," Detective Collier states.

Mr. Pearson gasps like she's just suggested that he cut off one of his arms. "Reschedule? That's not something we do. You don't just reschedule part of a funeral service."

Detective Andover steps forward before speaking. "Mr. Pearson, we apologize for this interruption. This has been an unusual day, following a death under even more unusual circumstances, and we have an investigation to complete. We were trying to allow the service to conclude, but that's no longer possible. We know it's an inconvenience, but it's what needs to happen. We appreciate your cooperation."

Andover's words snap Mr. Pearson back to his usual self. "Of course. I will dismiss the guests, and we will come up with an alternate plan for the interment. Do you need an office to use for your investigation?"

"Both of these gentlemen will be coming to the station with us, but thank you for your offer," Detective Collier states. Matt goes rigid, and Hanson jerks his gaze in her direction.

What? They're both going to the station for questioning? No, no, no! I don't even know if I can leave to see what happens. After my death, it was like I was asleep and then woke up here when my family arrived. I'm not sure if I'm tied to this place, to being within a certain proximity of my earthly body. I don't have a clue about how this ghost thing works. I have to be able to go to the station, though. I have to know that everything is okay. Perhaps I will finally find out exactly how I died.

Mr. Pearson exits the room, and I follow, hoping that Aunt Lill stays to help Hanson or get him an attorney, whatever it is he needs.

He clears his throat and speaks loud enough to quiet the crowd, "Excuse me! I'm sorry for the disruption but, due to unforeseen circumstances, the graveside service will need to be rescheduled."

Everyone starts murmuring at once, whispers echoing off the walls and filling up the space. "This is an unusual occurrence, and there's not really a protocol in place for how we will deal with the need to reschedule, but we will figure it out. For now, I need to ask everyone to exit the building."

Aunt Lill and Avery head toward Mr. Pearson instead of out the door. Monique, Vera, and Tiffany stay standing together near the windows. My mom is nowhere to be seen, which is probably a good thing. She probably had to lie down again because of all the stress.

"What is going on?" Aunt Lillian asks.

"The police need to take Matt and Hanson to the station for questioning. They demanded that we reschedule the rest of the service."

"What?" Avery gasps, and her hand flies to her chest. Aunt Lillian puts her arm around her.

"It's going to be okay, Ave. What happened?" Aunt Lill asks.

"I'm not really sure. I thought we had everything figured out until Hanson burst in the room, announcing that Matt killed Mackenzie. I thought there was going to be a fistfight, but the detectives jumped in and stopped it."

Aunt Lillian's face creases with worry, making her suddenly look about ten years older. "Why do they need to take Hanson?"

"I'm not sure, ma'am. You'll need to ask them," Mr. Pearson says. "Now, if you'll excuse me. I need to go figure out how to handle this change in plans."

Aunt Lill pulls Avery into a hug. Rather than to comfort Ave, I think she's doing it so she can remain standing. Monique walks over and waits for them to end their embrace before speaking.

"Everything okay?" she asks.

Aunt Lill doesn't seem to be able to find her voice.

"The cops are taking Dad and Hanson to the station for questioning, Oh, my God, I can't believe this!" Avery gasps, and tears fill her eyes.

"Lill, should we call an attorney for Hanson? Matt probably already has one lined up," Monique says.

"I don't know. I don't know what needs to happen. I can't think straight. This is all too much," Aunt Lillian says. I've never seen my aunt at such a loss before. She always knows what to do, when to do it, and how it needs to be done. My heart aches for her.

"Here's what we're going to do. Let's try to talk to one of the detectives when they come out of the room to see exactly what's going on. If they're going to question Hanson, he needs an attorney. I have a friend I can call to help with that." Monique takes Lill's hand in hers. "Babe, it will be okay. It will all work out."

This cracks Aunt Lill's façade, and her eyes fill with tears. "Why are they questioning Hanson? He didn't do anything. It was Matt. I know it. Matt killed her."

Everyone is so caught up in the conversation that no one notices Vera has joined them. "What do you mean? Daddy killed Mommy?" she shouts.

I stoop to comfort my baby girl but don't get to her before the past calls me back.

CHAPTER THIRTY-SIX
THEN

I'm again taken back to our house. A quick glance around tells me that it's only the kids and my younger self. No Matt, which is a relief. Hanson must be about eleven as the little boy chubbiness is gone, and his voice is at that stage in between boy and man. This was about the time he started going through puberty, and his mood swings were awful.

"Hanson, TV off! Avery, come down here!" younger me yells.

Avery bounds down the steps with a smile, and Hanson turns off the TV.

"What, Mommy?" Avery asks.

"Father's Day is Sunday, so I need you two to sit down to make Matt's card." Younger me points to the small table where the art supplies are laid out.

Avery, of course, complies immediately. Hanson refuses to get up off the couch, instead turning the television back on.

"Hanson, go make Matt a card, please," former me says, standing in front of the TV screen.

He doesn't say a word, rather cranes his neck to see around younger me as I turn off the TV and point at him. "Now, Hanson!"

"For what?" he asks with snark heavy in his voice.

"What do you mean for what? For Father's Day. Just like we do every single year!" younger me shouts. Despair and exhaustion fill every crease in my younger self's face. Vera is only three months old and, as I recall, still not sleeping through the night. I had such a severe battle with post-partum depression, which is apparent from my low patience levels.

"No!" Hanson says, crossing his arms across his chest and jutting his chin out.

"Perhaps you misunderstood me. I wasn't asking, I was telling you. Go. Do. It." As usual, when I got mad, hot tears built up in my younger self's eyes.

"Perhaps you misunderstood me. I said no."

Oh shit! I remember this day and what's about to come next.

"Calm down!" I tell my younger self, knowing it's pointless. My younger self's temper flares as made obvious by my reddened cheeks and bulging eyes.

Younger me grabs Hanson by the arm, trying to pull him up. He's already five feet, nine inches, a full four inches taller than me, and weighs about the same. He fights to pull his arm away, and former me slaps him across the face. Tears fill his eyes before he runs to his room, slamming the door behind him. Younger me falls to the floor, presses my head against my knees, and sobs, feeling like a piece of shit for slapping my son. Trying to pull myself together, I'm not sure whether to comfort my younger self or go after Hanson. Not that I'll make a difference in either place.

The commotion wakes Vera from her nap—her wails echo inside of my former self's already thundering head. Avery is distracted from her card-making and comes to sit on the floor next to younger me.

"Mommy," she whispers and pats me on the back. "What'sa matter?"

My younger self tries to speak, but the only thing that comes out is a sob.

"It's okay, Mommy." She puts her arm around younger me, resting her head on my back.

My sweet, sweet Avery.

Former me takes a deep breath, trying to regain some control, but the tears won't stop. It seems I am trying to let out decades worth of them all at once.

"Vera's crying, Mommy," she eventually says, quietly. As if the whole neighborhood couldn't hear her. I distinctly remember what's going through my younger self's mind. Vera's screams echo inside my younger self's head, competing for attention with the sound playing on repeat there. The sound of my hand smacking Hanson. Watching this from afar now, I know that it couldn't have hurt that badly, physically anyway. The wide-eyed look of betrayal, as my younger self's hand connected with his cheek, is one I've never forgotten.

"I'm gonna go get her," Avery says and walks away.

"You need to get up," I shout. Avery is only seven and great at holding Vera, occasionally carrying her around under supervision. But Avery is still so tiny. "Get up! She can't carry Vera down the steps. Get up!" I scream so loudly that surely younger me must be able to hear.

Alive me tries to speak but, again, the words can't get past the crushing guilt. The house goes quiet, which means Avery has Vera.

"Get up! Avery needs your help." I shout again and yank on my younger self's arm. I move to the staircase where Avery is starting to make her way down the stairs, holding Vera in her arms. "Now!"

Younger me snaps her head toward my voice and rushes to the stairs.

"Ave, wait! I'm coming. Sit down with her, please!" Former me seems like she's moving in slow-motion. I tremble envisioning the weight of Vera pulling Avery over, both of them tumbling down the steps.

Avery obeys and sits with Vera protected in her arms on the top step. Younger me takes Vera from her and tells her to go back to making her card.

"I need your help, though," she says.

"I need to talk to Hanson a minute. I'll be right there. Promise!"

"Did Hanson make you cry?" she asks with her brow furrowed.

"No, Mommy is just upset. I feel better now. Thank you for helping with your sissy!" Younger me pulls her close.

"I love you!" she says and kisses Vera on the foot. "I love you too, sissy!" Then she bolts down the stairs to make her card.

Younger me knocks on Hanson's door several times, but he doesn't respond. "Hanson, I'm coming in." He lies on his bed with his head buried in his pillow. His sniffles let me know he's crying.

Younger me sits on the edge of his bed, and I sit on the other side of him. "Buddy, I am so, so sorry that I smacked you. That was not okay."

No response. Younger me sits quietly for a few minutes before continuing. "C'mon bud. Talk to me. Tell me why you don't want to make Matt a card. What's going on?"

He pulls away and sits, draws his knees to his chest, and wraps his arms around them. "He's not my dad. I'm not making him a card."

"We've talked about this. He is your dad. He takes care of you and has been in your life since you were a little guy. He's your dad," former me says. I'm not sure if I am trying to convince him or myself.

"He. Is. Not." He glares at younger me from above his knees. "I want to know who my real dad is."

"I've told you. His name was Shane Talman. He died before you were born."

"Okay, fine. I want to meet his, I mean, my family then. I'm sure I have grandparents, cousins. Why have you kept me from them?"

I remember how my heart thudded in my chest, feeling like it was going to explode. Along with the absolute panic because I had no prepared answers for these questions. I had never thought it through this far. My former self's mind races with what to say that will be a good enough explanation to quiet his questions.

"Why don't you want me to know my family?" he shouts.

"Hanson, honey. I didn't try to keep you from them. I didn't know his family at all. I don't think they knew I was pregnant," younger me says, hoping my excuses come out as genuine.

"Why wouldn't you tell them? Don't you think they'd want to know that their son had a child?"

"I...uh...I...don't know. You're right. I don't know." Memories of his "father's" smell, his eyes, bombard me now as they did the first time this happened, taking my younger self's breath and words away.

"I want to find them. I want to find my real family," he says.

"Can we please talk about this later, bud? Please?"

"There's nothin' to talk about. I'm gonna find them," he says with a glare.

Bile rises in my throat, listening to this exchange. Why was I so unprepared? At eleven, he is old enough and smart enough to know how to research things. It hits my younger self while sitting there on his bed what a fool I'd been—my body slumps forward with the revelation. I hadn't even been smart enough to look up the name Shane Talman to see if there was anyone out there with that name. I'd failed to do the research to back up my story. The last thing in the world anyone needs is for Hanson to find out that he'd been lied to for all these years. I'd wanted to spare him from the truth so badly, yet I failed in so many ways. He can never know that his father was a rapist, and I have no idea who he is. A tremor works its way through my younger self's entire body.

Younger me looks at Hanson, and I know exactly what I saw back then. For the first time, I see the same eyes staring back at me that I'd seen so many years before. His father's. An urgency to get away from his gaze filled me. From the questions for which I had no answers. Younger me stands and walks toward the door. As it's almost shut, Hanson says, "I am gonna find my family!"

Younger me shuts the door and holds Vera tightly, trying to catch a breath. I couldn't then—and still can't now—wrap my mind around Hanson's declaration and all it would mean. Now that I'm dead, will he find out the truth? God, please! I beg, not knowing if anyone is listening to my pleas or not. Perhaps God can no longer even hear my prayers.

"Mommy, are you coming?" Avery shouts from downstairs.

Younger me takes a deep, steadying breath before responding, "I'm on my way!"

As I'm pulled away from my family and my house, I remember one thing clearly. From that day forward, Hanson refused to call Matt 'Dad' any longer.

CHAPTER THIRTY-SEVEN
NOW

I come back to the funeral home where Vera stands with her hands on her hips, waiting for Aunt Lill to answer.

"Oh, honey. I'm sorry. I didn't see you there." Lillian leans down so they're face to face.

"Why'd you say that? Daddy didn't kill Mommy!" Tears flow down her cheeks, but she doesn't change her stance of defiance. "Why'd you say it?"

Aunt Lillian remains silent. Finally, Monique intervenes. "Aunt Lill was upset. She didn't mean it, Vee!"

Vera glances from Aunt Lill to Monique, seemingly trying to determine the truth. I know she believes Monique when she drops her hands from her hips and wipes away her tears.

Aunt Lill pulls her into a hug as the doors open. Hanson is the first one out of the room, followed by two of the detectives, then Matt, with Collier at the rear.

"What's going on?" Aunt Lillian shouts, running over to them.

Hanson looks at Detective Andover, seemingly asking for permission to speak. The detective holds out his arm toward Lillian and walks over to her with Hanson trailing behind.

Hanson's lips tremble, and his face turns ashen. "I...uh, we need to go to the station to answer some questions."

"Why? What's happening, Detective?" Lillian asks.

"We have some questions to help with our investigation into Mackenzie's death. We need to speak with Matt and Hanson," he says firmly, not really giving an answer.

What the hell? Why do they need to speak with Hanson?

"Does he need an attorney?" Aunt Lillian points at Hanson.

"That's entirely up to him," the detective says.

"Can he ride with me to the station, or do you need to escort him?" Lillian asks.

"He's not under arrest, so that's between the two of you. We need him to come now, though."

"Thank you," Aunt Lillian grips Hanson's arm. "I know you have your car here, but I'm going to take you, okay?"

Hanson trembles from head to toe—there's no way he'd be capable of driving himself safely. He nods. I see the little boy hidden beneath the surface of the man he's become. He wears every insecurity, every fear, every failure, making him seem small even though he's six feet two inches tall. I want to wrap my arms around him and tell him that it will be okay. That Aunt Lill will make sure he's taken care of. For years, he's pushed me and everyone else away. For the first time, in a very long time, I can see how lonely and isolated he's become. How perhaps him pushing us all away was a cry for help. A way to show us how lost he really felt. And now, it's too late for me to do anything about it.

"I'm coming with you," Avery announces.

"I'll take Vee back to my house if it's okay with Matt," Monique says.

"Thank you, hon," Lillian says. "Okay, guys, let's go!"

I follow along, hoping and praying I'm able to leave with them. That I'm not stuck here in this funeral home. Relief floods me when Aunt Lill pulls out of the parking lot, and I'm still with them. Apparently, I'm tied to my family, more than to my empty shell of a body.

Once she's pulled out of the lot, Aunt Lill breaks the silence. "Hanson, Monique is calling an attorney for you, so don't worry."

"I don't need an attorney. I didn't do anything wrong," he says, staring out the window.

"It doesn't matter if you did anything wrong or not, you need an attorney if they're going to question you. I'm sure Matt will have one."

"Let me just see how it goes, okay? See if I need one."

Aunt Lill sighs. "I don't know, Hanson. Sometimes people can get tripped up in these interviews and not figure it out until it's too late. I'd feel better if you had a lawyer with you at all times."

"You really should have one, Hanson," Avery pipes in from the back seat.

Hanson runs his hands through his hair. "I don't know what to do, alright? I can't think!"

"Which is why you need someone with you," Lillian says.

"Go ahead and call someone, but I don't want them there right away. Let me see what they want. What they're asking. I don't want to look like I did anything wrong, because I didn't."

"Hanson, don't be stupid. Don't open your mouth until you have an attorney!" I scream, hoping that somewhere deep inside either he or Aunt Lill hear my demands.

"Okay, but I don't like it. You're an adult, so I have to trust you," she says instead.

"No! No! No!" I shout to deafened ears.

"As soon as you get uncomfortable with a line of questioning, you tell them you want an attorney and that I have one for you, okay? And, once you say that, don't say another word until your lawyer arrives. Got it?" she asks.

He nods.

"I want them to figure out the truth. Hopefully, this is a step in the right direction," Lillian says.

Again, Hanson nods but sits quietly, chewing his nails.

I can already tell that this isn't going to go well. I want Aunt Lill to insist on the attorney from the get-go. Hanson has never done well under pressure.

Far too quickly, we arrive at the police station. Aunt Lill puts the car in park and leans over to give Hanson a hug. "Ave and I will be in the lobby, waiting for you. Remember, ask for an attorney if the questioning gets out of hand."

"I will," he whispers. His nose reddens as though he's about to cry.

"I love you, Hanson!" Avery says from the backseat.

"Love you too, Ave!"

They get out and walk into the station together. I wish Hanson knew I'd be right there with him in the room. Perhaps he can feel my presence.

DETECTIVES Andover and Collier lead Hanson to a small interview room, complete with a camera in the corner but no two-way glass like is always featured in TV shows. He sits on one side of the table and clasps his hands together to try to stop them from shaking.

Detective Collier speaks first. "Thanks for coming to talk with us today, Hanson. Hopefully, we won't take up too much of your time. We're sorry for interrupting the service for your mother."

He sits silently.

"So, let's jump right in, shall we? I know some of our detectives already spoke with you, but we need to clarify a few things," Detective Andover says. "Take me back to the day your mom died. You were the one to find her, correct?'

"Yes," he says quietly.

"Oh my God!" I say with this revelation. I have no memory of the day I died. Everything is crystal clear up until that day. How awful that Hanson had to find me! How will he ever recover from that?

"Tell me about that."

"I went to the house to help Mom load up some boxes. She was moving out, ya know? I got there about one in the afternoon. The girls weren't home. When I got there, I found her," he stops talking, trying to choke back a sob as tears fill his eyes. He takes a deep breath and continues. "I found her in the kitchen. There was blood everywhere."

I gag and try to dredge up some memory of that day. There's nothing there. It's a blank.

"Was she alive at that point?" Collier asks.

He shakes his head. "I don't think so. She couldn't have been. There was too much blood. I panicked and called 911."

"Did you call immediately?" Andover asks.

"Yeah, I think so. I was kinda in shock. As far as I can remember, yes."

"Did you touch her, Hanson?"

He nods. "She was cold. I tried to check her pulse but couldn't find one. I held her hand until the police arrived."

"Could you tell at that point, how she had died?" Collier asks.

"There was a gun next to her, and the back of her head was missing, so I assumed she'd been shot."

"A gun? How did a gun get next to my body?"

"Did you touch the gun?" Andover asks.

He nods. "I know it was stupid, but yes. I was so shocked to see it there. My mom was very anti-gun. I pushed it away from her. I didn't want it near her."

"Do you know where she got the gun?" Andover says.

"I don't think she got it anywhere."

"What do you mean?" Andover leans forward.

"I think Matt got the gun and shot her because she was leaving him."

As much as I don't want to believe that Matt killed me, this makes the most sense. As Hanson said, I'm anti-gun—always have been.

"Has Matt been violent with your mother in the past?" Collier asks.

"Cruel, yes. Emotionally abusive, yes. He had never hit her, as far as I know, until the week before she died. He went off when she told him she was leaving."

Pain courses through me at Hanson's mention of this incident. The fear creeps up my neck and down my spine as I remember all of the events Hanson has no knowledge of.

"Did you witness that?" Collier asks.

"No," Hanson says. "I wasn't there. Avery called me crying and upset, begging me to come over. She told me that Matt had hurt Mom and that she was afraid."

"Did you go to the house at that time?" Andover taps his pen against the table.

"I was working. I had to finish my shift. I told Avery to stay in her room with Vera and that I'd be there soon. I got there within two hours."

This night is as clear to me as though it happened yesterday. Why isn't the day I died?

"And what happened then?"

"By the time I got there, Matt had stormed off. Mom, Ave, and Vee were on the couch watching a movie. Mom had marks on her neck and bruises on her ribs where Matt had kicked her."

"Why didn't she call the police?" Andover asks.

"I told her to. She wouldn't listen. She said she just wanted to be done. She wanted to move on with her life," he says as tears fill his eyes. "She'd gotten an apartment with some money from Aunt Lillian. It was small but big enough for her and the girls. I've been staying there and was planning on moving into my own place once she left Matt—which is why I was working, to save up money."

"I hate to be so blunt, but I have to ask. Do you believe your mother shot herself?" Collier asks.

I go still, anxiously awaiting his answer.

"No way! She'd never leave us. She couldn't wait to start over. Get a job. Be free of Matt. She'd never kill herself." Hanson's voice cracks as he speaks.

I ache for him.

Anders steeples his hands and rests his chin on his fingers, narrowing his eyes. "Were you aware, at the time you found your mother, that she had also been shot in the chest?"

Hanson shakes his head. "I don't think so. Like I said, I was in shock, and there was blood everywhere. All I could think about was Vee and Ave coming home and finding her. I didn't want them to see her like that."

My poor, poor boy. How is he ever going to get through this? How is he going to be okay?

"Tell me about Matt's reaction to your mother's death," Collier says.

"He's thrilled, I'm sure." Hanson unclenches his hands and rubs them through his hair. "He cried and sobbed. Put on a good show. He kept yelling he didn't know why she'd do this to herself."

"Have you and Matt spoken about her death at all?"

Hanson shakes his head. "I try not to speak to that bastard at all. I haven't been around him since it happened, other than at the funeral home. I can't stand him."

Andover stands and begins pacing, his brow furrowed. When he speaks, his tone is harsh. "Something I don't understand, Hanson, that maybe you can clear up for me. We know now that your mother was shot twice. Once in the chest and once in the head. The shot to the head could have been self-inflicted. There is no way she could've been the one to shoot herself in the chest. We didn't find Matt's fingerprints on the gun, but we did find yours," Andover stops pacing and leans to put both hands forcefully onto the table. "Help me understand that."

Hanson sits up straight and takes a deep breath. "I told you. I pushed the gun away from her. That's the only way my fingerprints could've gotten on it. I don't know why Matt's weren't on the gun. Maybe he wore gloves or something. I don't know," he stammers.

"Stop talking. Ask for an attorney!" I shout. It's obvious to me that they've switched gears into an accusatory line of questioning, but I don't think Hanson can see that.

"Okay, humor me," Andover says, pulling the gun from his holster. He removes the clip and slams the gun on the table. "Using my gun, show me exactly how you moved the one away from your mother."

Hanson physically recoils at the sight of the weapon. "I can't. I don't remember."

Collier speaks in a much calmer tone than Andover. "Just do your best to remember, Hanson. How do you think you would've moved it away if the gun were positioned exactly as it is now?"

"Don't do it, Hanson! Ask for a lawyer, dammit." I scream, but he doesn't hear me.

He sits and studies the weapon. Several times, he reaches forward as though he's going to comply, but draws his hand back each time before making contact with the gun.

Finally, he slumps back, dropping both hands in his lap. "I'm sorry. I don't remember. I wish I could, but I don't."

Andover slams the table with his hand. "Dammit, son. I don't think you understand how important this is. Your prints were found on the gun. We need to know how they got there. You said you moved the gun away. We need to know where and how you touched it. You 'not remembering' isn't good enough. You must remember."

Hanson clenches and unclenches his teeth. I'm sure he's about to demand an attorney. He's smart—he knows how badly it will look if he refuses to answer or if he answers incorrectly. After what feels like forever, he leans forward.

"Fine. This is how I moved it," he says, reaching forward.

I scream into the void.

He places his hand so that his finger lightly touches the trigger, his hand along the grip, exactly as he'd touch it if he'd been holding it. He picks it up, holds it to his own forehead, and then drops it back to the table, pushing it to the side. He slumps back in his seat.

"That's exactly what I did. I thought about shooting myself. I held it up to my head and almost pulled the trigger. Because without my mom, I have no one. Do you understand me? No one," he shouts as he finally sets the tears that have been building, free.

I go to my son and wrap my arms around him, holding him as he cries. I wish he could feel me, and I, him. I hope he knows that what he said isn't true. He may not have me, but he has Aunt Lill, Avery, and Vera. They will love him well in my absence. How I hope he knows this!

"So, why didn't you?" Detective Andover asks. I wish I could punch him. What in the hell kind of question is that to ask this obviously distraught kid?

"Why didn't I what?" Hanson says.

"Why didn't you shoot yourself?" Andover challenges.

Without missing a beat, Hanson replies, "Because there was no way in hell I could do that to my sisters. I can't leave them alone with that bastard. I wanted to pull the trigger, but then I pictured their faces, coming home and finding Mom and me both dead. So, I tossed it aside and called 911."

After a moment of silence, Collier, too, stands. "Hanson, thank you. Detective Andover and I need to speak for a few moments. Is there anything I can get you? Water? Coffee? Soda?"

He shakes his head. "I just want to go."

"That's not possible just yet, okay?" she says. "I promise we'll get you out of here as soon as we can. We will be back as quickly as possible."

They exit the room, and Hanson rests his arms on the table, burying his head in them. I want to stay with Hanson, to be able to comfort him and make sure he's okay, but I need to know what the detectives are saying. My suspicion is that they're going to question Matt. And I must be there for that. But, for now, I'm carried back in time to a place I'm certain I won't want to be.

CHAPTER THIRTY-EIGHT
THEN

I arrive in the empty living room of our house very early in the morning. The sun hasn't even begun to rise yet. Delicious smells waft in from the kitchen, so I make my way there. Former me is busy preparing a turkey. It must be Thanksgiving. My stomach drops—I know exactly which Thanksgiving this is. I watch myself work for a while—more carefree and happier than I'd been in a long time. It's the Thanksgiving—the last one I'd planned to spend in this house.

I had been planning for six months prior to telling everyone about my intent to leave Matt, for real this time. He had gotten to the point where he no longer even tried to hide his indiscretions. He'd come home at all hours of the night with hickeys on his neck, scratch marks on his back, and smelling like sex. I had honestly stopped caring. I was happy with anything that kept him out of the house, away from the kids and me. But he didn't like my indifference. He wanted a reaction, and the more I ignored him, the crueler he became. If he came home after one of his trysts and I was still awake, he'd make sure to do something to get my attention or shock me. One night it was shoving his fingers under my nose, asking if I could smell Charlotte on them. Another night, he stripped his shirt off and asked me to put antibiotic ointment on the scratches on his back.

If I was asleep, he'd leave clues for me to find. A condom wrapper on the bathroom counter. A slip of paper with a woman's name and phone number on the dresser. Sending me a text "by accident" that was meant for one of his lovers. He enjoyed causing me pain, but he'd lost the ability to do so because I no longer gave a shit. The less I cared, the more desperate he became. Higher desperation meant more cruelty.

I made the decision to leave the day Hanson graduated from high school. I knew that Matt would always make sure the girls were taken care of whether he and I were together or not, but he would be more than happy to write Hanson out of his life. At Hanson's graduation, as he crossed the stage to collect his diploma, I realized I could finally be free now that Hanson was an adult, and we had other survival options besides Matt providing for us.

The only person I told of my plans, in the beginning, was Aunt Lillian. She helped me search for affordable places to live around town. She helped me come up with a way to squirrel away money without Matt noticing. She bolstered my confidence in being able to do it on my own. The plan was to be ready to leave right after Christmas so that the kids' lives weren't disrupted during the holidays. I'd move to a small apartment close to Aunt Lill's shop and work there. She pulled ten thousand dollars out of her retirement savings to help me get on my feet. With that money, we rented the apartment and started slowly furnishing it so that it would be ready whenever I needed it.

Hanson moved out immediately after graduation, crashing on friends' couches until he could save enough money for his own place. He got a job in the office at a local correctional facility and seemed to love it. I tried to talk him into going to college, but he said it wasn't the path for him. He said his goal was to attend the Police Academy when he was old enough. Of course, once he moved out, I wasn't allowed to help him financially at all. Matt made that perfectly clear.

Hanson made sure to only visit when Matt was away. It was during one of those visits that I finally confessed my plan to him. Since I couldn't help him out with money without Matt knowing, I gave him the key to my apartment and told him to stay there until he could get his own place. I hated knowing he was essentially homeless and at the mercy of his friends for a place to rest his head. Hanson was reluctant at first about living in my new place before I got the chance, but I insisted. He was working so hard to better himself; I had to support him however I could.

That's why former me is smiling and happy this Thanksgiving Day. I thought it would be our last under the same roof as Matt. I was in the final countdown of escaping my prison. Hanson had been saving money and would be able to move into his own place by the time we left. I had enough money saved to get me through the first couple of months, in addition to the help from Aunt Lill. Having an escape plan made me feel something I hadn't felt in many, many years—hope. I felt so much lighter, as though I could finally breathe again. But, as always, Matt could sense it and became even more desperate to pull me down.

The plan for Thanksgiving was to have Hanson, Aunt Lill, and Monique over for dinner. This year, I was going to prepare the feast for all of us. I'd stayed up late into the night to cook. Former me whistles, which makes my stomach drop and my entire body starts to tremble. I try to walk into the other room because I don't want to witness what's going to happen next. Living through it once was bad enough. But I can't leave. It's as if an invisible force field holds me in place. I can't move out of the kitchen. Each time, it's like running into a brick wall. I'm stuck and being forced to bear witness.

"What the hell are you so happy about?" Matt squints against the bright lights.

Former me shrugs. "It's Thanksgiving. I'm thankful."

"Oh yeah. For what?"

"So much. Food, family, clothes, my health." My former self continues to cut up the sweet potatoes.

"What about your husband?" he says, moving closer to former me.

I tense along with my former self. "Of course."

"That didn't sound too convincing." He slips his hand inside my former self's shirt, grabbing my breast.

Former me flinches. At that point, he hadn't touched me sexually in a long time.

"Stop. I'm trying to cook," former me says, trying to pull away.

He refuses to move his hand and, instead, tightens his grip to the point where it hurts.

"Matt, you're hurting me. Stop it."

He stands behind former me and starts kissing my neck. Former me glances at the knife in my hand and has the strongest urge to plunge it into him. Instead, alive me drops it on the cutting board, figuring fighting him off was what he wanted from me.

"Get away, Matt!" I scream and try to barrel toward him, but I'm stuck. I can't move. "Stab him! Pick up the knife and stab him!" Tears stream down my cheeks.

He whispers. "Do you know why I fuck all those other women?"

Former me shakes my head.

"Because you're a sick, twisted, and hateful man!" I shout now, wishing I was strong enough to say it when he could hear me.

"Because you're a cold bitch!" he says, continuing to run his hands up and down my former self's body. "You have never been enough for me."

"So, why are you touching me?"

"Because I can. You belong to me. Don't you forget it," he says, his hot breath against my ear making me cringe. "Feel!" He moves my former self's hand to his crotch, against his hardness.

"Matt! Let me go! The kids could come down any minute," former me pleads.

He laughs—a bone-chilling and sadistic sound—and pulls down my former self's pants. He forces himself inside of me, covering my mouth with his hand when I try to scream.

I scream for my former self. So loudly that I'm certain my voice will break through whatever barrier separates current me from past me. But no one can hear me even though my entire body aches from the effort. I can feel him inside of me as he thrusts himself into my former self. The look on his face is one of pure evil. Tears stream down my former self's cheeks, matching the ones I now have.

Once he's finished, he pulls up his pants and pours himself a cup of coffee. Former me tries to resume cutting the potatoes through the tears because I didn't want to give him the satisfaction of seeing me cry.

He sits at the island across from where I'm working and chuckles. "What's wrong? You didn't like that?"

Former me doesn't look at him or utter a word.

"You sick bastard! I hope you rot in hell!" I shout for the both of us.

"You're the only one that doesn't. I have a dozen women I could call up right this minute who would be more than happy to be with me," he says and laughs. "But, not you. My frigid, uptight wife."

Former me puts the knife down and bolts toward the doorway, wanting desperately to get away from him. He grabs my former self's arm.

I lunge toward him, and this time I can move. I punch him as forcefully as I can, and he drops his hand.

"Where are you going?"

"To the bathroom. You left a mess,"

"You used to like those messes! What the hell happened to you? I'm surprised I can even get it up for you anymore. You've let yourself go. And you wonder why I sleep around!"

Former me yanks away. "Leave me the hell alone. I don't care who you sleep with; just don't touch me. I don't want you near me."

Former me again heads toward the bathroom. His next comment stops former me dead in my tracks and is one I will never forget. "That's what makes it fun."

"You're a sick bastard!" alive me shouts.

Once inside the safety of the locked bathroom, I wrap my arm around my former self as we both sob. I remember how my mind felt like it was going to shatter, trying to wrap itself around the fact that my husband just raped me. My thoughts whirled back then, trying to figure out how I was going to make it through the next month with this new level of cruelty. Another pointless thing to worry about because I didn't make it. I never got to leave—not alive, anyway.

I'm forced to sit through the family dinner as my former self struggles to make it through with a smile plastered on my face for the kids. Every time Matt catches my former self's eye, he smiles, looking happier than he had in months. He knew he'd found a way that he could still cause me pain.

Despair fills me, perhaps even more than when this happened. Being forced to relive this experience, I'm filled with doubt. I was convinced that Matt must have killed me, but now, I question if, in my desperation to escape, I killed myself. Perhaps it was the only way to be free.

As the family starts to leave, the living room fades around me, and I'm relieved that, at least for now, I get to escape my hell for a bit longer.

CHAPTER THIRTY-NINE
NOW

When I return to now, it's again as though I never left. I follow the detectives out the door even though I want to stay with Hanson. There's no point, though, since he can't feel my presence. The door shuts, and Collier turns to Andover.

"Well?" She raises her eyebrows with the question.

He shrugs. "Who knows? I can see him being upset and thinking about offing himself. He obviously doesn't have a great relationship with his step-father."

"Maybe talking with Matt will give us some more clarity," she says. "Hanson's statement is consistent with what he said previously. Well, other than the thoughts about suicide."

Andover chuckles. "True, but I doubt that talking with Matt will help with anything. He seems to be a bit of an ass. I'll be shocked if he doesn't lawyer up right away. He's an attorney after all."

I can't help but smile in relief that they can see the truth about Matt. They go into the fourth door on the left, and I follow behind. Matt sits at the table, calm, cool, and collected, as is his norm. He starts to rise when they enter, but Andover holds his hand out.

"You can stay seated," he says and takes a seat on the opposite side of the table as Collier sits next to him.

"Thank you for coming to the station today. We have a few questions and will try not to keep you long," Collier says.

"No problem," he says and smiles. I used to find his smile so charming. Now, it sickens me.

"So, let's go back to the day of Mackenzie's death, December twenty-ninth. Where were you that day?" Collier says.

December twenty-ninth? Four days after Christmas! The reality of this hits me again. I'd stayed so I wouldn't ruin the holidays for my children. That obviously didn't work out. My chest tightens—my babies will never be able to celebrate the holiday the same. I try again to pull up memories of that day, but nothing comes. As I suspected, I never did get to leave Matt and begin my new life.

"I've already answered that question but, I was in the office from eight in the morning until I got the call about the uh…the incident," Matt says.

"Can anyone confirm that?" Andover asks.

Matt thinks for a moment before responding. "I'm trying to remember if I saw anyone that day. A lot of people were still out of the office because of the holidays. Most of the staff take the week off between Christmas and the New Year, so…"

Andover interrupts him. "Did anyone see you in the office?"

Matt shakes his head. "I don't believe so, no."

"Okay, thank you. We understand Mackenzie was moving out, into her own place. Can you tell us about that?" Collier asks.

"We'd been having some issues, yes. We were going to separate for a while. She got a place across town."

"Issues? What type of issues?" Andover says gruffly.

Matt chuckles. "Are you married, Sir?"

Andover clenches his jaw and nods. "We are here to ask you questions, not the other way around. Got it?"

The smile leaves Matt's face, and he nods. "Can you tell us about the issues, Sir?" Collier asks calmly.

"Neither of us has been happy for a long time. We both stuck it out for the kids." Matt intently studies his hands resting on the table.

Collier nods while Andover glares at Matt.

"Speaking of the kids, what was going to happen with your daughters, Vera and Avery?" Collier asks.

"Naturally, they were going to stay with me in the home they've grown up in. There's no reason to uproot the children because we were having problems. Plus, apartment living isn't suitable for two active children," Matt says with a slight twitch in his right eye, which has always been his tell for when his anger is starting to build. I'd learned to study that eye closely over the years.

"And what did your wife think, Sir?" Collier asks.

Matt sits quietly for a moment before answering. "Uh, I'm not really sure."

Andover laughs, but there's no humor in it. "Let me get this straight. Your wife was in the process of moving out. Had actually started packing up some things, including your daughters' clothing, and you don't know what her intentions were? Bullshit."

Redness creeps up Matt's neck towards his lower jawline, another tell for his rage. "I'm sorry you don't believe that, but it's the truth. We had never discussed it. I didn't realize she was packing up our daughter's things until after everything had happened and I was finally allowed back in the house. I hadn't been home for a couple of days before the incident."

"Oh, really?" Collier asks. "Where were you?"

The redness now covers his entire cheeks, and his ears are flaming. "I have a girlfriend. I had been staying with her."

Andover chuckles and shakes his head. "You're a piece of work, aren't you? Who is this girlfriend? We need a name."

"I really don't want to bring her into this. She doesn't have anything…"

Collier interrupts. "Her name?"

Matt throws his hands up in the air and sighs. "Fine, Josie Lemmitz. She's my assistant."

"Funny thing is, I can probably already tell you what she's like. Mid-twenties, chesty, a bit ditzy. Young and dumb is probably exactly the way you like them. Could you be any more of a cliché?" Andover says.

Collier rests her hand on Andover's arm to indicate that he's said enough.

"You don't need to say anything about that right now," Collier says and smiles at Matt. "So, you were at work the day Mackenzie died. And then what?"

"I got a call from our neighbors, the Hudson's, to tell us there were police cars and ambulances at our house. I rushed home to a madhouse. By the time I got there, the house was a crime scene, and I wasn't allowed inside. The girls were home and obviously distraught."

"Where was Hanson?" Andover asks.

"He was with the girls when I got there. Trying to comfort them. He had blood all over himself, though. Once I got there, I took over with the girls, and the officers allowed him to go to the neighbors to get some fresh clothing. You guys took his clothing as evidence if I'm not mistaken."

Neither detective indicated whether or not that was the case.

"Were you abusive to your wife?" Andover asks with raised eyebrows.

The redness and eye twitch return instantly. "Heavens, no. I wouldn't ever lay a hand on a woman."

Andover slams his hand on the table. "Don't bullshit me. The autopsy showed three broken ribs and bruising around her neck, which was about a week old. If you weren't beating on her, then who was?"

Matt covers his face with his hands and sits quietly. Finally, he leans back, crosses his arms, and says, "Fine. Yes. I was violent with her once. Right before Christmas. She was threatening to take the girls and spend the day at her aunt's house because she didn't want to be around me. I got pissed. We'd agreed to keep everything normal for the girls until after Christmas. She hit me first, and I just lost it. I feel awful about that." Tears fill his eyes, and if I didn't know better, I'd think he was genuinely sorry. But I know better. It's all for show.

The fear and pain from that day fill me now. Of course, he left out all the parts that tell the true story about what happened that day.

"Yeah, they all do," Andover says only a bit louder than a whisper.

"So, humor me," Collier says. "What do you think happened to your wife?"

"We all know what happened to her. She shot herself," Matt says.

Andover steeples his fingers and leans forward. "Interesting, that you have it all figured out when we still don't have all of the answers."

"What do you mean? She shot herself in the head. How many more answers do you need?" This time Matt's shock seems genuine.

Andover leans forward as though he's going to tell Matt a secret but then continues in his normal, gruff voice. "Well, we've discovered some interesting things. For instance, a second gunshot wound in your wife's chest that was definitely not self-inflicted."

Matt's jaw drops open as though he's completely caught off guard. "Excuse me? Wh…what?"

"Your wife had a second gunshot wound to the chest that was not self-inflicted. Someone shot her. It's our job to figure out who that person was," Collier says.

Matt slumps back against his chair and loosens his tie, unbuttoning the top button of his shirt. Sweat breaks out across his brow.

"So, any ideas on that?" Andover asks with a smirk.

Matt twists his wedding band around his finger, studying it as though he's never seen it before. Finally, he stops and makes eye contact with Collier.

"I'd like to call my attorney."

I can no longer make out any of their faces. Matt, Collier, and Andover all merge together into a swirl of color as I'm carried away, yet again. Hopefully to somewhere in my past that can help me make sense of all of this. To help me figure out how I died.

CHAPTER FORTY
THEN

I'm in our bedroom; initially, I think I'm alone but then hear a noise in the closet and find former me, pulling clothes from hangers. This wasn't that long ago. Because of the boxes everywhere, my guess is it's about three days before Christmas. Former me picks up a handful of clothes and dumps them on the bed. There are no bruises on my former self, and it's then I'm certain of what day it is. One that was hard enough to live through the first time.

"Why are you doing this to me? Why am I being punished?" I shout to God, wondering if He can hear me. If He can, it certainly doesn't feel like he cares about me, or He'd never make me go through this nightmare a second time. My entire body trembles as former me meticulously folds each piece of clothing before putting it in the box at the foot of the bed.

At this point, I'd endured almost a month of Matt's newfound sexual cruelty, and I was counting down the days until I could move. My plan was to be out of the house by January first. Originally, I was going to just leave and not tell Matt where I was, but that wouldn't work with the girls. Why didn't I trust my gut and keep him in the dark? I'd started packing a box here and there, then Hanson would stop by to pick them up and put them in the apartment. Matt wasn't home often enough to notice anyway. And, when he was home, he was focused on the girls or making me suffer.

He hadn't seemed to notice things going missing. It helped that it was Christmas time, so the house was fully decorated, which meant some of our usual items were packed away to begin with. After Thanksgiving, I told Avery my plan and asked her what she wanted to do, where she wanted to live. She said she wanted to live with me but didn't want to hurt her dad's feelings. I lied and told her that I was sure he'd be fine with whatever she decided, knowing full well he most definitely would not. Hanson, Avery, and I decided that Vera didn't need to know anything ahead of time. She wasn't capable of keeping a secret.

Matt had been staying somewhere, with some woman, no doubt, for several weeks. He'd make an appearance a couple of times each week to see the girls and to sexually assault me, but other than that, he was pre-occupied. Which was perfect, or so I thought. We had planned on him coming home to spend Christmas Eve with the girls.

I hear the front door open before my former self does—probably because I know what's coming.

"Hanson?" former me yells downstairs, thinking he must have stopped by to take another load to the apartment.

There's no response. Former me keeps packing, not alarmed in the least, thinking he made a pit stop in the kitchen and didn't hear me yell. Former me heads back into the closet, standing on tiptoe to reach the sweaters on the shelf.

"Turn around!" I yell and grab my former self's arm just as another hand grabs me from behind.

Former me fights to get free, but the grip tightens. I kick and hit, trying to break the hold on me. Other me tries to twist to see who has me in their grips, but can't. Former me tries to scream, but a hand clasps over my mouth, despite my efforts to now pry that hand away. Absolute panic filled me at not being able to breathe, at my heart feeling like it was going to pound out of my chest. At the time, I had no idea who had me or if I'd remembered to lock the front door. Memories of my rape in college assaulted me. I shout at my former self, but my words don't penetrate. Former me struggles to take a deep breath through the nose as questions bounce around my mind. That's the moment my former self realizes who has me as Matt's musky smell permeates me, and nausea rises in the back of my throat.

"You sick, sick bastard!" I shout.

Former me stops fighting and lets my body go limp. I try to leave the room. I can't watch this again. I won't. If I can't make Matt stop, then I need to get out of here. But like Thanksgiving Day, I'm stuck right there next to the edge of the bed, unable to move.

As he whips former me around and forces his mouth onto mine, I try to shut my eyes to block all of this out. All I see in my mind is his tongue pushing past my tightly closed lips. Alive me doesn't kiss him back but also doesn't resist his roaming tongue or hands, thinking it was smart to not fight back because it's what he wanted. All of this plays out like a movie even though my eyes are closed. I force them back open.

"Fight him! Don't let him do this!"

He is being rougher than usual. My former self's eyes glaze over, and I remember how, in my mind, I was counting down the days until I'd be free. It was supposed to be only nine days. I remember chanting nine days over and over in my mind trying to tune out the pain, Matt's grunts, my nausea.

"Stop counting and fight! You're not going to make it out of here alive. Nine days doesn't matter. You need to fight!" I shout and fall to the floor, trembling.

When he finishes, it's as if he comes to and notices the mess of boxes everywhere.

"What the hell is this?" he shouts.

Former me ignores his question, grabbing a pair of sweats and pulling them on.

He grabs former me by the arm. "I asked you a damn question. What is going on?"

"Isn't it obvious? I'm leaving."

His right eye twitches as redness creeps up his neck into his cheeks.

Former me pushes past him, out of the closet, so that I won't be trapped there when he blows up.

I don't even try to shout warnings anymore. They're useless. I'm useless. Why do I have to come back to witness all of this if I can't change a damn thing? Why can't I just die? Be gone? Be free from this world of pain? I don't care anymore about how I died. I don't need or want to know.

"What do you mean you're leaving? Where the hell are you going to go?"

"Away from here. I'm done. With your games. Your bullshit. I'm done," former me says, in as steady a voice as possible.

He rushes over and pushes other me back onto the bed. "You aren't going anywhere. You hear me?" he shouts, spittle flying.

Former me turns away, refusing to make eye contact. He grasps my former self's chin and jerks my face back toward him. Former me still refuses to meet his eyes. Maybe things would've been different if I had.

"Look at me when I'm talking to you. You. Are. Not. Leaving. This. House." His face is only inches from my former self's, his hot breath turning my stomach, making me want to vomit. "Do you hear me?"

Former me stays silent. I didn't care what he thought anymore. I was leaving, regardless of what he wanted or demanded. There was no point in discussing it. My lack of a response is the final straw. He pulls other me to the ground and stands above me—above us really, since I'm laying right next to my former self. Being forced to look into my own eyes as this next part unfolds.

"This is the last time I'm going to ask. Do you hear me?"

Former me tries to pull up off the ground when the first kick comes to the ribs, knocking all of the air out of me. Pain rips through me, as though it's happening now. I see my former self's eyes roll back in my head with the second kick, on the verge of losing consciousness. I lose count after the third. My body aches more with each kick, but they just keep coming. I'd never felt such pain before.

The kicking stops, and he pulls former me to my feet. I stay huddled on the ground remembering the pain and how I felt like my ribs were sawing my internal organs in half. The pain was unbearable then, as it is now. His hands wrap around my former self's throat, tighter and tighter. It felt like my windpipe was being crushed beneath his fingers, and I really thought that this was it. That he was going to kill me. I was sure I was in my final moments as my vision started to go. Suddenly his hands relax, and he pushes former me back onto the bed. Other me curls into a ball trying to ease the pain in my ribs, in my neck. Just as I'm curled into the same position now on the floor.

The bedroom door closes, and Matt calls out. "Girls, hi! I'll be down in a second."

The girls are home. That's what made him stop. I didn't realize, at the time, what finally forced him to end his tirade. If they hadn't come home, I have no doubt he would've killed me this time.

"The girls! You can't let them see you like this. Get yourself together." I shout. But former me can't seem to move or put together what's going on. All I remember is how intense the pain was and then nothing until later. My former self's eyes drift closed, passing out from the pain. I lie on the bed next to my old self and pray for God to take me away from here.

I LAY there waiting to be carried back to the present for what feels like forever. Avery comes into the room, and her voice finally rouses former me.

"Mom! Wake up. Are you okay?" she says, crying and shaking my former self's arm. My heart breaks for her. Why the hell did I stay so long and allow this to happen? To let my girls think it's okay to ever let a man do this to them?

Finally, former me forces open my eyes. "Your dad?"

"He's gone. Did he do this to you?" Tears stream down her cheeks. Former me nods.

"I think I need to call 911. You're really hurt, Mom," she says.

"No, I'll be okay. I just need some ice. Can you get me some?" My voice is raspy.

"What happened? You need to go to the hospital. Your neck." She reaches out to lightly touch it.

"He found out I'm moving. He's mad," former me says even though it hurt so badly to talk. To breathe. To move. "Please, don't call. I'll be okay. I want to get through Christmas and then be done."

Avery sobs. As much as it hurt, other me pulls her close and cradles her. "I'll be okay."

"You're a liar. You won't be okay." I whisper. I reach forward and stroke Avery's back. "You're a sweet, kind, loving girl Ave. Don't ever change."

Finally, her cries quiet, and she goes downstairs to get ice packs and pain relievers. Former me begs her to make up some story to tell Vera because I don't want her to know that her father did this. She reluctantly agrees and leaves former me alone to sleep.

I'm finally being taken back to the present as I peer into my own eyes, my own soul, and tell myself what a weak liar I am.

CHAPTER FORTY-ONE
NOW

I'm yanked back to the police station just as the detectives leave Matt alone in the interview room and exit to the hallway.

"Well, that took longer than I thought it would," Collier says.

"He seemed genuinely caught off guard by the information about the shot to the chest. Don't ya think?" Andover replies.

Collier chuckles. "He's one hell of an actor. And, a narcissistic son of a bitch is what I think. We know that he beat his wife around a week before she's found dead. Enough so to break ribs and leave bruises around her neck. And, according to the autopsy, some of the bruises were probably only a couple of days old, so his story doesn't completely line up. We also know he didn't want her to leave him, that he was a controlling ass. It's all pretty clear to me."

Andover remains quiet for a few steps. "But, the evidence. The fingerprints."

"Which makes sense if Hanson really held the gun to his own head. It all adds up," Collier says. "Plus, Matt may be an ass, but he's smart. He would've known not to leave fingerprints behind."

I throw my arms around Collier into a hug, which makes her shiver. I'm so happy she's able to see through Matt's charming façade to the narcissistic man that lies beneath the surface.

"I agree. But Hanson's clothing came back with gunshot residue. Matt's didn't."

"Which also makes sense given the scenario. He admitted to touching the weapon and his mother's body. I think we have transfer at play here. Plus, Matt wasn't at the scene, which means he had plenty of time to change and dispose of his clothing," Collier says.

Andover nods. "I'm not sure we have enough to make an arrest," he says. "I'm gonna file for another search warrant. I feel like we may have missed something."

"Whatever you need to do," Collier says. "I am certain we've got our guy. But I want this to stick. He has motive. Obsessive, controlling, abusive husband whose wife was going to leave him and possibly take his daughters. Sounds like about a million other cases."

"Ain't that the truth?" He pushes open the door to the front waiting room.

Aunt Lill sees him and jumps up. "Detectives! What's going on? Can I speak to Hanson?"

"We're almost through with him. Everything is fine," Collier assures.

"Did he ask for an attorney? Because I have one ready for him if he needs one," she asks, breathlessly.

"No, he didn't, and that shouldn't be necessary," Collier says, placing a hand on Aunt Lill's arm. By this time, Avery has joined them. Her eyes are red-rimmed, and her nose is rubbed raw.

"Is my dad still back there?" Avery asks, sniffling.

Collier nods while Andover moves to talk to the receptionist.

"Hanson didn't do anything. It was my dad. I know it was him." She begins wrapping strands of her hair around her fingers. Aunt Lill puts her arm around Avery, pulling her close.

"I know you already spoke with a detective the day this all happened, but would you mind answering a few more questions for us, Avery?" Collier asks.

Avery turns to Aunt Lill, pleading with a glance for her to intervene. "Avery, would that be okay with you if I can be in the room, too?" Aunt Lill asks.

She shrugs, and tears spill down her cheeks. "I suppose," she whispers.

"Great. We have a few things we need to ask you about, and, of course, Lillian, you can join us," she says. One of the benefits, I guess, of Avery still being a minor.

Collier walks over to Andover, and Aunt Lillian turns to Avery. "You okay with this?"

"I don't know. I guess," she whispers. "I don't want Hanson to get in trouble for something he didn't do."

"I'll be right there with you. Just do the best you can answering the questions. You'll be okay; I promise." Aunt Lillian kisses her on the side of the head.

Andover and Collier walk back toward Aunt Lill and Avery. "Avery, thanks so much for agreeing to talk with us. Right this way," Andover says and opens the door for them. "You two can sit over there."

Everyone takes a seat. Avery clasps her hands together, trying to stop them from shaking. Aunt Lill rubs small circles on her back like she used to do to calm me when I was younger.

"We just have a couple of questions for you, Avery, okay?" Collier asks with a kindness I've not yet heard from her. "First off, you're not in any trouble."

Avery takes a deep breath, nods, and relaxes a bit.

"What do you think happened to your mom?" Collier asks.

"I'm so confused and don't really know. Up until this morning, I thought she killed herself, which I didn't understand cause she'd never leave us. But, now, I kinda think my dad killed her," she rambles.

"What changed your mind?" Andover says, still with his gruff tone. Collier reaches out and touches him on the arm as if to tell him to tone it down. He nods.

"I don't know. I feel so dumb. I didn't know he had all those affairs and stuff. Not until Hanson told me about everything today. Why didn't I notice? Poor Mom." Tears fill her eyes.

Collier leans forward, "Avery, look at me." Once Avery meets her eye, she continues. "It's not your fault that you didn't know. You're a kid, and you love both of your parents. They're supposed to take care of you, not the other way around."

For the second time today, I want to give Collier a hug. Avery nods and wipes the tears from her cheeks.

"They were having problems, and Mom was moving, but I didn't know all the details. The why. Now, I'm just so pissed at my dad for hurting her," she says.

"Hurting her how?" Andover asks a bit more gently than usual.

"By cheating on her. And he really hurt her the week before she died. I wonder if that had happened before, and I was too blind to see it."

Aunt Lill jumps in. "As far as we know, that's the only time he physically hurt her. So, don't beat yourself up."

Collier clears her throat. "I hate to ask this Avery, but do you really think your dad killed your mom?"

Avery picks at the skin next to her fingernails and studies the little bits of blood that appear. "It makes more sense to me that he killed her than her killing herself. After seeing what he did to her that week before she died, I think he was mad enough to kill her."

"Mad about?" Andover asks.

"Her leaving, I think. I don't really know."

"Did either of your parents talk to you about where you'd live once they split up?" Collier asks.

Avery nods. "Both of them. Mom asked me where I wanted to live, and even though I felt bad leaving Dad, I wanted to live with her. She's around more, ya know? Dad talked at me about it, telling me how he couldn't live without Vee and me, and he didn't think it'd be good for us to move out of the house. I could tell by the way he talked, he just assumed we'd stay with him. I didn't tell him anything different cause I felt guilty since I'd told Mom I wanted to live with her."

"Did Vera know about the incident between your mother and father the week before her death?" Andover asks.

Avery shakes her head. "Not really. She's too little to understand. Mom told her she wasn't feeling well. I don't even think she realized that we were moving."

"So, as far as you're aware, was your mom planning on taking you and Vera with her?" Collier asks.

"That was the plan. What's going to happen to us now? I don't even want to be around my dad." Tears fill her eyes again, and the picking of her fingernails intensifies. "Are you going to arrest him?"

Collier looks at Andover with raised eyebrows, a staring contest of sorts to see which one is going to answer. Finally, Collier breaks the gaze and responds. "We're still investigating, so I can't answer that for sure right now."

"Do you think she killed herself?" Avery whispers.

Without hesitation, Collier responds. "No. We know she didn't."

A satisfied grin pulls up the corners of Aunt Lillian's mouth.

"Then it was my dad," Avery declares. "There's no one else that would have hurt her."

I relax at Avery's declaration. Hearing her say the words is the confirmation I need to be certain that Matt truly is the one responsible for taking my life. She wouldn't say it unless she was absolutely sure. I lean forward and wrap my arms around her as everything in the room swirls together, and I'm transported back in time.

CHAPTER FORTY-TWO
THEN

I come to in our darkened living room with Tangled playing on TV. The girls and my former self are snuggled on the couch. God, how I wish I could spend one more night with them, snuggling and laughing. The front door opens. Former me immediately tenses, thinking Matt has returned, but my whole body relaxes as soon as Hanson walks through the door.

He flips on the light, making everyone squint against the invasion.

"What the hell happened?" he asks, barreling toward the couch.

"Vera, will you go upstairs for a few minutes?" alive me asks.

"I don't wanna. I wanna watch our movie!" She sticks her bottom lip out in a pout.

Avery stands and holds her hand out to Vera, "C'mon. I'll do your make-up so you can look like Rapunzel." Dear sweet Avery. Her eyes tell me she wants to stay for the discussion.

As soon as they are out of the room, Hanson sits on the couch next to alive me. "My God, Mom. Your neck."

My former self's hand instinctively rises to it, trying to block the bruises from his view.

"What happened?"

"Matt..." was the only word former me gets out.

Hanson jumps to his feet. "I swear to God, I'm going to kill him. He did this to you? Where is he?"

"Hanson, please sit down. He's gone. Please. Just calm down," alive me says with a still raspy voice.

"Calm down? Really? He could've killed you. It sure as hell looks like he tried," he shouts.

Former me doesn't say anything to that because, in reality, he did try, and he might have succeeded had the girls not come home when they did.

"You need to leave. Tonight!" he says, finally sitting beside alive me.

"You know the plan. I'm going to wait until after Christmas. Only nine more days."

"Screw the plan, Mom! You're not safe. The girls aren't safe. He's crazy! Have you seen yourself?"

Former me nods. "I know, Hanson. It looks worse than it is. We'll be okay!"

"God, Mom! How can you say that? Do you know how many women have probably said the exact same thing right before they end up murdered? Did you call the cops?" He runs his hands through his hair.

Alive me shakes my head, and he pulls his phone from his pocket. Former me lunges to grab it from him before he can push 911. The pain in my ribs makes me crumple to the floor. Hanson throws the phone down and rushes to my side, helping me back to the couch.

"Where else are you hurt?"

None of us have noticed that Avery is back in the room until she answers. "Her ribs. I think some are broken."

"Ave, tell her she needs to call the police and go to the hospital. She won't listen to me!" Hanson pleads.

"I have. She won't listen to me, either." Avery paces back and forth in front of the couch.

Disgust fills me, watching all of this now. Why the hell did I put my kids in this position, to serve as my protector? They saw clearly what I needed to do and the possibilities of what could happen if I didn't. They were right. I was a damn fool not to listen.

"Were you here when this happened?" he asks.

She shakes her head. "No, I think it happened right before we got home. Did it, Mom?"

Alive me nods. "I was in the bedroom packing, and he surprised me. I guess he knows now that I'm leaving."

Hanson chuckles, but his laugh holds no joy. "Sure, you are. If you live long enough to get the chance."

"I'm really scared, Hanson. What should we do?" Avery says.

"Mom should call the police and go to the damn hospital is what should happen!"

"Listen to Hanson, dammit!" I shout. "If you don't leave, you're not going to make it out alive."

Tears fill my former self's eyes. "I know, okay! I know. But I don't want this to be any more complicated than it needs to be. I just want to get the hell out of here. Soon, he won't be able to hurt me. I want Vee to have one last Christmas with both of her parents. That's it. Then I'm gone."

What I didn't say is how much it hurt to realize that I was going to break up my family. Or how afraid I was that I'd handle this even remotely close to how my mother would. I never wanted my kids to have animosity toward their father or to have a broken family like I did growing up.

Neither Hanson nor Avery speaks; they just stare at alive me with their mouths hanging open. Exactly as I'm looking at my former self right now. How could I have been so stupid? Giving the girls one last Christmas with their father obviously cost them the life of their mother. Why didn't I listen to Hanson? Why can't I make myself listen now and change this whole path? And why was I stupid enough to take any blame for breaking up my marriage? That was one hundred percent Matt's doing.

"Please," alive me pleads.

Again, they remain silent for what feels like forever.

Finally, Hanson speaks. "Fine, but I'm moving back in until you're ready to leave. And I swear to God, if that asshole lays another finger on you, I'm killing him. I'm not a little boy anymore that he can push around."

The thought of Hanson and Matt being under the same roof again spiked my anxiety out of control. "Hanson, that's a bad idea. That will just make things worse, and you know it."

"Then call the police. Get him out of the house," Hanson chides.

I can see the wheels spinning in my former self's mind, racing to come up with another plan. One that will ultimately be a total failure. "How about this? He won't do anything to me when the girls are here," former me says, even though it's not entirely true. How many times had he raped me when the girls were upstairs? I thought that he wouldn't hurt me in other ways, though when they were here. "They're on break through the first of the year, so I won't be alone. Today was their last day of school."

Avery nods. "That's a good point. We'll be here, except after Christmas, I have cheer camp every day, and doesn't Vee have a girl scout overnight thing?"

"Okay, so through Christmas, everything should be fine. How about after Christmas, when the girls are gone, you stop over each day to make sure everything is okay. Would that work?"

Finally, Hanson relaxes his jaw a bit, and some of the visible tension leaves his shoulders. He sighs deeply and sits back down on the couch.

"Fine. I don't like it. At all. But, fine," he says. "Ave, make sure to hang out here and not off with your friends, okay?"

"Tell me no, Hanson. This plan fails. Please tell me no," I plead.

Avery nods.

Hanson continues. "And, if there is any problem at all, call the cops first and then me. Regardless of what Mom says, okay?"

My wishful thinking convinced me that Matt would stay away other than Christmas, and none of us would have to worry about it. I had no doubts he had a variety of women he could choose to spend his time with.

"Okay, I will. Mom, do you understand? Even if you tell me not to, I will call the police if anything else happens, okay?"

Former me nods. Vera's footsteps pound down the stairs.

"Look at me! I'm a princess!" she shouts.

Everyone turns toward her. She has make-up smeared all over her face, her hair is a ratted mess, and she has one of Avery's far too big dresses and pair of heels on. Everyone's laughter fills the room at the raggedy little princess before us.

Hanson picks her up and tickles her. Her giggles fill the room. For only a moment, I remember that it felt like everything was right with the world. I thought that soon it would be. How wrong and stupid I was.

The sound and my living room fade away. It's time to go back to the present to try to figure out more about exactly what happened.

CHAPTER FORTY-THREE
NOW

I'm back in the interview room, with my arms still wrapped around Avery. Collier and Andover escort Avery and Lillian out of the interview room and back into the lobby.

The receptionist calls the detectives over.

"We've got the search warrants." She hands them a small stack of papers.

"That was fast! Thanks for your help, Joan!" Collier says and turns to Lillian and Avery. "Do you have access to your house?"

Lillian and Avery both nod. "Why?" Aunt Lill asks.

"We've got another search warrant," Andover says, holding up the papers. He turns back to the receptionist. "Have Phillips, Montgomery, and Nelson head to the Bartholomew household." He points to Aunt Lill and Avery. "One of them can allow entry into the property."

Aunt Lillian nods as she and Avery stand.

"We're going to serve them now, so we should be set by the time they get to the house. If there's a problem, I'll call Phillips."

Collier opens the door to the back, but Aunt Lill's voice calls out right before they leave the room. "Can we just let them in and come back here? I want to be here when Hanson leaves."

"Sure thing!" Collier answers. "We shouldn't need him much longer."

Aunt Lillian and Vera head out the front door as Collier and Andover disappear into the back. A huge part of me wants to go back to the house and see what the search uncovers. If they find any evidence to help them make an arrest. But I can't leave Hanson here by himself, so I move to the back to find Collier and Andover standing in the hallway, chatting outside of the doorway to Matt's interview room.

"He's gonna be pissed," Andover says and smiles.

Collier smacks him lightly on the arm. "You are enjoying this far too much! I assume you want to do the honors, right?"

"Hell yeah," he says and pushes the door open.

Another man sits at the table with Matt. He rises when the detectives enter, holding out his hand. "Bruce Farber," he says. "Mr. Bartholomew's attorney."

The detectives quickly introduce themselves, and then Andover hands Matt the stack of papers.

"What's this?" Matt asks, shuffling through them. "A search warrant? You already searched the house!"

"We need to do another search of your house and have a team on the way there now. As you can see, we also have one for your office and your car. Which, by the way, is your car here?" Andover says with a gleam in his eye. He's enjoying making Matt squirm.

Matt jumps to his feet. "What the hell? You already searched the house. This is harassment and…"

"Mr. Bartholomew," Mr. Farber shouts. When Matt doesn't respond, he tries again, louder this time, "Matthew! I'd advise you to sit down and let me see the warrants."

Matt tosses them onto the table but doesn't sit. He paces back and forth on his side of the table while Mr. Farber reviews the documents. Finally, his attorney places them back in a neat stack on the table. "Everything is legit. Is your car here, Mr. Bartholomew?"

Matt sighs and nods.

"It will be easier if you give us the keys, but, either way, we're searching it," Andover says.

Matt hesitates a moment before reaching in his pocket and tossing his keys to Andover. "Am I free to go?" he asks.

"We can't force you to stay at this point if that's what you're asking. However, it would be better if you stayed as I'm sure we'll have more questions," Collier says.

Matt looks at Mr. Farber, his brow scrunched with indecision. "Can my client and I have a few moments alone, please?"

Andover smiles. "Sure thing! We'll get the team working on the car." Andover and Collier walk out of the room. I stay behind to listen in on the conversation between Matt and his attorney.

"Well, do I have to stay? I want to get the hell out of here and out of these clothes." Matt still paces while tugging at his tie, finally removing it altogether.

"They haven't arrested you, so you can leave, but I'd advise you to stay," Farber says.

"Why? What the hell's the point?" Matt shouts.

"Well, first of all, they are searching your car, your house, and your office. Where are you gonna go?" Farber asks.

"Trust me, I have plenty of places to go."

"Let me re-phrase the question. Where do you have to go that's not going to make you look worse than you already do? I wouldn't advise going to hang out with a girlfriend at this point."

Matt finally slumps into the seat, his ego deflated a bit. "I suppose you're right."

"Secondly, the more you cooperate, the better you look. And, trust me, right now, you need to seem like a grieving husband who wants the truth. Understood?"

Matt nods. "I understand. They're not going to find anything, so I suppose it doesn't hurt for me to stay here for a while. Answer any more questions they have."

"Glad you see my point," Farber says. "If it's okay with you, I'm going to head back to the office since it's close by, and you don't want to have to pay me to sit here with you. Have them call me back before you answer any additional questions. I'll leave a message at the front, too."

Matt nods. "Sounds like a plan. Maybe I can lay my head down and sleep for a bit. It's been an exhausting few days."

"Good idea," Farber says. "I'll see you soon."

ANDOVER and Collier are back in the room with Hanson, who hasn't seemed to relax one bit since they left the last time. He never did like to be in confined places. I'm sure being trapped with his thoughts hasn't helped.

Collier is the first to speak. "Sorry to leave you in here so long. Would you like a drink?"

Hanson shakes his head even though he must be dying of thirst.

"We have a couple more questions, for now. We talked with Avery, and she told us about the incident with your mom and Matt the week before her death. Can you tell us any more about that?"

"Besides what I already told you? No."

"As far as you know, were there any other incidents over the next week between the two of them?" Andover asks, no longer playing the bad cop with Hanson.

Hanson chews on his lower lip. One of the tell-tale signs that he's nervous. "I don't think so. I stopped by every day that the girls weren't home to check in. They were on break, which helped. Besides, I don't think Matt was around much."

"Would your mom have told you if something else happened?" Collier asks.

Again, he bites his bottom lip. "I doubt it. She knew I'd call the cops. I mean, you guys."

"So, you didn't notice any new bruises or injuries?" Andover asks.

Hanson shakes his head.

"What about Christmas Day? Were you all together then?" Collier asks.

Hanson answers so quietly that it's impossible to hear. "I didn't go."

"What'd you say?" Andover leans in closer.

"I said I didn't go. I was supposed to but changed my mind at the last minute. I couldn't deal with being around Matt. I feel awful about that now…"

Collier reaches out her hand and places it on Hanson's. "You didn't know, okay? Sounds like you were all just doing your best."

Hanson nods but doesn't raise his eyes from the table. I have no doubt that he will carry the guilt of missing my last Christmas for many, many years.

"I hate that I missed her last one," he says, his voice weighed down by sorrow.

"I'm sure she understood," Collier assures him.

"Yes, I do. I know how hard it was for you to be around Matt and don't blame you one bit. None of us should've been there."

"Yeah, I guess."

"Anything else remarkable between your mom and Matt over that next week? Anything at all?" Andover asks.

Hanson's face scrunches in thought. I try to remember if there were any more but draw a blank.

Finally, he shakes his head. "Nah. That's it. I thought everything was going okay. And that she'd be out of there soon."

Collier turns to Andover with raised eyebrows. Andover nods. "Okay, well, thank you for coming in today. We may have some additional questions for you but, for now, we're set."

Hanson raises his eyebrows, and his mouth drops open in shock that they're letting him leave.

"Oh, we do have a crew at your house now with another search warrant, so you can't go there. Your Aunt Lillian and Avery went to let them in, but they should be back anytime to pick you up," Andover says. "You can sit in the waiting room if you'd like."

"Oh, okay. Yeah," Hanson says and stands.

They escort him to the front lobby. He sits and takes a deep sigh of relief. He pulls his phone out of his pocket, and a slight smile crosses his face.

I sit next to him and lay my head on his shoulder. Within a minute, I'm whisked away from Hanson and the waiting room, back to the past.

CHAPTER FORTY-FOUR
THEN

This time, I get to revisit one of my favorite last memories with the girls. It's Christmas Eve, and alive me is in the kitchen with Ave and Vee making the last batch of Christmas cookies. The stereo is blaring Christmas music, and there's a mess of flour and eggshells all over the kitchen.

Former me doesn't hear Matt until he walks in the front door with arms full of presents, like Santa Claus, acting like nothing is wrong. He has the biggest smile, and, for a moment, I catch a glimpse of the man he used to be. Or rather, the one he'd convinced me he was.

Alive me is so startled by him showing up, I drop the half-empty bag of flour on the floor, covering everything in a coat of white.

"How are my girls?" he says, smiling.

Vera runs over to him with her cookie-dough covered hands and wraps her arms around his waist. "Daddy! You've got to try our cookies. The dough is really good!"

"Are you sure any dough made it into the cookies? It looks like it's all over your fingers," he laughs and lowers his mouth to her hand, pretending to nibble her fingers. "Let me taste!"

Vera's giggles fill the room, a sound I love more than anything.

Why couldn't this be the real Matt? The loving, doting father. The charming, handsome man making our daughter giggle.

"How are my other two girls?" he asks.

Former me doesn't bother to stop cleaning up the floury mess. My plan was to not be rude to him, for the girls' sake, but to also not be overly-friendly.

"I'm fine," Avery says flatly as she scrubs the cookie sheet.

"Kenzie? How are you?" he asks.

I didn't want to speak to him. Why couldn't he just pretend I wasn't there and be content spending time with the girls? But I knew if I didn't answer him, he'd take it as a challenge and be more persistent.

"Good," former me finally says, without making eye contact. "Just cleaning up this mess I made."

He walks over and reaches out his hand. Does he seriously think I want to touch him?

Former me leans back and wrinkles my nose. He must get the hint because he clarifies his gesture. "I wanted to help you clean up! It looks like you've been busy."

"It's okay, I've got…"

"Kenzie, let me help. I'm sorry I wasn't here to help make the cookies this year. It's the least I can do."

Alive me hands the broom over to him and steps to the other side of Avery to dry the dishes and get as far away from him as possible. In that moment, his offer of help was almost like an apology of sorts. As he sweeps, Vera chatters away, rattling off the names of all the cookies we made, botching half of their pronunciations.

Before long, Matt begins dancing with the broom, singing along with the stereo. Vera can never pass up the opportunity for singing and dancing, so the broom gets pushed to the side as he takes up his new little dance partner. Traces of flour are left in their wake as they two-step around the kitchen.

Despite all that had happened, the hell he'd put me through, in that moment, I couldn't help but laugh along with my former self. And soon, Avery joins in, too. This moment of seeing my girls laughing and enjoying their father at Christmas time makes staying through the holiday worth it. No matter what happens between the two of us, I knew at that moment that he'd take care of them. I was left with no doubts. Matt was an awful husband, but he was a good daddy.

THE GIRLS GO to bed a little after midnight, a moment former me had been dreading. I follow my old self to Hanson's room after goodnight kisses, hoping to avoid any interaction with Matt, without them there to act as a buffer.

Former me changes into pajamas before the knock on the door comes. The soft rap nearly makes alive me jump out of my skin.

"Yes?"

"Can I come in?" he asks.

The fact that he asked, instead of barging in, caught me off guard back then. Alive me goes to the door and opens it a crack.

"What's up?"

"I wondered if you wanted me to sleep in here?"

Former me cringes. "Umm, no."

He chuckles. "I didn't mean with you. Like, do you want our room, and I'll sleep in here?"

I remember the relief that flooded me. "Thanks, but you can have it. I'm already set up in here."

"Okay. Anything else you need me to do tonight?" he asks.

"We're all set."

He takes a couple of steps away and then stops. "Kenzie, thanks for staying until after Christmas. Tonight was fun. It felt like old times."

Former me tries to respond, but words can't squeeze out past the lump in my throat. A mixture of bittersweet memories and painful moments are lodged there. Finally, alive me says, "It was good to hear the girls laugh."

"Goodnight," he says and flips off the hall light.

Former me shuts the door, allowing a finger to linger over the lock for a few seconds debating on whether or not to lock it. Former me finally presses the button after remembering the crazed look in Matt's eyes as he tightened his hands around my throat. I knew that a lock wouldn't stop him if he wanted to come in and hurt me, but at least there was more of a chance I'd wake up if he tried to get in.

Matt's kindness was more unsettling to me than if he'd come in and given me the cold shoulder as I'd expected. Avery was caught off guard, too, but even her walls came down as the night wore on. I couldn't let mine down at all. I had to protect myself and my heart. He'd gotten past those walls far too many times over the years. I'd decided to put on a happy face for my girls to get through the holiday.

I SPEND the night wandering around the house, but most of my time is spent in the girls' rooms, watching them sleep. Savoring every second I can get with them. Vera comes into the room to wake former me at seven, just as the sun is starting to peek over the horizon. Former me convinces her to snuggle for a few minutes before the smell of coffee makes its way up the stairs.

"Vee, did you wake Daddy first?"

"Yes. It's Christmas! I wanna see what Santa brought," she says, bolting upright.

Former me stretches and yawns. "Okay, I'm going to text Hanson. You wake sissy up, okay? I'll be down in a minute."

Alive me chuckles as Vee pushes out of bed and scurries down the hallway to wake Avery. Avery is not a morning person, not even for Christmas. Former me pulls out my phone to text Hanson but decides to call instead. He'd agreed to come over to open presents with the girls. The phone rings four times and goes to voice mail. Instead of leaving a message, alive me calls again immediately, thinking that the day would have two grumpy teenagers from being woken up so early.

"Yeah," Hanson says, sleep still heavy in his voice.

"Merry Christmas! Vee just came in to wake me up and is dying to open presents."

He yawns. "I changed my mind."

"About what?"

"Coming today. I just can't do the whole put on a happy face and pretend everything is okay. If you can, more power to you. I don't want to be anywhere near Matt."

"Hanson, please, it's…"

He interrupts. "Mom, don't start with me. I can't be around him after what he did to you. If you want him there, fine. But, I'm not gonna sit back and pretend like everything is cool."

"Please, just one day! I want you all here for our last Christmas together in this house, as a family." Tears well in my former self's eyes.

"We stopped being a family a long time ago," he says with sadness. "Merry Christmas, Mom. I hope you enjoy your day." He hangs up.

Former me instantly dials his number again, but the phone goes straight to voice mail. I remember how deflated I was because I would've much rather had Hanson here than Matt, but I didn't know what to do. How much worse I would've felt if I'd known it would be my last Christmas ever with my children. The whole reason I'd stayed this long is so that the girls could have a nice Christmas with both of their parents. Hanson knew that. I didn't understand why he couldn't just suck it up, bite his tongue, and come spend a little time with me. With his sisters. Former me wipes away a tear. I knew deep inside that no amount of begging and pleading was going to change his mind. This was my first Christmas morning without my son in nineteen years.

"Mommy! Come on!" Vera's voice rings out from downstairs.

Former me wipes my nose and shouts, "Be right there, honey!"

I remember talking to myself as I worked my way down the steps, reminding myself that this was the last time I'd have to fake a smile and pretend like everything was okay for the benefit of my children. After this, I wouldn't have to pretend that we were a normal, happy family. I thought that in one week, I'd be in my new apartment. Instead, I'm in a casket with my spirit being dragged back and forth across time. I no sooner think this than, once again, I'm carried away before I reach the bottom of the stairs.

CHAPTER FORTY-FIVE
NOW

I come back to the exact same place and time where I left off. Sitting in the waiting room of the police station with my head leaned on Hanson's shoulder. Hanson texts Avery to see when she and Aunt Lillian will be back. Avery says they'll be back shortly—they had to run by Aunt Lill's store first. I sit next to Hanson as he scrolls through Instagram. I don't even realize someone has come in the front door until the receptionist offers her greeting.

It is my father. He's walking towards Hanson.

"Hanson," he says and offers his hand.

Hanson reluctantly takes it, and then my father sits across from him.

"Ummm...you were at the funeral," Hanson says.

My father nods. "We didn't get the chance to talk. I heard they brought you here, so I thought I'd stop by to check on you." He nervously laces and unlaces his fingers.

Hanson raises his eyebrows. "Okay. Umm...who are you?"

A slight smile pulls up the corners of my father's mouth. He's got a nice smile. "Oh, sorry. I'm Calvin Sanders. Your mom's father. Your grandfather."

Hanson's mouth drops open in shock. He sits back without saying a word.

"I hope it's okay that I came by. If not, I'll go," he says, still working his fingers.

"No, it's fine. I'm just shocked. I've never heard much about you," Hanson says as he runs his hand through his hair.

Calvin chuckles. "And, I'm sure what you have heard hasn't necessarily been kind. Or true for that matter."

Hanson shakes his head. "No, I haven't heard anything terrible about you. Mom said you took off when she was around two and that she's never heard from you since. It broke her heart."

The words hit my father like a punch, and he slumps back in his seat. His eyes glisten with tears. "Yeah, I figured."

"So, why are you here now? It's a bit late, isn't it?" Hanson's face reddens, flushed with anger on my behalf.

"Calm down. Take a moment to listen to what he has to say." I'm not sure if I say this because Hanson needs to hear it or I do.

"That's exactly why I'm here. It is far too late. I should've reached out to your mother a long time ago. But I didn't. Now I have to live with that." He looks up at the ceiling to keep the tears at bay.

"So, why didn't you?" Hanson crosses his arms over his chest. He's not about to let Calvin off the hook so easily.

Calvin clears his throat several times before answering. "Listen. I don't want to talk badly about your grandmother, but she did a number on my relationship with your mom. She made some things up that never happened to ensure I left them alone. Sadly, I let her plan work when I should've been man enough to fight it. To be a father to her."

"Yes. You should have," Hanson says.

Calvin nods. "I guess that's why I'm here now. I don't want to miss the chance with my grandchildren that I missed with my daughter. From what I gathered at the funeral, you could really use some people in your corner."

Tears waterfall down my cheeks. Calvin reaching out to my son, trying to be here for him, means more to me than if he'd tried to reconnect with me before I died to have a relationship. Hanson needs as many people as he can get to support him, especially another man. I want Hanson to be able to hear me when I tell him to ease up on my dad, to let him in.

"That's putting it mildly," Hanson chuckles.

My father smiles. "So, listen. Are you allowed to leave? Do you want to go grab lunch or coffee or something?"

"Uh, yeah. I'm done. Let me call Aunt Lill real quick to make sure it's okay with her," he says.

Hanson goes outside and lights a cigarette while he calls. He fills Aunt Lill in on the visit from my father. I can hear her excitement standing next to Hanson. She is thrilled and goes on and on about what a wonderful man my father is.

Once he finishes his call and cigarette, he peeks his head back in the door. "I'm good to go."

My father gathers his things and exits.

I get in the car with them, excitement flooding me. Whether he knows I'm here or not, I get to go to lunch with my father. Something I've wanted for a lifetime. But before I get to enjoy getting to know my dad, I must again revisit my past.

CHAPTER FORTY-SIX
THEN

I come back just as former me steps off the bottom step to find Matt in a Santa hat with a steaming mug of coffee in his hand for me. The scent of cinnamon and butterscotch hangs in the air from the Monkey Bread in the oven, our yearly Christmas morning tradition.

"Merry Christmas, Kenzie!" Matt says as he hands over the cup of coffee. "Go ahead and sit. The girls and I will get the gifts passed out."

Vera is already half under the tree, digging through the presents to see what Santa brought her. Matt did a lot of his own shopping—the number of gifts under the tree have tripled from last night before bed.

"Vera, I promise you'll get all of your gifts. Now help Ave and me get them all passed out," Matt chuckles.

Avery and Matt each grab a handful of presents and divide them into piles. Vera gathers handfuls of her gifts and stacks them near her bean bag chair.

"Mom, where's Hanson?" Avery asks.

Former me takes a sip of coffee before responding. "He's, uh, not able to come today."

"What? He has to. I'm going to call him," Avery says.

"No, leave him be, Ave. He's not feeling well and just wants to sleep," former me says, hoping she won't see through the lie.

She studies my former self's face for a moment; her eyes scrunch with questions. Alive me whispers a prayer that she'll just let it go, so Matt doesn't get riled up. Finally, she says, "Let's put Hanson's gifts over here, and he can get them when he's better."

Former me breathes a sigh of relief.

"Great idea, Ave!" Matt says and adds to Hanson's pile.

Almost all the presents are distributed and, before the opening frenzy begins, former me goes to the kitchen to refresh my coffee. I stay in the living room and watch as Matt places a beautifully wrapped package in my chair. My former self's eyes go wide with surprise at seeing the gift.

Former me puts the coffee cup on the end table and picks up the gift. "Matt, what's this?"

He waves his hand dismissively. "Oh, just a small something I picked up for you. No biggie. I saw it and thought you'd like it."

"Thanks, but I didn't get you anything. I'm sorry," former me says and weirdly enough, actually feels a bit of remorse.

"This," Matt says, spreading his hand out toward the girls, then the tree, finally to me, "is enough of a present."

The next hour flies by as the girls tear into their presents, littering the room with wrapping paper and empty boxes. Matt bought Vera a new bike, her first without training wheels, a Barbie Hotel complete with furnishings while I got her all of her requested Barbies and rollerblades. I got Avery clothing, all name brand, of course, make-up, gift cards, and a new necklace with an infinity symbol. Matt surprised her with a new laptop and cell phone. He's always been an extravagant gift buyer, but this year, it makes me sad. Alive me comes to the realization, watching my girls smile with glee, that this will be the way things are from this point on. I'll have less income and get the girls smaller, less expensive gifts. While Matt will be the one to buy them big items, like their first cars, prom dresses, et cetera.

I recall all the thoughts swirling in my mind as the realization flooded me with doubts. As I watch my former self, I can almost hear the questions. Questions, it turns out, that don't matter. What am I doing? How am I going to survive and provide for my girls by working

at my aunt's store? My former self looks around the house as the questions continue assaulting me. How can I make them leave their four
thousand square foot home, where they've lived their entire lives to go
live with me in a thousand square foot apartment? Am I selfish for
leaving? Am I stupid to give all of this up?

"You okay, Kenzie?" Matt asks.

Former me swallows the lump in my throat and wraps my arms
around myself. "Yeah, sorry. I'm good. You did a great job with gifts."

"Thanks. You know how I love spending money on my girls," he
chuckles. "Speaking of which, did you open your gift?"

"Oh, shoot. I forgot." Former me digs through the piles of trash on
the floor to find it. Finally, alive me finds it and rips it open.

It takes my breath away. It's the perfect gift—a painting of the
girls, Hanson, and me, recreated from a picture Matt took of us on the
beach during our vacation to Jamaica. It was one of my favorite vaca-
tions and fondest memories. Tears fill my former self's eyes, along
with mine now.

"Do you like it?" Matt asks.

"It's…it's perfect, Matt. I absolutely love it," former me says as a
tear slips past my eyelid. "But you lied. You said you just happened to
find the perfect gift for me. You had to work to get this made."

He laughs. "Okay, okay. I may have embellished a bit. Someone at
work had a painting done by the same artist, and I thought it would
make a perfect present for you. That's my favorite picture of you and
the kids. I thought you'd like to hang it in your new place."

I remember how my head swarmed with so many conflicting
thoughts, feelings, and questions. Who is this man? What happened to
the violent, abusive person he had been only a few days ago? He was
so calm and loving last night and today. He acted like the man I had
fallen head over heels in love with so many years ago.

Former me leans the painting against the wall and embraces him. I
couldn't recall the last time I'd affectionately hugged him. Instead of
my skin crawling with his touch, former me actually relaxes in his
arms. Was this his way of getting my guard down before he killed me?

"Thank you, Matt. Really. It's the best gift ever," I whisper.

Avery walks in the room, prepared to model one of her new outfits. "What the hell?"

Matt and former me break our embrace. "Ave, language," Matt says.

"Sorry, that just caught me off guard. You guys hugging. What's up with that?"

Former me points to the painting. "I was thanking your dad for my gift. Isn't it lovely?" Avery nods. "And, you, my dear, look amazing in that new outfit."

She twirls, and a smile beams across her face. "I love it! Do you wanna see the next one?"

Former me laughs. "Of course!"

She runs up the stairs, taking them two at a time.

"Daddy, I wanna ride my new bike. Can we?" Vera asks.

"Let's eat first. Monkey bread is calling my name," Matt says.

The next several hours go by quickly with Avery modeling her new outfits, Matt teaching Vera to ride her bike and attempting to teach her to rollerblade, and with me unburying the living room from the piles of wrapping paper. My heart aches seeing Hanson's pile of presents sitting under the tree. Alive me tries to call him several more times, but each time the phone goes to voice mail. That morning, I hated that he missed our last Christmas here. Now, I'm filled with grief that he missed our last Christmas morning ever.

As great as the day was, alive me still felt uncomfortable all day. I didn't know how to relax around Matt anymore when he wasn't torturing me mentally or hurting me physically. I felt like I was in some alternate universe or like we'd gone back in time to the man he used to be.

It is late afternoon by the time Matt leaves. He asks the girls to give us a few minutes to talk, and my former self instantly tenses, wondering if the switch is going to flip once they leave the room, allowing the evil Matt to return.

"I just wanted to thank you again for staying through Christmas. I had a wonderful day," he says.

"Yeah, me too. The girls enjoyed it," former me says.

"So, what's the plan? When are you leaving?"

"I should be gone by New Year's Eve. That's the goal anyway," former me says, shocked because this is the first time that we've rationally discussed my move.

He nods a few times. "Okay, I'll try to stay out of your way."

"I appreciate that."

My body goes rigid as he walks to the front door. He turns back toward alive me as he twists the knob. "Oh, and Kenzie. Just so you're clear, the girls are not going with you. They're staying right here." He smiles. "Understand?"

My stomach drops as it did that day. With one simple statement, the past two days made perfect sense. He had been buttering me up and being kind as a lead up to this moment. As usual, it was all an act. A way to get what he wanted—our girls.

Former me doesn't answer him because, although a million thoughts race through my mind, none of them will make a difference.

"Did you kill me to get what you wanted, you bastard?" I shout and push him. "I hope you rot in hell!"

He rubs his arm where my punch landed, as though he can feel it. "Bye, girls!"

Avery and Vera both come running and give him a hug.

"I love you both. I'll be back home with my two favorite girls next week," he says and flashes former me a smile. One that says he'll go to whatever lengths necessary to make sure our daughters stay exactly where they are. With him.

I lunge toward him one more time but never make it. The house, Matt, and the girls fade away as I'm carried back to now.

CHAPTER FORTY-SEVEN
NOW

I'm in the car with my father and Hanson. Hanson directs him to Café LaMont, which is a small, French-style bistro down the block from Aunt Lillian's store. There are only a few customers since it's late afternoon, and the lunch rush has already passed through. My father asks the hostess for a booth tucked into the back corner.

Once they're seated, and their orders are placed, an awkward silence settles over the table. My father clears his throat a few times and says, "So, tell me about your mother."

Hanson twists his napkin around and around in his hands. "She's a great mom. I mean, um, she was." Hanson's eyes glisten with tears that threaten to fall.

"And you have two sisters, right?"

"Yeah. Avery is fifteen, and Vera is seven," Hanson replies, offering no more information than is necessary.

The waiter drops off my father's steaming mug of coffee and Hanson's soda. Each takes a drink. "I'm assuming Matt isn't your father based on what happened earlier."

Hanson puffs out a breath of air. "Hell no. Thank God! He's a bastard."

"I kinda sensed that myself. Were he and your mom happy? How long were they married?"

"Mom was getting ready to move out, so no, they weren't happy. He was a mean, sick asshole," Hanson spits out, stirring his soda with his straw. "That's why he killed her. Because she was leaving."

My father leans forward and lowers his voice. "Do you really think that's what happened?"

Hanson nods. "No doubt about it."

"My God, that's terrible." Calvin slumps back against his seat. "So, why were you at the police station?"

Hanson runs his hand through his hair and chews on his bottom lip. "Cause I found her. They had some questions, I guess."

My father leans forward and rests his hand on top of Hanson's. "I'm so sorry. How terrible for you."

Hanson shifts uncomfortably in his seat at the physical contact. He sighs deeply and withdraws his hand as the waiter arrives with their meals.

"Well, this looks tasty. I'm starving," Calvin says as they both dig in.

They eat ravenously as though it's been days since they've tasted food. I laugh because they have many of the same mannerisms. The way they chew. How they study each bite before it goes into their mouths. They even tend to take a drink at the same time. Genetics is certainly a powerful thing.

"So, do you have contact with your dad?" Calvin asks. Hanson goes rigid with tension.

"No, and I don't wanna talk about him," he says. "In fact, let's talk about you. Why the hell didn't you ever try to get in contact with my mom?" Hanson has always been a pro at deflecting when conversations get uncomfortable.

Calvin takes a drink of coffee, puts his napkin on his plate, and sits back. "I suppose you're old enough for the truth. Linda and I split up when Mackenzie was two, as I'm sure you know. I tried to make our marriage work for our daughter's sake, but Linda was bound and determined to move on to her next man. One she deemed more successful or wealthier, I suppose. She wanted me to leave, and I refused, at least I wasn't going to go without my daughter.

"Linda wasn't a very good mother, and Mack would've been better off with me. I knew that, and she knew it. But she wanted my child support and alimony. I hate talking badly about your grandmother. Are you sure you want to hear this? Are you okay?"

Hanson nods. "We're not close. At all. Mom wasn't really close to her either. So, yes, I'm fine. Aunt Lill was really more of a mother and grandmother."

I'm so relieved that this is his answer because I need to hear this story. I need to know what happened.

"Ah, Lillian. She is such a lovely person. I'm so glad she was there for you both." He smiles. "Anyway, when I refused to leave, Linda went psychotic. She accused me of being an alcoholic and sexually abusing Mackenzie, both of which were complete lies. I should've fought it. I know that now, but I was so scared then. I was a high school principal back at the time. Allegations alone of substance abuse could've cost me my job. Speculation of sexual abuse would have ruined me. So, I left."

Hanson pushes his plate away and clenches his jaw. He's not about to let my father off the hook that easily.

"That's shitty, and I kinda get why you left and all that, but why didn't you ever contact her when she was an adult? She needed you," Hanson says.

My dad pinches the bridge of his nose and sits for a few seconds before responding. Tears glisten in his eyes. "Trust me. That's one of my biggest regrets. One I'll never get over. I guess I assumed that your mother believed all the lies Linda had told throughout the years. I thought she'd want nothing to do with me."

Hanson laughs with no humor in it. "Well, you were wrong. She doesn't believe half of the shit that comes out of grandma's mouth. We all know she spins whatever story she thinks will get the most attention."

"I guess some things never change. Sadly," my father says.

The waiter brings the bill, and my dad hands over his credit card.

"Anyway, I'd love to spend more time with you. Let you get to know my wife and kids. If that's okay with you, of course," Calvin says.

Hanson's expression is blank, and I wonder what words are going to come out. With him, it could go either way. "Yeah, sure. Mom would like that."

I want to shout with joy. Yes, I would love that. I want Hanson to have a sense of family, and God knows he needs all the support he can get now that I'm gone.

"Great!" My father hands Hanson his business card. "Here's all of my information. I put the house phone and cell number on the back."

Hanson studies it. "You're an engineer now. What happened to being a principal?"

"The whole thing with Linda shook me to the core. I got tired of living on pins and needles, wondering if she was going to come up with some kind of crazy story that would get me in trouble. I drove myself half-mad. So, I went back to school and changed careers. I didn't want that woman to have any power over my life."

For the first time, it hits me just how alike Matt and my mother are. I can't believe that I've never made this connection before. Both of them are so self-serving that they don't care who they destroy to get what they want.

Both men stand, and my father pulls Hanson into an embrace. Hanson finally relaxes and gives him a genuine hug in return.

"You mentioned you like Aunt Lillian. Her store is right down the street. Would you like to see it and her?"

"I'd love that!"

The three of us take off towards Aunt Lill's store. I never knew I could feel such contentment in death.

HANSON and my father walk into the store. Avery is sitting on one of the couches by the fireplace, her nose buried in a book. Aunt Lill is nowhere to be found.

"Ave," Hanson says, and she peeks over the top of her book. She drops it on the couch and runs over to Hanson, throwing her arms around him.

"Are you okay? What happened? Did they arrest Dad?" The questions spill out.

"I'm okay. They just asked some questions. Not sure about Matt." Hanson holds his hand out toward my father. Avery hasn't noticed him before then. "Um, Ave, this is Mom's dad. Our grandfather. Calvin Sanders."

Avery's brow furrows as she looks him up and down. She's frozen in place, trying to figure out the appropriate reaction. Her sweet nature wins, and she holds out her hand.

"Hi! I'm Avery."

"Pleased to meet you. Finally," he says. "You look just like your mother. At least what I could tell from the pictures at the funeral home."

Avery wraps her arms around herself. She never could take a compliment. "Thanks, but Mom was way prettier at my age."

"Where's Aunt Lill? He wanted to see her," Hanson says.

Avery grimaces but doesn't respond.

"What Ave? What's wrong?" Hanson says.

She shakes her head. "You guys should probably leave because…"

She's interrupted by my mother's voice screeching from the doorway into the office. "What in the hell is he doing here?"

Calvin, Hanson, and Avery all snap their heads in her direction.

"I should go," my father whispers.

"No," Hanson says. "Go sit with Avery. I'll be back."

Avery links arms with my father, and they walk toward the couches. Hanson storms off towards my mother who's now shouting for Lillian.

"Grandma, lower your voice!" Hanson insists as Aunt Lill pushes past her out the doorway.

"What in God's name is wrong, Linda?" Lillian asks.

"That bastard is here with my grandchildren. Of all the nerve." Her hands tremble, and her nostrils flare.

Aunt Lillian furrows her brow and shrugs. "Who?" She glances around the store, her gaze finally settling on my father and Avery. "Oh!"

"We had lunch, and he wanted to stop to say hi. I thought it would be okay," Hanson says.

Aunt Lill grabs Hanson's hands. "It's perfectly fine. I haven't seen your grandfather for years."

My mother's mouth drops open, before slamming shut into a scowl. "I cannot believe you, Lillian. How dare you say it's okay after everything he put me through! And Mackenzie. He's a monster," she says and raises her voice loud enough for my father to hear. "I don't want that pervert anywhere near my grandchildren."

"Enough!" shouts Hanson. "We're all sick of your lies and your bullshit. He stayed away because of you. You made him out to be this awful person when really, you're the awful one!"

My mother physically recoils as though she's been punched. "How dare you! After everything I've done for you. For your mother. You should be thanking me. Neither of you would've survived without me."

Hanson shakes his head and walks away, toward Avery and my father.

"Hanson, get back here! Where are you going?" my mother shouts.

He glances over his shoulder and says with a smirk, "It's pointless."

"Lillian, do something! How dare he! I've done so much for him. How could he choose that bastard over me?"

Aunt Lillian clenches her hands into a fist, ready to explode. "Linda, Hanson's right. He has every right to be here. If you don't like it, you can leave. You've kept him away long enough. It's too late for Mack, but let him have a relationship with his grandchildren. It's what she would've wanted."

"No! You don't know that! She wouldn't have wanted that after everything he did to…"

Aunt Lill cuts my mother off. "Get out! I'm done with the lies. The games. The manipulation. You didn't do shit to save Mack or Hanson. Everything you did was for you! I can't do this anymore!"

Tears waterfall down my mother's cheeks for what seems like the thousandth time today. She stomps into the back room, gathers her purse, and pushes past Aunt Lill.

"I can't believe you're doing this to me. Choosing him over your own flesh and blood!" she screams.

"Any choice I make is for your flesh and blood. Your grandchildren!" Lillian shouts in return. She must be steaming mad because I've rarely heard her raise her voice.

My mother continues toward the door, doing nothing to hide her tears. She stops and points at my father. "You have ruined everything. My relationship with my daughter and, now, my grandchildren and sister. I hate you!"

"Linda," he says calmly. "Can you please calm down so we can talk?"

She shakes her head. "I've got nothing to say to you. Or any of you!" She points at Hanson, Avery, and Aunt Lillian. "You no longer exist to me. This is the ultimate betrayal."

She walks out, the only sound left in the room is the jingling of the bell on the front door as she leaves.

I'm so glad that Aunt Lill finally stood up to my mother. She's needed to for years. The jingling bell explodes into a thundering noise in my mind as the bookstore fades away.

CHAPTER FORTY-EIGHT
THEN

I'm in the car with my former self and Vera, outside of Girl Scout camp.

"Bye, Mom!" Vee shouts as she bolts from the car.

Former me waves and waits until she makes it to the door before pulling away.

The entire ride back toward home, I presume, based on the route, I scan my memories for this moment. I come up blank. I don't recall any of this. A lump rises in my throat. Is today the day I died?

"Turn around. Go back and hug Vee. Tell her how much you love her!" I shout, realizing I didn't even say a real goodbye to her. If I'm going to go home and meet my death, the last words she needs to hear me say is how much I love her. Former me doesn't respond and keeps heading towards home. Fear grips my chest, wondering what I'm going to find waiting for me there. Or rather, who. But the biggest part of me already knows.

"Remember!" I shout at myself and think back to the days after Christmas. The first few days were quite peaceful, but a gnawing feeling lingered in my gut, knowing that Matt was not going to let me take the girls with me. At least he wasn't without one heck of a fight. Beyond packing, Hanson stopping over each day to check on me, and being happy that I'd soon get to leave, nothing comes to mind.

All this time, I thought I wanted to know exactly how I died, but as former me pulls into the garage, my instinct is to flee. I don't want to know anymore. I don't want to witness my own death. I try to walk out the garage door as former me enters the house. Again, it's as though an invisible tether pulls me toward my alive self, keeping me from escape.

In the kitchen, Matt sits at the island with a scowl on his face.

I jump right along with my former self. "What are you doing here?"

"It's my god damn house, in case you forgot," he slurs, the smell of alcohol permeating the air.

A tremble works its way through my former self's body, as it does the same in mine. A sober Matt is scary enough. A drunk one is downright terrifying.

"Of course. I just thought we had an agreement. I'll be out in three days," former me says with a shaky voice.

He slams his hands on the counter. "You don't get to make all the rules. I don't care what your plans are. This is my house. My life."

His face is red with rage. He needs to calm down, or I need to get the hell out of here.

"Calm him down!" I shout. Alive me must hear me.

"I know, Matt. I'm sorry. How about I give you a bit of time? I need to run to Aunt Lill's." Former me backs toward the door to the garage.

I think my former self's plan has worked because I've almost made it to the garage door when Matt lunges, pushing alive me flat against the door with the knob digging into my back. I try to wriggle away from my former self so that I don't have to gaze into Matt's deranged eyes. Smell his alcohol-laden breath. Hear his heavy breathing. But I'm stuck right next to my former self to live through this again.

"Where the hell do you think you're going? I'm not done talking to you," he shouts, inches from my former self's face, his spittle flying everywhere.

"Matt, please. Let me go to Aunt Lill's. Please."

His response is to tear off my shirt and pull down my pants. He wraps his hand around my former self's throat, tightening it as he plunges into me. I feel my own breath constrict as well as each push of his body into mine. Former me, along with dead me, claws and kicks at him but, it only energizes him more, provides further fuel for his rage. Finally, former me goes limp, struggling just to breathe. I have no energy or will left to fight him off. My former self's eyes close, and I have no doubts that I'm about to witness my death.

"Get up!" I shout. "Please get up! Your kids need you. He's going to kill you!"

I'm so caught up in trying to rouse my former self that I lose track of Matt, who's apparently now finished with me. I lay cheek to cheek with my former self, closely watching my chest to see if I'm still breathing. Do I die here on the kitchen floor from this attack? I think back to some of the conversations at the police station, though. There's no gun. No blood. Does Matt come back with a gun and finish me off?

The questions linger in the air around my former self and me as everything grows blurry, and thunder echoes inside of my head. I'll have to wait a bit longer for my answers, as now, it's time to go back to the present.

CHAPTER FORTY-NINE
NOW

My entire body trembles as I reappear in Aunt Lill's store.

"I'm sorry about that!" my father says after a few minutes of silence.

I'm so rattled from what happened back in the kitchen that it takes me a few seconds to absorb what he's saying. My mother. Her fit about him being here.

"No! Don't apologize. You did nothing wrong," Aunt Lill says.

"She wouldn't have blown up if I hadn't come here. It was a stupid decision on my part."

Aunt Lillian sits on the sofa across from my father and Hanson. "You are, and always have been, welcome here. I'm so sick of her drama and lies."

"That means a lot, Lillian. Really," my father says.

Aunt Lill's cell phone buzzes in her hand. She walks away to take the call and is only gone a few moments.

"Well, that was Detective Collier. They asked us to return to the station," Lillian says.

Hanson shifts in his seat and chews on his cuticles. "Why? Did they say?"

Lillian shakes her head.

"I'll let you guys go. It was great seeing all of you," my father says.

"Uh, would you like to come with us?" Hanson asks, fear filling his eyes.

"If you'd like, sure. I just need to let Tiff know."

"We'd love for you to," Aunt Lill says.

After Dad checks in with Tiffany and Lillian informs the staff, they load into Aunt Lill's car and head to the station.

AS SOON AS WE ARRIVE, I search for the detectives. I find Detective Andover and Detective Collier sitting in an interview room with the Lieutenant when I arrive.

"We've got him," Collier says. "All the boxes check off. We've got motive—he didn't want Mackenzie to leave him and take the girls. Opportunity—he knew she'd be alone in the house since the girls both had activities that day. And means—we don't know where or how he got the gun, but he'd definitely have the ability."

Andover nods. "With the results from the lab showing his semen in her, fresh bruises on her neck and back, and finding Matt's bloody shoes today, we've got more than a circumstantial case. I have no doubt in my mind he's guilty. I can't wait to knock that smug smile off his face."

The Lieutenant nods as he ruffles through a notebook, which I presume to be the case file. "Okay, make the arrest," he says.

Collier and Andover exchange glances. Collier smiles, and Andover takes a deep breath.

"My pleasure," he says. "The family should be here any minute."

Relief floods me, along with sadness. Matt's getting arrested. My girls and Hanson are safe. I can't believe he really killed me. Why couldn't he just let me go? Why did he have to do this to our children? Perhaps now I'll be able to move on. To rest in peace. The thought of leaving my children for good brings me to my knees.

I rise as Collier and Andover leave the room. I follow them into the interview room with Matt and his attorney. I can't break down now, before I have all of my answers.

"Please stand, Sir," Collier says.

"What's going on?" Mr. Farber asks.

"We need your client to stand up," Andover says.

Mr. Farber nods at Matt, and reluctantly, he stands.

"Put your hands behind your back." Collier slaps handcuffs on him as Andover reads him his Miranda rights.

Matt stiffens and narrows his eyes. "What the hell? I didn't do it. I swear."

Collier laughs. "Yeah, okay. That's what they all say."

"I'll be at the hearing next week. We'll get you bailed out," Farber says as Andover leads Matt toward the door.

"My girls. Make sure they know I didn't do this," Matt shouts as they cross the threshold into the hallway.

"We'll make sure your girls know the truth," Collier says. "That you're the bastard that killed their mother."

I throw my arms around her, so thankful she can see through Matt's bullshit. She disappears from my embrace as I'm carried backward in time again for what I believe will be the final time.

CHAPTER FIFTY
THEN

I'm confused when I come to sitting next to my alive self on the couch at home. There are blackened bruises all over my neck, but I'm still alive. I didn't die on the kitchen floor after Matt's rape, as I'd suspected. My former self texts Hanson, asking him to come over to help get the rest of my stuff moved. He doesn't respond. I follow my former self around the house to get the girls ready for camp and shuffle them out the door to their rides. Once they're gone, former me scrambles to finish packing.

My alive self's nerves are shot; I jump at every little noise, fearing at any moment, Matt will bust through the door and rape me again. I know he has worse planned, though. The next time he comes through the door, it will be to kill me. I'm witnessing my final moments left on this earth, at least those where I'm not a ghost. Former me lugs box after box down the steps into the foyer so that everything will be ready to go when Hanson arrives.

Around noon, former me is in Vera's room, grabbing the last of her things, when the front door opens. Former me drops the box I am carrying, its contents spilling onto the floor. I freeze, next to my former self, trying to listen for footsteps on the stairway. Former me scans the room, probably in an attempt to see if there is anything to use as a weapon. It seems like, in my former self's gut, I know that if he gets to me today, I won't make it out of the situation alive. I shake my head. My death is inevitable. He's going to get me. He's going to kill me. There's no way out of this.

Finally, when no noise comes from downstairs, former me yells. "Hanson?"

"Yeah. It's me," his voice echoes up the stairs.

My shoulders instantly relax. I'm not going to die yet. "Oh, okay. Good. I'll be down in a sec."

Alive me quickly picks up all the scattered items and shoves them back in the box. Vera's room is done. I exit the room with my former self, who shuts the door. There are enough of her items left in her room so that it'll still feel like home when she comes to visit Matt on the weekends. What will happen to her now? Where will my girls go now that I'm dead and their father's been arrested? My heart aches for my daughters. Former me lugs the box downstairs and deposits it in the pile.

Hanson sits at the kitchen island, staring out the window.

"Hey, thanks for coming! I wasn't sure you got my message."

Former me is met with silence. Hanson's jaw is clenched, and his hands are balled into fists.

"You okay?"

He laughs, but there is no humor in it. "Yeah, sure," he says.

Former me grabs a bottled water from the fridge and turns to him. "What's wrong? You seem upset."

"Gee, Mom. You're observant," he says sarcastically, reminding me of his early adolescent years.

"Enough with the games. Tell me what's wrong so we can get out of here."

He looks toward the ceiling and rubs his hands through his hair. "Well, gee. I don't know where to start," he says. "How about with the fact that I stopped by yesterday to check on you and found you half-naked on the floor?"

What? My heart races, and my head throbs with this information. "Oh, God, Hanson. I'm sorry." My thoughts spiral. He had been here? Had he witnessed the rape? If he was here, why didn't he do anything to help me? Why'd he just leave me like that on the floor?

"Wait, there's more! Your darling husband was still here, zipping up his pants when I came in the kitchen. We had a nice little chat."

How did I miss that? Hanson was here as Matt was leaving? Why didn't I see him? Did Matt hurt Hanson?

"About?"

"I was a bit upset at realizing the bastard had just raped my mother. I saw you lying there and thought you were dead. I pushed past him to check on you. When I realized you were still breathing, I charged him. Told him I was going to kill him."

Oh, God! I knew in my heart there had been some kind of physical altercation. There was no way Matt would overlook Hanson confronting him like that. "Did he hurt you?"

He laughs a dry, mournful chuckle. "That depends on what you mean."

He stands and paces back and forth like a caged animal. "So, I told him he was a sick, rapist bastard and was ready to punch him. I'm not a kid anymore and have no doubts that I could take him. For once, the asshole didn't use his fists to stop me. He did something worse."

My mind races. What could he have done that was worse? Former me takes a drink of water as Hanson paces back and forth, back and forth. From the island to the windows and back again. When he gets like this, it is always best to give him time and space. To let him talk when he's ready.

"Yeah, he spilled your dirty little secret, Mom. Well, maybe more like my dirty little secret."

"What are you talking about? What dirty little secret?"

He stops and glares at me. "You're really gonna keep up this game? The lies?"

My hands start shaking, although I have no idea why. Perhaps it is the rage I see in Hanson's eyes. The questions swirling round and round in my mind. I've never seen him so angry at me.

"Please tell me what you're talking about. I really have no idea."

"Let's talk about my father. You know, Shane Talman." He makes air quotes when he says the name.

My heart sinks. Oh, God. What did Matt do? I look to my former self to come up with something to say to calm Hanson. To protect him from the ugly truth.

"Okay," former me says. I don't want to know what's going to come next.

"You're a liar. Matt told me the truth. That you made that nice little story up. That my real dad was a rapist!" He resumes his pacing. "Imagine my surprise when he told me that I had no right to chastise him for having sex with his wife when my real father was a rapist. That I'd probably turn out just like him."

"Oh my God, Hanson. I'm sorry. I never meant to…"

That bastard! Hurting me is one thing, but doing this to Hanson is unforgivable.

"Stop. Just stop! Is it true?" He makes eye contact with my former self for the first time today. I still see my little boy somewhere beneath those hardened eyes.

"Please, let me explain, okay?"

"Answer the question. Is it true?"

Alive me nods and buries my face in my hands, unable to meet his eyes with the confession hanging in the air. Tears spill down my former self's cheeks. Bile rises in my throat. I never wanted Hanson to learn the truth. I knew it would crush him. I wish I could go back and erase all the lies I'd told but, at the time, I did what I thought was best. What I needed to do to protect him.

"So, all those times you told me those wonderful stories about my 'dad.' That was all just bullshit?" he yells.

His words pierce like an arrow through my heart.

"Hanson, I'm sorry. I just wanted to protect you from the truth. I didn't want you to ever think I regretted having you. I didn't want you to carry the burden of knowing," former me says, my voice quivering.

"You let me believe a lie! You think that was better?" he shouts. "Do you realize how many times I dug for information on Shane

Talman? Or how many times I questioned why his family wanted
nothing to do with me? I wanted to know if I looked like him. If I had
the same interests as him. If I had aunts and uncles out there that I
knew nothing about. Grandparents! And, all of it was a lie? How was
that supposed to help me, Mom? And you told that bastard the truth?
But not me. Your son!"

The truth in his words stings. He's right. I understand his feelings
of betrayal—they are completely justified. He has every right to be
angry with me. To hate me. To never want to speak with me again. All
the justifications I'd come up with over the years feel hollow now.
Meaningless. I want to comfort him. To apologize. To make him understand. But from this side of death, there's nothing I can say that he will
hear. There's no way to fix this.

"You've got nothing to say?" He starts pacing again. "How about
the truth? The real story. I guess with a mom like Grandma Linda, lies
come naturally."

That hits me like a punch to the gut, and all of the air leaves me. I
owe him an explanation. Memories of a thousand moments rush into
my mind. Those when Hanson looked at me, doe-eyed, trusting every
word out of my mouth. I'd betrayed him. I was the one person he had
in this world, and I'd let him down.

"Fix this! Say something to fix this! Tell him the truth! "I scream at
my former self. Former me takes a step back.

"I know it doesn't make it any better, but I'm sorry. I did what I
thought was best. I know that might not be enough. I didn't want to
hurt you. I never wanted you to feel the pain and doubt you do now,"
former me says, sobbing.

Hanson paces. Back and forth. Back and forth.

"You're right. It's not enough," he finally says, barely louder than a
whisper.

"I promise. I'll tell you everything. The whole truth," former me
says. "We can do it now. Or later. Whatever you want."

He huffs. "Whatever I want? I want the mom I thought you were.
The one I could trust. That's what I want."

In this moment, that's all I want, too. To be the person I pretended to be. To be the mother he'd thought I was. To not leave him wondering how I could betray him so deeply.

The room swirls into an array of colors, and I'm plunged forward into now.

CHAPTER FIFTY-ONE
NOW

The detectives escort Matt to the holding cell to await his ride to the county jail. It's hard to leave him because I am thoroughly enjoying watching him squirm. Now that I'm aware that he told Hanson about the rape, I hate him more than I ever have. But I want to hear the conversation between the detectives and my family so, eventually, I give in and join them in the front lobby. Everyone sits quietly, lost in their own thoughts. Avery picks at her cuticles; some of them are starting to bleed. Hanson sits and stares at the floor; then gets up and paces—an endless cycle, back and forth, over and over again. Like that day in the kitchen. My father scrolls through the news on his phone. Aunt Lillian holds a book in her hands and pretends to read, but she's been on the same page for ten minutes.

After what feels like a lifetime, Detective Collier opens the door to the back of the station.

"Hi! Thank you all for coming and for waiting. We'd like to meet with you for a few minutes."

Without saying a word, everyone gathers their things and follows her to the back. Collier leads them to a conference room where Andover is waiting.

"Have a seat," Collier says, holding her hand out to the table and chairs.

Once everyone is seated, Andover speaks. "We won't take much of your time, but we wanted to give you an update."

Aunt Lillian nods. Hanson's eyes grow wide. Avery continues to pick at her cuticles.

"We've placed Matt under arrest. He'll be held in the county jail awaiting his arraignment," Andover says, unable to hide his smile.

"Really?" Aunt Lill says with excitement creeping into her voice. "How? Why?"

"We're not able to divulge all of the details at this point, but with the results of the Coroner's report and the findings of the search today, we have sufficient evidence to make the arrest."

Hanson's hands start shaking so badly, he clasps them together to try to stop it. When that doesn't work, he places them on his lap, underneath the table. Avery continues staring at her fingers; she's no longer picking at them, rather watching the blood pool and trickle down her hand.

"Wow! This is great news," Aunt Lillian says. "Right, kids?"

She looks at each of them and realizes they aren't as excited as she is about this prospect.

She pulls Avery close. "Are you okay?" she whispers.

Avery shrugs as a tear falls down her cheek. "I don't know. I mean, I'm glad they arrested him but sad, too, if that makes sense."

"Oh, honey, I'm sorry. It does. It makes perfect sense," Aunt Lill says.

My father clears his throat. "So, what happens with the children? Was there a will?" He shifts his gaze from the detectives to Aunt Lillian to Hanson.

Finally, Aunt Lillian speaks up. "I'll reach out to the attorney she was talking to about her divorce. Perhaps she knows something."

Thank God Aunt Lill is smart enough to think of this. The information they need will be with my attorney. I recently had a new will drafted, one that Matt isn't aware of.

"What do we do until then? Where do we go?" Avery asks, her eyes filling with tears.

"Sis, I can come stay at the house with you or, if you don't want to be there, you and Vee can come stay with me," Hanson says. "I promise I'll take care of you guys."

"I will take care of all of you, including you, Hanson," Aunt Lill says. "You aren't ready to raise two girls—you're still barely an adult yourself."

My father clasps and unclasps his hands, staring at the table. He clears his throat. "I understand you just met me, but I'll help however I can. With money or whatever you need," he says.

My heart melts. Why did my mother keep him from me? Perhaps if I'd had him in my life, I wouldn't have ended up with a man like Matt.

"That is so kind of you, Calvin." Aunt Lill reaches across the table to pat him on his still clasped hands.

"I just wanna help. I feel horrible that this all happened without me ever having the chance to get to know my daughter," he says and rubs his forehead. "I want to know my grandchildren, at least. I have enough regrets for one lifetime."

Collier shuffles the papers on the table, stacking them into a neat pile. "It sounds like you all have some things to figure out. From our end, we need to know that the minor children have an adult to care for them, so we don't have to get Children's Services involved. It sounds like you all have that worked out."

Aunt Lillian and my father nod.

"Any additional questions for us right now?" Andover asks.

"Are you sure?" Avery says barely above a whisper.

"Sure? About what?" Andover says.

"That my dad did this? That he killed my mom? That she didn't kill herself?" Avery asks.

"We are as sure as we can be, Avery," Collier says kindly. "I'm sorry."

Hanson takes a deep breath and slumps back against his chair. It's as if all of the fight has left his body. He can finally relax.

Avery nods.

"What happens next?" my father asks.

"Since it's a Friday, the arraignment won't take place until early next week. We will keep you posted about the details so that you can attend the court hearing if you'd like," Andover answers.

"I'm not sure how all of this works," Aunt Lill says. "Can Matt be bailed out before his arraignment?"

Collier shakes her head. "He'll be locked up at least through the weekend. Which will give you all time to figure some things out."

Lillian takes a deep breath, realizing she has a few days to make decisions. "That's my only big question. The rest of the answers I hope to get from Mack's attorney. Kids, do you have any more questions?"

Both of them shake their heads. Avery is as white as a sheet and probably in shock. Sure, she knew before today that her father had a temper and that our marriage was falling apart. She's been bombarded with a lot of truth in a short amount of time. Her brain probably can't process any of it. I long to be there with her to help her navigate these new truths.

"Alright. You have our cards and numbers. Call us if you have any more questions," Andover says and rises. He reaches out his hand to each of them as they exit the room. Collier offers a hug to Avery as a way of comfort. Avery falls into her arms and relaxes against her. I pray that she can feel my touch and love in Collier's hug. I want her to know I'm here.

"Thank you," Avery whispers.

"For what?" Collier asks, breaking their embrace.

"For figuring out that my mom didn't kill herself. I didn't think she did, but…" Avery says and lets her voice trail off.

Collier places her hands on Avery's shoulders and looks in her eyes. "Listen, I didn't know your mother, but I've heard a lot of conversations today. The one thing that's clear to me is how much she loved you guys. You children were her world. She wouldn't leave you on purpose."

Avery sucks in a deep breath as a single tear falls down her cheek. She then nods. I am so thankful Collier took this moment with Avery. I am even more grateful that Avery believes, beyond the shadow of a doubt, that I didn't take my own life. That I didn't leave her on purpose.

CHAPTER FIFTY-TWO
THEN

I come back to the past and am, once again, in the kitchen with Hanson.

"I need some space. I'm going out for a smoke," Hanson says and heads out through the garage.

Former me hesitates, debating about following him outside.

"Just give him some time," I say, even though my heart breaks for him. He always needs his space when he's this upset.

Alive me heads upstairs for a last once-over of all the bedrooms, and I follow behind.

Vera's room is done. Avery's is packed. Previous me glances in our bedroom and pauses before shutting the door to take in the room one last time. I'm flooded with memories. The day we moved into this house and how full of hope I was. I had a husband that adored my son and me. My utter joy at having a nice home to make a better life for my child than I ever had. I had dreams of growing old with Matt. How different things had turned out. Had the signs been there all along about Matt's narcissism, his rage? Had I been so desperate to escape my mother's house that I overlooked it all? Or was it possible that underneath the monster he'd become, he actually did love me at one time?

I shake my head, trying to clear the questions. Entertaining them and the memories do no good. None of that matters anymore. Bottom line, he had become a monster, and all the thinking or questioning in the world wasn't going to change that fact. He killed me. He took me from my children. Alive me shuts the door and heads back downstairs.

Hanson sits at the island, drinking a soda. His posture isn't as rigid, and he seems to have relaxed a bit. Alive me walks in and places a hand on his back. He doesn't try to pull away.

"I love you, Hanson. I'm sorry," former me says as I kiss him on the head.

He takes a deep breath. "I love you, too. Let's get your stuff packed up and get the hell out of here. I've waited this long to find out the truth, a bit more won't hurt. We can talk about this later."

A tear falls down my alive self's cheek. "Okay. I promise to tell you whatever you want to know."

He nods and stands.

"Can I have a hug?" former me asks, holding my arms open.

He pulls me into a hug. I'm reminded of when he was no taller than my thighs and would squeeze me so tightly around the legs. Now, my head barely reaches his shoulder. Former me pats him on the back and freezes, my hand lingering on his waistband. He jerks away.

What in the world is going on?

"Hanson, is that what I think it is?" alive me asks with a shaking voice.

"Mom, let's get your stuff packed," he says, backing away.

"No. Show me what's in your waistband. Now!" I shout.

"Leave him alone. Just get the hell out." I yell even though it's pointless.

"Damn it, Mom!" He reaches around to his back and pulls out a gun.

My heart sinks.

"Oh my god! Why do you have that?"

"Please, just let it go, okay? Please," he pleads.

My head feels like it's going to explode with the confusion.

"Let it go? Really, Hanson? You know how I feel about guns. Why the hell do you have one?"

"Can we please talk about this later?"

Former me crosses my arms and stares at him.

"Fine. You want the truth?" he asks. "After I drop you off, I'm going to find that bastard and kill him. For hurting me all these years and for the hell he's put you through. Seeing you like that yesterday broke something in me. I realize how easily he could kill you. Even after you leave him, you're not safe. The only way you'll be safe is if he's dead."

What is he even saying? My mind can't comprehend.

"Hanson, he's not worth it. If you shoot him, you'll go to prison for a long time. Your life will be wasted. I will be okay."

"I've already made up my mind, Mom. I'm not asking for your permission. I'm telling you," he says. "You can pretend like you've got it all under control and that you'll be okay, but he's never going to set you free. Don't you get that? He's crazy, and he will kill you." The veins in his neck throb as he clenches his jaw.

My mind whirls. He can't do this. I understand that he is angry at Matt, and scared for me, but there is no way in hell my son can go to prison and ruin his life over my stupid choices. Matt simply isn't worth it. My pain is insignificant compared to the thought of my son spending the rest of his life in prison. I'd rather be beaten and raped every day than see that happen.

"Get the gun!" I shout in my alive self's face. "Don't let him do this."

Former me puts down the water bottle and lunges towards Hanson. My hands latch around the gun, and alive me tries to wrestle it free from his hands. The entire scenario plays out before me in slow motion. My alive self's hands slip as Hanson pulls backward on the gun.

A shot rings out. The noise is deafening. I fall to the ground next to my former self.

I'm carried away, back to the present.

CHAPTER FIFTY-THREE
NOW

M y head is still reeling with what happened in the kitchen. I can't comprehend what I just witnessed. That Hanson had a gun, not Matt.

My focus is pulled to the present as Aunt Lillian drops my father off at the hotel. He must've texted Tiffany to let her know he was on his way because she's waiting out front.

"I know now isn't the best time, but I, at least, want to introduce you to my wife. Hopefully, we'll be seeing a lot more of you all," Calvin says and opens the door.

He says something to Tiffany, and she leans in. "I'm so sorry for all you've gone through. I wanted to say hello and let you know we'll stay in town for a few days. If you need anything, we're a phone call away." She hands Aunt Lillian a piece of paper. "This has all of our numbers on it."

"Thank you," Aunt Lill says. "We'll be in touch. Perhaps you can come over tomorrow for lunch or something."

Tiffany nods and looks at Hanson and Avery. Avery gives a slight smile, and Hanson nods.

"Okay, I'll let you go. Talk soon." She shuts the door.

She and my father embrace, and the love between them is apparent.

How I wish I could've given my children that type of love to see as an example. Perhaps, they will get to experience it through my dad and Tiffany.

Aunt Lill pulls the car out of the hotel lot. "So, we have to go pick up Vera at Monique's. Do you guys want to go home? To the apartment?"

"Not to the house. Please. I just can't," Hanson says. "Not yet, anyway."

"Of course, Hanson. How about we hang out at Monique's tonight? She's got plenty of space and loves you guys. Plus, her cooking is divine."

"Sounds good." Avery attempts a smile, but the sadness lingers. The pain in her eyes will possibly be there for a lifetime. She's lost both of her parents.

The drive to Monique's is silent. Everyone is lost in their own thoughts, hidden behind their own pain.

WHEN WE ARRIVE at Monique's, she and Vera are sitting at the kitchen table coloring. Vera's carefree spirit is refreshing. All that matters to her at this moment is choosing the prettiest colors for her unicorn and trying to stay inside the lines. How I am going to hate not being able to watch her grow up, become a woman. She's such a spunky little girl; I have no doubts she'll accomplish great things.

"Hi!" she says. "Do you like it?" She holds up her partially colored picture. "I made it for Mommy. I wanna put it in her casket, so she has it with her."

My dear, sweet baby.

"It's pretty," Avery says and smiles.

"Great job staying in the lines, Vee. Your mommy will love it," Lillian says as tears pool in her eyes. Monique rises and pulls her into a hug.

"Do you like it, Hanson?" Vera asks.

"No," he says, and Vera's face falls as though she's about to burst into tears. "I love it!" He laughs and tousles her hair.

She breaks into a smile. "Color with me! We can all make Mommy a picture! Daddy, too!" She looks around the room. "Where is Daddy?"

"Let's talk about that later, Vee. Right now, we all have pictures to make!" Avery says and sits next to her.

Hanson sits on the other side, and they both start flipping through coloring books. It reminds me of when they were younger. Those blissful days when I thought anything was possible and that our futures were full of hope.

"And, I'll make lasagna," Monique announces. "I bet you're all starving."

"We sure are," Aunt Lill says. "And you guys will absolutely love Monique's lasagna. It's the best on the planet. Say, can I make Mack a picture, too?"

"Yes! She would love it," Vera shouts.

Aunt Lillian takes a seat, and, for a moment, the people I love most in the world sit together, smiling, laughing, and coloring. It makes me believe that despite everything, they may all be okay, after all.

I whisper a prayer that I can stay right here with them. This is where I want to spend eternity, surrounded by their love. But first, I must go back and see how my life ended.

CHAPTER FIFTY-FOUR
THEN

Former me doesn't realize I've been shot until the blood seeps through my shirt. It spreads across the green cotton, turning it an ugly shade of brown. My mind swirls back to what I heard at the police station. I was shot in the chest, and the police knew that it wasn't self-inflicted. Hanson stands frozen, and there is silence for what feels like a lifetime. The clatter of the gun falling to the floor snaps him out of his shock.

He runs to former me, placing his hands on the wound in my lower chest.

"Oh my God, Mom. I'm so sorry. I need to call 911. Oh my God!"

I feel pain in my own body as though I'm lying there for the first time. Horror rises in my chest at realizing the consequences my son will face as a result of this accident. I want a rewind button. To go back in time to when he was two and Matt walked into the restaurant, charming me with his smile. If I couldn't have that, one that would at least take me back ten minutes in time so that this whole thing never would've happened. This accident that is going to destroy my son's life.

Former me tries to sit up but can't, and it's getting harder to breathe. I gaze into my former self's eyes and see a knowing there. I have no doubts that I knew that I was going to die on the floor of my kitchen, in the house I so desperately wanted to get away from. The irony doesn't escape me.

"Hanson," former me says and grabs his arm. My voice is breathy, no louder than a whisper.

He leans down, putting his ear to my mouth.

"I love you," former me manages to get out. "You need to make it…"

"What mom? Please be okay. I need to call 911," he shouts and tries to pull away. I raise my hand to my former self's arm, tightening my grip.

"He can't call 911," I say. "He can't let the police know what happened."

Former me nods as though my voice is audible and forces the rest of the sentence out. "Make it look like Matt did this."

"What? How?" he shouts.

I try to remember some of the true-crime television shows I'd seen and what would make the police lean toward Matt. I whisper into my former self's ear.

"Shoes. His shoes. My blood. Hide them." Each word is a struggle. I breathe a sigh of relief. It seems former me heard my command.

"Mom, I need to call 911. They can help you. I don't want you to die," he cries, tears streaming down his cheeks.

Former me smiles. "No. Go. Get shoes. Now."

Hanson is no longer a man. He's reverted to a little boy, trusting his mommy and that everything I tell him to do is the right choice, the better choice. I wish there was another option. That it didn't have to be this way, but it does. I see it clearly now. How to fix this. Hanson doesn't deserve to be locked up for a mistake. An accident. Matt had tortured and abused us both for years. He is the one who deserves to be behind bars for his intentional cruelty. Hanson can't pay for my mistakes—the mistake of marrying the wrong man. Of not seeing the truth until it was far too late.

I tell my former self what needs to happen. Again, former me nods and peers into my eyes. An understanding passes between us, as if the veil between the real world and the spirit realm has been torn. We can see each other. I'm no longer a spectator, but an active participant.

"Sit up," I say.

Former me tries to scoot to a sitting position but can't.

"Get the gun. You have to get the gun!" I shout.

Again, former me tries to reach it. "I can't! The pain. Help!"

I leave my former self's side and look to the heavens, begging that just this once I can impact something physical in the real world. I push with all my strength, summoning every bit of pain and anger within me. The gun moves a few inches. Just within reach of my former self.

Former me picks it up. I'd never held a gun before.

"Your blood. Rub it on the gun to smear the fingerprints."

Former me complies, rubbing my bloodied hands over it, trying to conceal whatever fingerprints remained. I need my former self to erase any trace of evidence that Hanson had touched the gun.

A million thoughts race through my mind as my former self does what needs to be done. Former me raises it and puts it in my mouth. Alive me and dead me merge into one. I feel the things I did that day, in that moment. I don't want to die and leave my children. I want to see them grow up and get married, have children of their own. I want the quiet, joyful moments with them of snuggling under a blanket, watching a movie, or taking a drive through the countryside. I want Sunday dinners at Aunt Lillian's house, full of laughter and love. I want to experience life without Matt.

None of that is possible, though. Matt destroyed it all. I know now that Hanson will do exactly what needs to be done to make sure Matt pays for every little thing he put us through. I don't care who fired the shot—all of this lies squarely on his shoulders. I hate that I'm leaving such a monumental, impossible, and heart-breaking task for my son to take care of.

I close my eyes and picture each of my children's faces. In my mind, I say, "I love you" to each of them and pray for God to protect them all, give them a happy life, despite all of this.

Then my finger tightens, pulling the trigger.

The world around me goes black and silent. Is this it? Is this death? Did I need to witness this final scene before I could move on? The only thing surrounding me are the questions. Did I come back to make sure I did what needed to be done? My mind swirls into a world of color, and thunder booms inside of my head. There's still no peace in death.

CHAPTER FIFTY-FIVE
NOW

Noise penetrates the silence and light illuminates the darkness. I'm back at Aunt Lillian's.

She and Monique sit at the kitchen table, enjoying a cup of hot tea in the quiet house.

The kids are settled into bed. Avery and Vera share the pull-out sofa in the living room, and Hanson is in the guest room.

"So, I've been thinking," Monique says quietly.

"About?" Lillian says.

"These kids have a long road ahead of them. I know we have to see if Mack had a will and what it said, but what do you think about moving in here? Letting them move in with us?"

Aunt Lill's eyes grow wide as she takes another drink of her tea. "Wow! You sure you mean that? About me? And them? Talk about a big change!"

"I'm one hundred percent sure. I love those kids. And," she says and grabs Lillian's hand, "I love you."

Aunt Lillian blushes, which is cute. I've never seen her blush before. "And I love you, too. But this is huge. I want to make sure you know what you're getting into."

"I know it won't be easy. But they can't go back to the house where their father killed their mom. Your house is too small. I don't want Hanson to try to be a dad to his younger siblings at his age. And, I think we're ready for this step. Living together. We practically do, anyway." Monique laughs. "In fact, we could get married."

Aunt Lillian smiles. "I suppose you're right. I kinda do want to spend the rest of my life with you, so why the heck not?"

They both laugh and embrace. It is tender and beautiful. I burst with joy for both of them.

I move into the living room where both girls are lost in the land of sleep. I watch them for a few minutes trying to soak up every detail of them. The shape of their lips. The sound of their soft snores. The smell of them. I haven't been gone long, but I already miss them so much. I hope they know how loved they are. I pray they never find out the truth —that it remains hidden, buried for the rest of their lives. Pangs of guilt assault me, realizing that, in a sense, I've sacrificed my daughters to make sure my son is okay. I have no doubts that they'll eventually forgive their father as neither of them has a spirit of anger or resentment. As awful as Matt has been, he loves his girls. It's truly his only redeeming quality. But if they knew the truth of what I'd done—how I'd betrayed them—I don't know that they could ever forgive me.

I lean forward to kiss each of my daughters on the forehead and pretend I can feel the warmth of their skin. Avery stirs in her sleep, almost as if she can feel me. She opens her eyes and, for a moment, stares right into mine.

"Mom?" she whispers.

"Yes, love. I'm here."

She rubs her eyes, shakes her head, and rolls over. I smile, thinking maybe, just maybe, she got a glimpse of me.

I move into the spare room where Hanson lies staring at the ceiling. I sit on the bed next to him.

His voice breaks the silence. "Mom, I don't know if you can hear me, but I'm sorry. I'm so sorry. I didn't mean to hurt you."

Tears spill down his cheeks onto the pillowcase beneath his head.

"I know, son. I know."

"I don't know how to do life without you. You're the only one who's always had my back. I don't know how to live with this guilt. That I killed you. I took you away from Vee and Ave." Sobs wrack his body.

"You didn't kill me. Matt killed me. His abuse. His torture. He destroyed both of us."

"I understand why you did it. Shot yourself," he says. "So, that I wouldn't be the one to take your life. You made sure of that."

I nod. He's exactly right. The shot that Hanson fired couldn't be the one that killed me. He'd never forgive himself for that. This way, I have at least assumed some of the burden. I also needed to be gone by the time he called for help. To protect him from the consequences of what happened. I'm so thankful he was smart enough to do what needed to be done to make Matt pay.

"I wanted to kill myself. I still kinda want to," he says. "But I won't. I promise you I won't. I gotta be here for Vee and Ave. I'll make sure they're okay. I promise."

I lie on the bed next to him and cuddle against him as I used to do when he was small. With Matt locked up, I know he will be okay. He feels alone now but, with Aunt Lillian, Monique, Vera, Avery, my father, and Tiffany, he'll be well-loved. I trust that they will work together to make sure all three of my kids are okay.

"I love you, Mom," he whispers.

"I love you too, Hanson."

I close my eyes, and peace washes over me. A peace unlike anything I've known before. Hatred toward Matt no longer consumes me. I take a moment to think of my mother and feel nothing. No anger. No resentment. Not even sorrow. I do, however, feel hope. Hope for a new beginning with my dad and Tiffany for the kids. I also feel love. Love for my Aunt Lill, for Monique, and especially for Avery, Vera, and Hanson. Something else lingers within me. A feeling that's foreign to me, but one that fills me with a sense of closure. It seems I'm no longer bound to this world, stuck somewhere in between truth and lies, life and death.

I am finally free.

———

Two families, forever linked by tragedy.

Ruby Dunkin is in an abusive marriage. Her best efforts aren't enough to shield her two children from an abusive father whose cruelty knows no bounds. Their volatile situation ends in tragedy when Ruby's eldest son, Billy is torn away from everything he loves. Consumed by hatred and self-loathing Billy becomes the thing he hates the most—his father.

Chelsea Wyatt, a senior in high school, goes missing after work one night, never to return. Her parents are devastated, only knowing this kind of tragedy from the news. Crimes like this are unheard of in their quiet, midwestern town. Consumed by the tragic fate of their friend, family member and neighbor, their lives and futures are forever altered.

For over eighteen years, no one knows the connection between Ruby Dunkin and Chelsea Wyatt. A journey through time reveals the common thread stitching their heartbreak together. Yesterday echoes throughout each character's life as they decide how, and if, they will break the chains of the past.

Will they continue to leave a legacy of pain and loss for future generations? Will they break the cycles of abuse that have destroyed so many lives?

———

Mosaic is a collection of very short stories, ranging from scary pieces to those full of hope. Through these stories, I hope to provide glimpses into what it means to be human. Each of us is made up of many different pieces that, when fit together, make a beautiful, messy whole. Those tiny pieces in and of themselves don't mean much and are easily overlooked. But, when we put them all together, a full picture of what it means to be human starts to form.

___

Bits & Pieces

Tessa was born with a gift. Through a simple touch she picks up pieces of others. A chance encounter with a stranger traps Tessa within the mind of a madman. A "flash" of color devours her—the only indication that she's gained something new from another person. Will she be able to find the killer and help save the next victim without losing herself in the process?

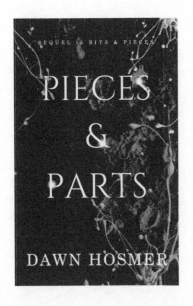

The highly anticipated sequel to *Bits & Pieces*, the psychological thriller that kept readers up at night.

For the past five years, Tessa has lived a normal life, the kind she always dreamed of. One without her gift and the flashes that tormented her for as long as she can remember.

All of that changes on a winter's day when, out of nowhere, the flashes return. Only this *time they're different.*

Along with the flashes, Tessa makes a gruesome discovery on her property. Images haunt her. Voices from beyond the grave plead for her help. She is thrust into a quest to find and stop a murderer. Time is running out.

Tessa scrambles to fit all the pieces and parts of this hideous puzzle together before someone she loves becomes the next victim.

***Pieces & Parts* is a spine-tingling psychological thriller with a touch of the supernatural that will keep you guessing and turning the pages until its chilling end.**

ACKNOWLEDGMENTS
SOMEWHERE IN BETWEEN

I spent many hours alone writing and editing this book, but I could not have done it without the help, support, and love of so many others along the way. I'd like to take a moment to thank some of the people who have been instrumental in making my dream a reality.

First and foremost, I'd like to thank my husband, Steve, and children—Krystyna, Jesi, Dominic and Gabriel. You have been by my side, cheering me on, every step of the way. You are my why, the reasons I carry on. I'd also like to thank my mother, Joyce. Your love and support are a constant in my life. I wouldn't be who I am without your love.

Thank you to Gestalt Media for publishing the first edition of *Somewhere In Between*. I'm grateful for the support and effort you put forth to help me get this book into the world.

A huge thank you to Rebecca at Black Cat Graphic Design who has helped me beyond words with getting my books re-uploaded, with formatting, with graphics, with my website, and for your friendship and support. I would be seriously lost without your assistance. I am forever indebted to you.

I would like to thank Jen Yan and Carol Beth Anderson for taking the time to beta read this book and for offering me your valuable insight and feedback. You helped this book become so much better. Also, thank you to Bambi Sommers for the amazing job you did with editing. You helped make this book the best it could possibly be.

I would also like to thank the Writing Community on Twitter for all of the love, encouragement, and support you've given me over the past several years. You've all inspired me to keep pursuing my dream and have shown me more support than I ever could've imagined. In addition, a special shout-out to Booktok and the Kind Valkyries for welcoming me with open arms. Your friendship, love, and support has been such a blessing. You keep me laughing and keep me spending way too much money on books to add to my enormous To Be Read pile.

Also, a special thank you to Kate Minear Sorenson for your friendship and for using your mad photography skills to do my author photo. Also, much gratitude to Rachel Hopmoen for convincing me to join Twitter.

Thank you to every single person who lets me into their life by reading my words. I cannot describe for you what an honor it is that you invest your time, energy, and money to support my dream. I am touched beyond words.

While the subjects in this book are heavy, I hope readers leave with a sense of hope. No life is beyond repair. One person can truly make a world of difference in another person's life. Our tragedies and hurt do not have to define us. We do not have to take our pain and use it to hurt others. There can be healing.

Independent Authors rely on reviews to help spread the word about our work. Please take a moment of your time to leave a quick review on Amazon and/or Goodreads. Reviews are one of the few ways we, as writers, know whether you enjoyed (or hated) what we wrote. Thank you so much!